*BOOK ONE: THE BINGHAM CHRONICLES*

# THE BEATING OF SARAH STRONG

*The Beating of*

# SARAH STRONG

*Book One: The Bingham Chronicles*

## T.B. STONER

LUMINARE PRESS

WWW.LUMINAREPRESS.COM

The Beating of Sarah Strong
Book One: The Bingham Chronicles
Copyright © 2020 by Terri B. Stoner

Printed in the United States of America

Cover Design by Melissa K. Thomas

Author Photograph: Jessie Flori Photography

Luminare Press
442 Charnelton St.
Eugene, OR 97401
www.luminarepress.com

LCCN: 2020914322
ISBN: 978-1-64388-444-8

*All your works shall give thanks to you, O Lord,*
*and all your saints shall bless you!*
*Psalm 145:10*


*This book is dedicated to my husband, Mark,*
*whose confidence in me and his encouragement*
*are the reason it was written.*

*And to Emily, Cameron, and Samuel who have*
*taught me more than they will ever know.*

# CHAPTER 1

Quigley passed through the overgrowth with familiar ease. The crowd long since dispersed. His goal—a discarded bottle of bourbon. It had been known to happen. A Boy will steal from his father's liquor cabinet. Then in bravado and braggadocio, with friends laughing and goading him—*chug, chug, chug*, he drank. Not realizing the potency, the bottle, half of its liquid remaining, is discarded while the drinker, in shame, loses the first half. It was the rhythm of the male adolescent chant that put the idea in Quigley's head an hour before. Bingham's football fans, gone home, he searched behind the bleachers on the south side of the field. The same spot their parents gathered with friends and their parents before them. Darkness was a blessed comfort. Quigley wore it like a cloak while conducting his nightly raids. His large overcoat, worn in every season, was placed on its hook before his excursion. He would feel the darkness as always; believing his skin absorbed the anonymity that is night. The daylight exposed him, leaving him vulnerable to every sideways glance and the quickness with which a mother snatched a toddler's hand when he passed. Late August in a Missouri river town mimicked a cosmic embrace of sticky humidity Quigley welcomed. He conducted his search to the music of cicadas and tree frogs. The full moon gave adequate light but he still made use of the flashlight Lowell's boy left last week.

Bingham High's first game of the season yielded nothing but a dollar and some change. Quigley was used to disappointment. It wasn't as if he needed a drink but he did have an occasional taste for good bourbon and knew the men of Bingham to have it also. Nights were long, living alone in the abandoned factory, and on hot August nights, it was hard to sleep. He resigned to returning home after pocketing his booty. As he squeezed back through, he heard the scream. It was loud and terrifying. He moved his thumb over the switch on the light and held his breath, stock-still in the middle of the hedge. The scream came from near the front of the factory. There were few choices, wait until whatever it was—was over, or try to intervene. Intervening, would be out of the question any other time, but his pounding heart and the accumulating sweat on his palms and forehead cemented a conviction that spread throughout his whole being. He could not hide or run from this. A force greater than his fear or typical indifference seemed to overtake him. Inching to the other side, another scream traveled through the nerve endings of his spine. He recoiled. Quigley used to the play, taunts, and language of children, and adolescents knew this was nothing to do with childish pranks. The scream was unmistakable and terrifying.

The third scream louder than the first two echoed off the old factory. It forced him further through the hedge. A man, tall and bald, the street-light casting a glare off his head, stood above a small crouching figure. One hand gripped hair; the other landed on her face. A weak cry escaped her lips before a second blow. Then silence—except for the sickening thud of fist meeting flesh.

There was a smooth rock at Quigley's feet, smooth and round like a baseball. With the light of the moon and a distant street lamp, he knew he could hit his target. He rarely missed. Caressing his weapon, remembering, knowing. Once, he heard them comment, *could have been ninety*, but Quigley thought they were being generous. When he drew his arm back and felt his bicep stretch, and strength travel from the crook of his neck through his shoulder to his elbow and then to his wrist, where the momentum collided with the movement of his fingertips, Quigley knew there was one thing he could do better than any man in Bingham. They knew it too. The rock left his hand. The man dropped the limp figure he roughly held and stumbled, holding his head. Had Quigley been ten years younger, the villain would not be standing. The stranger drew a gun and pointed it in the direction he dropped the girl. Quigley knew he must do something.

The yell was feral, frightening even Quigley. His voice was seldom used and to hear it like this brought him to the ground. It was as much a shock to himself as to the stranger. The gun turned his way and footsteps drew near. He closed his eyes tight and waited. The shot never came. Headlights from a passing car on highway Seventy-Nine froze the moment.

The bright lights shone over Quigley's head. He lay still crippled by fear, not knowing if his heartbeat was audible. Another car passed. Two passing cars, after eleven were rare. A third could be categorized as a miracle. Approaching footsteps forced Quigley's head to the dirt. The damp smell of earth brought him back—for an instant—to his mother's garden, her hands digging for new potatoes while he held her apron strings wishing to be inside under the stairs. His brothers and sisters at play in the nearby lot, their laughter drifting over his head like the clouds. Only a very small part of him wished to join them, but even as a child, he knew it was not possible.

The hedge provided camouflage. Lifting his eyes; he could see a pair of black loafers directly in front of him. Quigley stopped breathing, craning his neck a little higher. Tattoos on a thick forearm, a broad torso connected to trunk-like legs met his glance. He dropped his head in despair catching the movement of the loafers as the light from the lamp disappeared. Inches away, the unmistakable sound of a gun's chamber drawing back to accommodate the bullet sent a wave of nausea over Quigley. He shut his eyes, willing his body to shrink, hoping the shot would miss his vital organs. Silence. In the distance, he heard it but could hardly believe it—another vehicle approaching. The man swore, then dove in the ditch to avoid the head-lights. Again, Quigley braced himself but was relieved at the sound of another engine—squealing to a stop—a voice screaming, *'Get in now!'*

Quigley kept still until the car engine faded. His shaking legs barely able to carry him the four flights to his room in the factory, he collapsed trembling, muttering to himself in disbelief.

He sat in the corner rocking back and forth, wringing his hands. The girl lay out there alone. Quigley's whole life had been self-preservation. He had little trust for anyone, even his own family. Running to the safety of his corner, he forgot the reason for his fear. The girl could be dead, he reasoned, but if not, what suffering might she be enduring? She needed help and he was the only one who could help her. The weeds in the parking lot were tall enough to hide a small person from the road. It was up to him and him alone. He felt his insides rise to his throat as he crawled to the only window that still had the glass intact.

Movement in the tall weeds somewhere in the middle of the lot close to the road compelled Quigley to go down. It was a slow process getting to the girl; he stopped several times agonizing and cursing himself. His lifelong cruel companion held him so tight it was as if he struggled through chest-high water; light from his flashlight swinging like a heavy pendulum as he walked.

Finding her, Quigley dropped to his knees and whispered, "You alive, girl?"

No answer. He inched closer; he knew her. It was Sarah, who worked for Ben. When Ben wasn't around it would be Sarah giving him his coffee and cookie. Disappointment always accompanied his grumbled gratitude. He preferred that Ben hand him his breakfast. Sarah's disdain was evident.

Maybe if he said her name, "Sarah?"

Her hand moved. Quigley touched her forehead; it was warm and perspiring. Bruises and swelling were beginning to surface and blood formed a pool on the cracked asphalt. Pity compressed his heart. He rose and searched for her bike; she always rode past the factory on her way home to Sutter's Grove. It must be nearby.

Mumbling instructions and reproof to himself, he summoned courage out of the recesses of his being. He looked across the road. Lang's Grocery had a few cars in the lot. There were few people in town Quigley could tolerate and fewer he spoke to, going to Lang's Grocery was almost as frightening as what had just happened. It would have to be the bike. There had been no cars since the one carrying the villain away. Another one passing at this point seemed an impossibility, but Quigley decided he would take a chance. If it didn't work, he would have to go to Lang's Grocery.

Finding the bike at the edge of the lot, he rolled it to the middle of the highway; it was risky but it would stop a passing car. Back in his room, he watched. It wasn't long before he saw the lights. Flashing, red, and blue, sweeping the side of the factory, briefly blinding Quigley, he observed the sheriff's car pull to the side of the road. Mike Reynolds was one of the few people who knew he lived at the factory; there would be questions. Quigley let out a sigh of despair as he watched Reynolds carefully exit the patrol car, hand on his holster. Examining the bike for what seemed like an eternity, he finally turned his gaze to the area where Sarah lay.

"Imogene, it's Mike, I just found Sarah Strong's bike in the middle of the road." The sheriff crept cautiously toward Sarah, holding his walkie. "We may need an ambula…," his voice escalated, "we will need an ambulance. Seventy-Nine, in front of the glass factory."

Quigley watched as the sheriff bent over the girl. Mike Reynolds was up in a moment running to his car to retrieve a blanket all the while calling orders to Imogene.

"Get Karl out here, someone needs to tell Joe. What? I don't know, she's breathing, but it is pretty bad. No, not hit by a car, her bike is fine. She's beat up, there's a lot of blood. Yes, I feel a pulse. We may need air transport. Tell Karl to get Joe now."

Bingham, Missouri had nothing more than a small clinic. They would take her somewhere else, St. Louis maybe or St. Charles. He had done his duty. Before turning from the window, he caught the sheriff glancing up. Looking around, Quigley packed his things quickly. There wasn't much; he had no idea where he would go, but he knew he must. The caves maybe? An old barn? He had lived in both but the factory had been a real home to him. Sheriff Reynolds would come looking for him, probably tonight. He would question him and try to make him go to the nursing home again or live with Lowell's boy, his nephew. No, that was out of the question. Quigley slipped out the back door of the factory and disappeared into the night.

# CHAPTER 2

Ann Fletcher stood on the sidewalk watching each oncoming vehicle like the horde of fatigued airline patrons around her. She nervously flicked the ID badge on her Samsonite while observing a mother struggle to pull a toddler out of a horizontal meltdown. The child reaching his limit, an act of desperation and defiance. Whatever their journey's stage, he wanted it done. She bit her lower lip, leaning further into the drive that brought relatives, indifferent cabbies, and friends for happy, sad, or dreaded reunions. What would her own be? Looking down at the luggage, she recalled receiving it one year for Christmas, her freshman year in college. Given to her by her mother, intended for travel of a nature different than what had occupied it the last three years. The familiar blue SUV crawled behind a hotel passenger bus. Exhaust assaulted her nostrils as she mustered an apprehensive smile and wave. Her mother, Nancy, sat in her usual stoic attitude glancing at Ann with a return wave and uncertain smile. Her father, Stuart, ran from the driver's side, gave Ann a quick hug, grabbed her suitcase, and urged her into the vehicle.

Stuart Fletcher hated the airport pickup and was keenly aware of waiting cars and impatient cab drivers. They sped away before Ann could say hello. The barrage of questions would come soon; Ann prepared for full-on-rapid-fire from both parents but especially her mother. An hour's drive would be tough. There hadn't been much conversation when she broke the news she would be coming home, just a warning her things would be shipped and she would be on a flight in a week.

Small talk transpired as Stuart navigated the traffic on Interstate Seventy to Highway Sixty-One where they would turn north to Bingham. The assault of questions and accusations did not surface, to Ann's surprise and relief. Bouts of silence, the price of gas, an observation of construction on the bridge, and various comments about the weather in a strained yet concerned tone from her father were the backdrop to the familiar scenery flying past. Her mother broke her silence with the news concerning Rachel's upcoming wedding. Rachel, Ann's sister, would marry soon to the great relief, she was sure, of Nancy. The right man had come along to sweep her off her feet. It was all Rachel had wanted. Nancy's disappointment in the planning was evident and Ann was relieved by it. It was a godsend, so to speak, to take the focus off her homecoming and circumstances and put it on Rachel's choice of a Baptist ceremony—they were Presbyterian, the lack of reception venue and various other things not getting done. Ann relaxed for the moment. Rachel being the object of their mother's disappointment was new and reassuring. It was a rare occurrence; Rachel always being just what she should. She finished college, had a job teaching Bingham's kindergarteners, chose a solid fiancée, and still lived at home. Ann propped her feet on the back seat and relaxed. She loved her sister dearly, but it was tiring always being the source of conflict in the family.

Nancy continued, with a tone of sarcasm, "I guess we can pitch a tent in the yard if we have to. I'm not sure where they can book this late. The wedding is in less than two months. I told her to wait until spring but she wouldn't have it."

Ann noticed her father's glance in the mirror. She was smiling as if getting away with something. Stuart frowned. Ann knew he would change the subject; he did that to diffuse any potential words between her and Nancy. The three of them in the car for over an hour was probably not ideal for him, especially after Ann's three-year absence.

"Fannie," he interrupted using her childhood nickname. "Do you remember Sarah Strong?"

"She was years behind our girls, they wouldn't know her," Nancy interjected annoyed.

"I don't know her," Ann admitted, "Should I?"

"They found the poor child beaten almost to death; night before last."

Ann shivered, "Here in Bingham?"

"Yes, and she's hardly a child," Nancy corrected. "I believe she's nineteen."

"They found her in front of the factory barely breathing… brought her down south to ICU. She works for Ben at Level Grounds. You know Ben."

"No, I don't, who is he?"

"Must have come after you left. Bought the old bakery next to your mother's shop, turned it into a coffee shop, does pretty well, I think. He said she was the best worker he's had yet," Stuart said with emphasis. "Must have been on her way home, lives over there at Sutter Grove Mobile Home Park. Rode her bike everywhere, shame really…" His voice faded and he went into a time of silent reflection. Her mother too, stared out the window, her thoughts a secret.

Ann enjoyed the reprieve. Her mind drifted from Sarah Strong to her homecoming. Bingham had been home to her family for at least three generations. The Fletcher's were not of the founding families, the Binghams and Wesleys, they were the second tier—as it were. Her great grandfathers, on both sides, came for work in the glass factory around the turn of the century. Growing up, Ann could not wait to leave. Leaving meant freedom, no longer under the watchful, critical eye of her mother. Coming home meant failure. She had tried to re-adjust her attitude in the weeks before leaving Colorado, convincing herself it would be different and temporary, just enough time to find another job and move on. Making a mental to-do list, she inventoried her talents and skills; she never finished college, which was a negative—at least for her mother but her experience in the hospitality industry in Colorado covered many positions. The last being in public and guest relations. She loved it. It suited her. Too bad Josie's father had to sell. She had been offered a position by the new owners but renovations would take months. Ann could not wait. No money, the demise of her Jeep, and the situation with John drove her home.

Her father, stirring from his reflection, decided to regale Ann with Bingham gossip the remainder of the trip. It was a pleasure Stuart often indulged in; gossip about the eccentricities of the town. Her mother thought it unchristian but never hid her amusement. He began with the last town council meeting, in which there were heated discussions regarding booth placement at the upcoming Apple Festival. JC of JC's Garage and Bike Rental claimed a prime spot near the Bluff Trail which did not go over well with many business owners. The evening ended with a foam cup of coffee hurled across the room at the Festival Committee.

He continued with, "Last spring Prom-goers dyed the fountain waters blood red and Josephine was hit by a car." Josephine, belonging to JC, had been a fixture in Bingham for so many years no one remembered her as a puppy. To Ann's relief, she survived.

Josephine was very un-dog-like in her character, as her loyalty to JC waned anytime there was a better offer from one of the townsfolk. As a result, she seldom stayed home and considered Bingham a free and open territory in which she could explore and forage. JC tried a kennel one year during the Apple Festival but Josephine howled so loud her containment was worse than her presence. On her release, she roamed the rest of the festival weaving in and out of booths and tourists, sniffing every inch of ground. Josephine never bothered anyone and went unnoticed by adults. Children, who didn't know any better, ran to her expecting the usual exuberance one gets from a dog but they were disappointed and eventually left her alone.

Stuart continued, "She still managed to make her rounds thanks to the sixth-grade class and a dog stroller. JC was grateful and gave them each a free hour on a bike. Old Levi Brooks ran her over; the council pressured Sheriff Reynolds to take his license but the sheriff said it was only a matter of time before Josephine got hit and it could have been anyone in Bingham that did it."

Ann believed that, despite Levi's 90 years, many near accidents have happened because of Josephine.

"That dog is a nuisance and JC should obey the leash laws like everyone else. Those kids, with her in that ridiculous stroller, only encouraged her bad behavior. She thinks she owns the town and can go into shops and peoples' yards without question and we all allow it." Ann's mother interjected.

Ann, knowing Nancy as she did, felt the remark was indirectly for her. Nancy Fletcher was a woman of order, discipline, rules. It would not do to have the rights of others infringed on by an inconsiderate dog owner and an unruly dog. It would not do to have a daughter with the same character.

Stuart shifted uncomfortably and adjusted the air conditioner, "Your mother has been mad at Josephine since she knocked over her favorite ceramic planter out front and broke it to pieces; in JC's defense he offered to pay for it."

Nearing town, her father exited the Avenue of the Saints, as it is called, a stretch of highway connecting St. Louis and St. Paul. They took Seventy-Nine the rest of the way and Ann was glad; she would see the river almost all the way home. The Mississippi represented home as much as anything to Ann. Bingham was a river town. It was also home to a population of unique and enigmatic characters. Located between Hannibal and St. Louis, it boasted the best view on the Mississippi set high on bluffs; one could see into Illinois for miles.

Most, who lived there, grew up there with a lineage that traced back, at least, to the opening of the Silver Glass Factory in 1927. Some even further, the ancestors of founder Josiah Bingham and his in-laws the Wesleys. Josiah and his brother Albert left their father's farm in Maine around 1840 seeking their fortune in the west. They crossed the Mississippi in Hannibal and proceeded south getting as far as the current town limits. Having lost two wagon wheels and one horse they were compelled to shoot, Josiah, the less ambitious of the two, settled on the bluffs of the Mississippi River and bid Albert goodbye. Josiah left Bingham—which he named after himself—only once; to marry and bring his bride from St. Louis. A bride Albert had procured for him by exaggerating Josiah's character and industry. Betsy Wesley's parents were so impressed they decided to sell their Mercantile, pack up Betsy's seven brothers, and move to Bingham also. Josiah and Betsy then produced their own family of mostly males and thus sprung the town's current substantial population of Bingham and Wesley. These have been divided and subdivided into groups identifying familial quirks and idiosyncrasies. The George Wesley's have always had heart trouble; the Cotton Bingham's were cheap, and so on.

Josiah lived to the ripe old age of 96 and saw Bingham rise from a one-man town to a prosperous, bustling one street municipality that provided the only ferry across the river for miles. The industrial revolution came at the turn of the twentieth century with the Silver Glass Company, which employed most of the town until its closure in 1975. The mayor, who was a Wesley, went immediately to work to save the town. Committees formed and Main Street was made a small-town showpiece. The factory converted to an antique mall and the addition of two bed and breakfasts kept Bingham in the black for a few more decades. A municipal park with a bike trail along the bluff boasting a magnificent view year-round was developed.

With some savvy marketing, a popular Midwest magazine named Bingham in its *Favorite Small Towns* issue. Bingham commerce sailed through the rest of the eighties up to Y2K. The world did not crash as predicted but Bingham's progress leveled off. The Silver Glass Antique Mall and one of the bed and breakfasts closed. Bingham limped along until a prudent, local apple orchard owner brought forth the idea for the annual Apple Festival. Complete with every kind of product an apple can produce—it brings enough retail revenue to last until Christmas. After Christmas, the eagle watchers come. It was discovered by one Rudolph Bingham in the late nineties that a population of eagles began favoring Bingham's riparian territory. Seizing on this discovery, Rudolph sent photos and press releases to multiple Missouri news outlets and from that, grew the eagle watching past time that brings no little income to local café and businesses in an otherwise slow, dead of wintertime. While Bingham boasts no wineries like other parts of the state; it oozes quaintness other small towns do not.

This town Ann and Rachel Fletcher grew up in and knew. Their childhood was unremarkable, other than some minor dysfunction and drama. They were carefully provided for, brought to church and Sunday school, taught the golden rule, and then left to run free in a place where neighbors rarely locked their doors and shopkeepers left merchandise on the sidewalk overnight. Their friends and acquaintances had much the same experience. Unlike many Missouri small towns, Bingham was prosperous and its inhabitants wanted to keep it that way. If you don't own a business in town, chances are you drive almost an hour each way to work. Nancy Fletcher owns the only florist shop on Bingham's Main Street and Stuart drives forty-five minutes to teach economics at a community college. A life they are both satisfied with and it seemed to Ann, her sister Rachel would soon slip comfortably into the abyss of small-town existence too. But for Ann, Bingham never had a place on the timeline of her future.

After a few miles of river view, there is a curve on the highway that bypasses Main Street and the town square. The country club, adorned with homes on either side of the fairway, is the first thing you pass. Crossing Church Street and continuing up Seventy-Nine, you will see schools on both sides of the road. The baseball diamond is next to the elementary school and then Lang's Grocery and gas station. Opposite them are the glass factory turned antique mall and Sutter's Grove Road. A few hundred yards passed that; Bingham Place is on your right.

Ann was glad her father didn't turn on Church and take Main. She was not ready for the stares and waves; it was still daylight and she was sure most of the town knew of her homecoming.

Bingham Place looked the same, neatly organized homes of the old, affluent, stately type protected by ancient slate roofs. Grand, columned porches leading to grander entryways and old, giant oak trees standing guard in front, gave one the impression they had stepped back in time. The Fletchers occupied the smallest of these—some believed at one time it was guest quarters to one of the bigger homes. Purchased when Ann was five, for the better part of her childhood she witnessed its transformation to a modern-day grandeur without sacrifice to its historical beauty. This street—populated mostly with the remaining descendants of the founding families—was the only home Ann had known, other than a college dormitory, until three years ago when she left for Colorado, determined never to come back.

The fattened calf would survive another day. There would be no fuss to this homecoming. Expecting words from her mother, words of reproof mingled with, "*all we want is what's best for you*", Ann determined to say as little as possible. The discussion, argument, conflict had existed from her earliest memories. *I told you so...what are you going to do now...you really didn't think it through,*

*it's time to settle down and get serious...if you would only...*
were phrases and questions all too familiar to Ann and
she expected they would come at any moment. She had
no answer or comment. Not ready to delve into her life in
Colorado, she communicated to her family scant updates
and mundane events throughout the last three years. Rachel
was privy to a little more than her parents. There was no
need to get into a life-style they disapproved of and would
only upset them. Ann lived without future plans most of
the time and found ways, throughout most of her life, to
be where she wanted and do what she wanted. That's why
she found it impossible to stay in Colorado. Doing what
she wanted, was how she landed in a risky relationship that
proved difficult to break free.

John's last meltdown scared her enough to cut off all
ties. She left town while he was on assignment fighting fires,
going home seemed her safest option. And with the close
of the resort, it confirmed her time to go. Josie invited her
to California, and it was tempting but she missed her sister
and with an upcoming wedding, felt she should be home.
After all, she missed Rachel's graduation last spring because
of her involvement with John, something she deeply regretted. Rachel's greeting as she burst through the door assured
Ann there were no hard feelings and her anxiety about the
reunion melted away.

Dinner was savory, creamy tomato bisque with a salad
of greens and side of Nancy's homemade bread. Surprised
by her appetite, she devoured two bowls as Nancy pensively
glanced her way. A few times Nancy opened her mouth as
if to speak and then thought better of it. Rachel and Stuart
finishing first, cleared plates to the kitchen, and murmured
in low tones. Ann complimented Nancy on the soup and

excused herself to her room to unpack. She found it virtually the same except the Christmas wrap box and a few odds and ends that had taken up residence in her closet. Everything from her books that occupied one whole wall to her poster of the Eiffel Tower remained unchanged.

As she was putting the last of her clothing in a drawer, Rachel bounced in and plopped on the bed expectantly, "Well...?"

"Well, what?"

"What happened?"

Ann ignored the question and continued wrestling her suitcase next to the plastic cargo box of wrapping paper. Rachel's stare was determined. "I ran out of money, that's what."

"I'm not buying it and neither is Dad, you've always been able to find employment and land on your feet. Is it that John guy?"

The reference to John irritated her. It was over, a bad decision in a stream of many, he was the main reason she left. Still processing the whole relationship in her mind, telling Rachel would have to wait. John had been an irresistible dream when they first met, saying all the right things, and looking all the right ways. Her fall was fast and impulsive, barely a thought to what she was doing. Her self-restraint gone; not realizing the power John had when he spoke, touched or looked at her. How she escaped, she was still piecing together. But that's what it was, an escape. Shuddering at the memory, she considered Rachel sitting patiently behind her, she turned and smiled, thankful for her sister being safe and marrying a good man.

"Just ran out of money, I guess." She answered hoping that would be enough.

"I would've lent you some until you found another job."

"Just what I want to do, borrow money from my little sister."

"Why not? If living in Colorado is where you want to be, I could've helped you out."

Ann sat beside her sister and tried to fill in the blanks without mention of John.

"It's not Colorado, and I'm not even sure that's where I want to land. It's a lot of things. Not sure I can explain it, I've run out of money before and have always managed, just this time it was everything at once. My Jeep, the resort suddenly closed its doors, and most of my friends moved away or went back to school. I found myself in an empty efficiency apartment barely bigger than this room with no plan, no money, and no transportation. The plane ticket home was paid for by the proceeds of what was left of the Jeep. It just suddenly seemed like the time to come home."

"How has Mom been?" Rachel changed the subject.

Ann shrugged, "Very quiet. Scary quiet, in fact. What's up with that?"

"Maybe she's giving you space."

"That would be a first." Ann forced one more sock in a drawer and pushed it closed. "Space was something I could have used most of my life but she never gave it." Ann didn't finish the thought, her leaving had much to do with getting space. Space between herself and her mother. Their relationship could be defined as difficult at best. Ann loved her mother; she was her mother, after all. Very few people can say they don't love their mother but she had never wanted to share all her secrets with Nancy or shop on the weekends or get a manicure together. The older she got, the less she wanted to reveal anything about her life because seeing the disappointment on Nancy's face sucked the fun out of it.

"You saw her at dinner, barely a word to me. No questions about my future, no questions about what I've been doing, who I've been seeing, nothing. She didn't even mention the Jeep, which I thought would induce her to a lecture on responsibility."

"Maybe she's decided a different approach with you…" Rachel turned her gaze from Ann's, without finishing.

"What? A different approach, what does that mean?" Ann said defensively, never considering she required a special approach.

"Nothing,"

"Don't be afraid to tell me. Whatever it is, I won't be offended."

"It's just that, sometimes, you make it hard to know you." Rachel's look was one Ann knew well. When compelled to say something difficult to hear, her forehead creased above her nose. "We are always guessing at what you could be thinking or doing, maybe it would be nice to let us in on something before we have to ask."

Ann went to a discarded sweater and began folding. This was something new, Rachel was not one to point out defects, but now she thought Ann should communicate better. Ann turned to her sister.

"I'm not sure what you mean by guessing, it's not a mystery what I've been doing or where I've been." She argued as her door burst open.

"There!" Stuart peeked in smiling broadly. "My two girls under the same roof again. What more could a dad want? Glad you're home Fannie, I sure did miss you."

He reached her in one step, his arms circled her—the smell of dandruff shampoo and dryer sheets enveloped her. There was always comfort in those arms but at times, they were met with resistance. How many times had she pushed them away when they tried to coax and calm her in the heat of an argument or draw her in—in a joyful occasion? Joy everyone felt but her. While they celebrated a family moment she thought of her excuse to exit, be with her friends, find a place to be herself.

Not telling them everything, like her sister implied, had always been her modus operandi. The less they knew the fewer questions, or so she thought. Backing away from her father, she observed the lines on his face. He had grown a little fatter around the middle and earlier when he lifted her luggage from the car, she noticed his hand on his back and a slight groan escaped his lips.

"Thanks, Dad," her voice caught.

Stuart backed out of the room with an ill attempt at disguising his concerned look. Ann caught a tear roll before he abruptly turned and exited. During her three years away, she thought little of her parents. What they must have felt or thought never crossed her mind. Hiding her life from them, feeling the freedom from their set of rules was what she wanted. Yet, she was conscious—in parts of her mind she kept locked—they thought of her, prayed to their God for her, worried, and lost sleep over her. Those thoughts she quickly put back in their place. The thought of family and even Main Street, Bingham, Missouri would hinder her freedom and the life she wanted. Short texts, a few emails, and some trips home for holidays were the breadcrumbs she tossed their way. Ann flinched at her unfeeling attitude. Seeing her father and hearing Rachel's remark was bringing some things into focus that she preferred stay in the blurred background. It was a hard truth. Especially excluding Rachel from the details of her life and not sharing in her recent joys. She watched her sister finger a loose thread on a pillowcase.

"I'm sorry." Ann blurted.

"Hmm?" Rachel looked up.

"Sorry for not being at your graduation in May, I should have been there for you."

"It's okay…really."

"No, it's not. Dad would've flown me home. I know he would've. I was too proud to ask and too proud to see you do something I couldn't." Ann sat back on the bed and taking Rachel's hand, rolled her thumb across the engagement ring. "I am proud of you and am truly sorry I wasn't here for one of the most important days of your life." Ann wanted to say more, more about why she wasn't as transparent as others but, like always, she couldn't find the words.

"Don't say you couldn't, we both know that's not true. You'll finish someday, that is if you want to. Besides, you didn't miss much, I think I saw Nana dozing off and Millie was looking at her phone the whole time." The girls laughed.

"How are they?" Nana and Millie, their grandmothers, both widowed long ago; lived together in Hope Village across from the golf course.

"Intolerable! They laughed at Connor's proposal."

Ann had seen it on social media and chuckled a little at the time herself; balloons and strangers enlisted to hold signs, it was quite a spectacle.

"They're not used to such intimate things being broadcasted for the world to see. I'm surprised they know how to work any social media."

"Millie has it all." Rachel waved her hand in the air.

"I'm sorry they laughed at him…How is he?"

"He took it all in stride; he's in Chicago this weekend visiting some college friends, so I thought you and I could do something."

"Sure, what is there to do? Count cars on Main Street?"

"For your information, we have quite a hip establishment on the top floor of the Wesley Building."

# CHAPTER 3

Wesley, Wesley, and Hinkle, Attorneys-at-law, occupied one side of the building and Bingham Medical group the other. The division stopped before reaching the top floor where a vast area, complete with exposed brick walls, industrial fixtures, and hip artwork met your first glance. There was a large bar in one corner and tables full of diners scattered throughout. Outside seating on a balcony that overlooked the river, drew the sisters. A band playing soft rock renditions serenaded couples with their wine and appetizers.

"There is a private room that holds about a hundred and fifty on the other side of the bar." Rachel motioned with her hand in the opposite direction. "We are thinking of having the reception there."

Ann ordered a white wine, Rachel raspberry lemonade.

"Is this the Baptist thing?" Ann pointed to her drink as the server set it down.

"Oh, Mom told you. You would think I ran off and joined a cult. It is just easier; Connor's uncle is the pastor and he has married everyone in the family. Mom said Doctor Francis would be happy to have him officiate at Bingham Pres but I don't care which church, if it makes Connor's mom happy, then I'm happy."

That was Rachel, accommodating, good, helpful. Ann was different, fighting for her own way most of her life. Rachel was happy when those she loved were happy. Connor was a lucky man. Ann looked around Top Floor—the name of the establishment. Nothing was familiar in the upscale, trendy place except the people and the view of the river. Tommy Short tended bar, his sister Amy waited tables, Evie Camden sang with the band. Everywhere she looked she knew someone.

Evie caught her eye as she ended a folksy ballad; she slid the mic in the stand and made her way over. "Fannie, when did you get back?" She didn't wait for an answer; "I haven't seen you in years! How are you?"

Interrupted before her mouth opened, Tommy approached, "Fannie Fletcher!" he said with a towel over his arm and a tray of drinks tottering above his head. "Let me get this table served and I'll be right back."

His sister Amy waved from across the room which caused heads to turn and before Ann knew it, hugs, handshakes, and questions came at her in rapid succession.

"Fine, just needed to come home and re-group, I guess. No, sadly my Jeep had to be put to sleep. How are you? No, haven't seen him yet…Oh how is she…A baby, wow…oh and she had twins…no, no one serious…not sure what's next, employment, I guess…oh he did, that's great." And so it went for an hour and a half until Rachel pulled her out the door and down the steps.

"What a homecoming! You were always the popular one."

Ann smiled; she had felt welcomed and it warmed her. The very people she couldn't wait to leave three years ago, the people she had known since the time she picked up her first crayon in preschool. These people knew everything about her, who her parents and grandparents were, who and what her firsts were…kiss, job, car, date. She was Ann (Fannie) Fletcher, riding through town with the top off the Jeep, mud on the sides from going off-road into a farmer's field. She was the 'hard to handle' daughter of Stuart and Nancy, 'the troubled one', 'the one you had to watch'. That's how some viewed her, others just wanted to be around her. She was popular, carefree, happy but never content, always thinking of ways to entertain. The more bored she became the more trouble she could get into. The mastermind of the senior prank, it was legendary.

The aftermath of the Flamingo incident, as it was referred to, surprised Ann as much as anyone. Ann watched the truck for hours, no one claimed it. Piled high in the bed of the truck were plastic pink flamingos, the kind attached to a wire rod. To her, they had no choice. Bruno, her boyfriend at the time, coordinated the pick-up at midnight. They transferred the flamingos from the truck outside of JC's garage to Bruno's. Transporting them to the first hole of Bingham Country Club's award-winning course and strategically placed them between the tee and the green. It was, by Bingham High School standards, one of the best pranks in history. Unfortunately, the neighboring jewelry store caught everything on camera. To make matters worse and unbeknownst to Ann and company, The Bingham Charitable Tournament was to begin at seven that morning. The tournament was delayed a full two hours as greens keepers and volunteers painstakingly removed the flamingos and flattened the divots. An angry truck driver threatened to file charges, VIP's and highbrow Bingham Country Clubbers swore punishment to the fullest extent. Ann escaped with com-

munity service at the nursing home. Nancy was morti-
fied and went to her room and wept. Stuart gave a slight
reprimand while turning his face and clearing his throat.

Ann tried to sleep in Saturday morning but couldn't
ignore the familiar sounds from the kitchen beckoning
her. There would be bacon, eggs, toast, possibly a box of
donuts, all enticing and all the last things she needed,
having returned to Bingham out of shape and a few pounds
heavier. Food had become her go-to comfort and despite
early morning runs her waist stubbornly stayed. In yoga
pants and long t-shirt, she sat at the bar nibbling a piece
of bacon.

Her mother entered pulling her hair back in a barrette
wearing her work posture. "I'm going in this morning for
a few hours, Josh Bingham is getting married at two and I
have to get the flowers there by noon."

"Do you need help?" Ann had no idea why she asked,
it felt as if someone standing behind her said it. She was
tempted to turn and look. By the look on Nancy's face, she
was just as shocked.

"Yes, that would be nice, if you wouldn't mind." She
responded suspiciously.

Nancy Fletcher uncomplicated and keeping things simple,
named her shop, The Flower Shop. It smelled the same, a
mixture of carnations, roses, and lilies with an underlying
dampness. Her mother was at work on the groomsmen's bou-
tonnieres. A simple white rose surrounded by baby's breath;
the stem wrapped in a fine, thin ribbon. Ann looked around;
there were vases full of white lilies, with some white roses
mixed in, just the right amount of green and baby's breath
subtly spread throughout—simple but elegant. There was a
reason her mother did every wedding in town.

"What should I do?"

Nancy looked up and thought a moment, "These need a box, a medium one in the back, and grab some green tissue paper." Ann returned. "Could you also put together an arrangement in that small vase over there? Some of the more colorful lilies maybe the stargazers, some white carnations, and yellow daisies maybe...just get creative."

Bewildered Ann went about gathering the arrangement; her mother had never trusted her to put together a simple bouquet let alone something larger. She worked a full fifteen minutes without looking up, poking flowers here and there pulling out and cutting stems and putting them back in. It was intense labor. Her mother's praise broke her concentration.

"That's very pretty; you have a knack".

Ann examined the colors and then looked at the wedding flowers. There was something amiss. "Does this go to the wedding too?"

"No, no that goes to the nursing home." Nancy checked a list near the cash register. "That is for Mrs. Lindhorst. Will you bring it to her? But first I would love it if you went next door and got me a coffee; you know how I like it. Get one for yourself too."

Ann left the shop in a daze. The hour in the shop with her mother left her wondering at the lack of criticism. Where was the confrontation, the dig, the 'wasting your life speech'? Atypical of their relationship, it was not surprising Ann felt discomfort mingled with relief. The possibility of change was not wholly unthinkable, her mother had been known to back away in the past, but it was never for long periods and today would have been opportune for Nancy to unleash. Volunteering today, Ann assumed the matter would be done and behind them but instead, she made a flower arrangement to her mother's satisfaction.

Level Grounds was right next to The Flower Shop. When she opened the door the smell alone brought pleasure that extended to the other senses. Coffee, the only thing she and Nancy had in common. They both loved it with a generous amount of half and half and sometimes sugar. She ran her fingers over the display of old-fashioned coffee tins and took in the hip but casual décor; an earth-toned couch layered with colorful, throw pillows and two overstuffed chairs sat at one end with a coffee table full of books in the middle. A beautifully framed photo of a mountain surrounded by mist hung above the couch. Some framed vintage photos were placed throughout with some eclectic signs about the sublime joy of coffee. An old coffee grinder with a handle sat on the counter where orders are taken.

There was a jar, the type known to plead for funds for some unfortunate. Taped over the front was a picture of a beautiful dark-skinned girl with sorrowful yet inquisitive eyes and long wavy hair. *"Proceeds go to Sarah's medical expenses."* She ran her hand over the picture gently; Rachel filled her in a little more on the beating. Sarah was in an ICU in St. Charles and had not awakened yet. There were no leads. Justice moved slowly in Bingham and this proved to be a challenge for the local police. The Fletchers were friends with Mike Reynolds, her father played golf with him occasionally. It had always seemed to Ann that he wasn't all that interested in his position, particularly when she had past run-ins with him. The girl stared up at Ann with a pleading look making her skin turn to bumps. Seeing her face made the crime all the more real and caused anger to well up. Ann looked away and around the coffee shop for signs of life.

The front of the shop was empty so Ann perused the menu and decided on her and Nancy's usual. Minutes ticked by; she craned her neck to look in the backroom and with impatience yelled, "Hello?" It sounded as if a box dropped and there was a slight groan.

"Be right there," he came out from the dark doorway, tall, broad-shouldered, wearing a blue t-shirt covered with a white apron, hair un-kept and un-parted with a slight wave, it was brown, his eyes blue. Ann looked away and pretended to read the menu.

"Hi, how can I help you? Sorry about that." He waved in the direction of the back room. "I'm short of help, didn't hear you come in."

Ann ordered two coffees with enough room for a generous helping of half and half. The barista smiled broadly.

"I only have one customer who orders that way and you look a little like her. You must be Nancy's daughter; I heard you were coming home."

"Yes, I am," Ann couldn't tame her smile. "I'm Ann."

"Oh," he looked perplexed. "I thought…"

Before he finished, she clarified, "Fannie is a nickname."

"I'm Ben, pleased to meet you."

"You're short of help?" She wondered if he would give her a job, one day in The Flower Shop was okay but she couldn't see working with her mother indefinitely.

Ben looked down and tightened the string on his apron. "I have help, she just has…well, there has been a horrible acci…not accident. She was a victim of a crime." He nodded toward the jar.

"Sarah Strong? Yes, I am sorry to hear that. How is she?"

"Still in ICU, I went down there last night, still unconscious. Joe, her Dad, hasn't left her side. He is taking it pretty hard. I'm doing what I can." He turned and poured two cups. "Law enforcement around here doesn't seem to think it's an urgent matter."

"You have no idea if she had any enemies, an old boy-friend maybe?" Ann again reminded of John—winced on the inside.

"No, if you knew her you could not have even asked. She didn't…" He seemed as if he wanted to finish with something but thought better of it. "Did you know her?" His voice went considerably softer.

Ann shook her head.

"She was very much liked, a kind kid, worked hard here, always got good tips, went to school, and took care of her dad. He had Sarah when he was older." He put two coffees in front of Ann, "Enough room for half and half, it's over there." He waved to a table full of carafes and everything necessary to make a specialized coffee.

"So, was she on her way home from here when the attack happened?"

"No, she had the night off. She was at the game and I guess she and some friends hung out after, down here on Main. They said she took off on her bike around eleven. Reynolds found her around midnight. Her friends deny anything odd or suspicious happening."

"Can't believe a thing like that would happen here in Bingham," Ann turned to say goodbye.

Ben's expression hard and mysterious softened when he caught her eye. "Yeah, hard to believe," he said barely audible.

Nancy thanked Ann for the coffee and took a grateful gulp. "The card is finished and this is ready to go. If you want, you can help me load the van for the wedding, and then you can take this beautiful arrangement you made to Mrs. Lindhorst."

The nursing home hadn't changed since she did her mandatory service which consisted of reading to the residence and getting them coffee. The girl at the desk pointed to Mrs. Lindhorst, who was sitting by herself near the piano. Her mother gave her strict instructions to personally give the flowers to only her. The old woman hardly noticed the approaching Ann until she was almost in front of her. Looking up slowly; a smile spread across her face as she reached for the flowers. "What's this?" she whispered.

"For you," Ann said surprised at the pleasure she felt from the whole experience.

"Will you read the card? I don't have my glasses."

*"Dear Mrs. Lindhorst, Thank you for being kind and always doing for others. You are very much loved and appreciated."* Ann turned the card over, "There is no signature, I'm sorry. I don't know who sent them."

The old woman's eyes beamed. It didn't matter. An aide arrived to wheel her to lunch. "Would you like me to put those in your room, Mrs. Lindhorst?"

"Oh, no, I'll keep them with me all day."

Her mother returned home after Ann, the house empty except for the two of them; Stuart at his weekly golf game and Rachel with her future in-laws on wedding business.

"I put in a pizza for lunch, you want some?" Ann watched her mother put her things away, tidy the kitchen, and wipe the breakfast crumbs. Nancy nodded yes to the pizza and began emptying the dishwasher. *Idle hands…,* Ann was reminded of the old proverb she heard growing up. Ann rarely remembered her mom sitting still at home, one of the things that annoyed her. Where was the fun in constantly doing housework? Old judgments and resentments surfaced regarding her mother's expectations about what Ann should be. Ann wondered if Nancy ever actually enjoyed herself, it seemed she had today working at the shop. Ann had too, come to think of it. Almost twenty-four hours home and no criticism or questions about her life; Ann wished it done and over with.

That she was a disappointment to Nancy was no secret, so why did she want the reminder? Maybe Nancy would let her be, something Ann found unbelievable. She hadn't let her be any time she left the house in clothing Nancy disliked or whenever she failed to turn in homework or when she had a date with Bruno. And Ann knew she would never hear the end of it when she decided to quit school. That's why she waited until the day before she left for Colorado to tell her parents. Amidst the yelling and screaming, her father just stood there, hurt and dazed. As she pulled out of the driveway the next day, tears rolled down his face. Her mother stood in the upstairs window with a look of hopelessness. Could it be possible Nancy had given up on her? Ann doubted it, however, Nancy seemed different. The desperation to set Ann straight had not shown in her brow as it had before. Her demeanor calm, Ann wondered what this meant and how long it would be before things fell apart.

The pizza was typical frozen fare. Ann regretted the third piece. Shoving the paper plate away, she studied her mother. There were some gray strands in her hair that hadn't been there before, no doubt her fault. The silence between them was unnerving. She wasn't used to it. If there was to be no confrontation or questioning there had to be something to talk about. Ann searched for a topic, thinking of Sarah's picture on the jar at Level Grounds.

"So, this Sarah Strong What do you know about her?"

Nancy looked up thoughtfully, "I only knew her from the coffee shop. She has lived here for most of her life with her father, Joe. You remember Joe…used to mow lawns over here and he has a regular job at the golf course. He is a little slow, some kind of accident, I think. Anyway, his wife left them, she wasn't from here," her mother clarified as if a Bingham woman would not leave her child, " It's been just the two of them…he must be beside himself, I'm sure. No one really knows what happened. Mike found her, said her bike was parked in the middle of the road, not lying down but up balanced on the kickstand as if someone put it there. He suspects Quigley. He lives in the glass factory, well I should say lived, he was gone the night it happened. Mike has been looking for him since."

"Do you think Quigley did it?" Ann felt a flush of guilt. She knew Quigley lived on the top floor of the glass factory. She and her friends used to throw rocks at the windows to see if they could get a glimpse of him. Childish pranks, Ann never thinking of the harm of disturbing an already disturbed man's peace. She felt it keenly now with regret.

"Oh, no, you know Quigley is harmless. But if he saw something it would be like him to run away. Anyway, she is still unconscious with a fractured skull, has multiple bruises and a broken bone, her wrist I think, not sure what. They did surgery on her head to relieve the swelling. It will take weeks, maybe more, to recover if and when she does wake up. I cannot imagine that kind of hatred…" Her mother's voice faded. "Are you finished?" She began clearing before Ann could answer.

# CHAPTER 4

James Johnson peeled off from the crowd, ran through the overgrowth, and walked to school on 'the wrong side of the road', according to his grandmother.

"You cross at the crosswalk with the other children," she shouted to him as he walked out the door. James knew he would disobey so he pretended not to hear. Walking slowly, looking down every step of the way, he made his way across the old glass factory parking lot. Looking, as usual, for treasure lost and forgotten. James already covered Lang's Grocery parking lot and hadn't been this side of the road for a while; not since poor Sarah. His Gran had an uncanny knack of knowing when he had an idea in his head, she knew this morning. James smiled thinking of it.

His eyes scanned as he walked and listened to the shouts and laughter of his friends across the road, taking the usual route to the elementary school. The Bingham School Board cut bus service to anyone within a mile of the school, so, most town kids walked. A crosswalk from Sutter's Grove Drive was installed to reach the sidewalk in front of Lang's Grocery. This stretched to the school and beyond to Church Street then turned onto Main. It was as safe as any place for children to walk to school. Every day a volunteer grown-up would cross with the children and watch them until they arrived. Today it was Edgar Ditch. James knew Edgar would not pay any attention and his best opportunity would be today to walk on the other side of Seventy-Nine. He hoped to scan the outskirts of the high school football field too. Once he found an unopened box of gum, the kind that comes in the plastic-looking cup. He was careful not to let Gran see it for fear she would throw it away.

James stopped at the place they found Sarah, he knew because he watched the sheriff and his deputy Karl search the area the day after it happened. They spent a whole ten minutes going over it. James, who watched his share of crime stories, waited for the yellow tape to go up and for a photographer to come and take pictures. None of that happened and he was highly disappointed. They gave a cursory look and left. Sketchy police work even to a nine-year-old. So, James thought he would conduct his own investigation as he passed on the way to school. There would not be much time; James searched for footprints in the gravel or signs of a scuffle and spotted some broken weeds. He looked down and saw the blood, it seemed like a lot to him. His grandmother told him Sarah was still asleep. They prayed every night she would wake up. James looked around for a weapon, that's what they did on the crime shows. He walked in outward circles around the place where the blood was. He was out about five feet when he noticed something glittering in the morning sun; he moved closer, it seemed as if the sun was pointing it out to him.

James didn't know what real gold looked like but he was pretty sure this was it. Prepared as any young detective, he used the clean tissue in his pocket his grandmother placed there that morning and fished a plastic sandwich bag out of his other pocket; he picked it up with great care. A gold clip, stuck in the ground as if someone had stepped on it, he pulled it up and to his surprise it held money. James gingerly used his tissue to examine the treasure. He counted twice; there were three one-hundred-dollar bills. Looking around, he could hardly believe his luck. No one would believe him but he couldn't give his secret away. This was a crime scene. He should bring this to the sheriff, but then again, who would believe a kid, and besides, he wasn't supposed to be there. And he reasoned, if the sheriff had done his job, he would have found it and maybe, someone dropped it after the beating. The boy stood alone in the parking lot arguing with his conscience. He looked around one last time. He thought he might go closer to the factory; he dropped his treasure in his backpack. The booming voice of Edgar Ditch stopped him. The boy turned, crossed the road, and ran to school.

"Ann." Nancy raised her voice, "Ann! Don't you need to be next door?"

Ann looked at her phone. "Yes, I'm not finished, sorry."

"It's beautiful," her mother walked around the bright, alstroemeria arrangement. Ann used every color in the cooler. "It just needs this bow and it's ready. I'll bring it this week."

Ann looked suspiciously at her mother, grabbed her bag, and left. As she donned her white apron emblazoned with Level Grounds across the front, she pondered the weekly trips to the nursing home. This would be the third Saturday since she had been home, last week it was Ida Wesley, again with a card and no signature. The arrangements were mid-price but giving every week would be about two hundred dollars a month, by Ann's calculations. It was a curious situation and Nancy never expounded on it, avoiding Ann's questions with vague answers. The past two weeks working part-time with her mother Ann had a change in attitude. It was a transformed relationship; nothing was mentioned about her future plans or any questions about her time in Colorado. Ann's communication with Rachel was still selective even after their conversation her first night home. Ann suspected what little she told her sister was passed onto their mother but Nancy uncharacteristically kept silent on the matter. Ben hired her a few days after they met; so far, they were a good team. Ann was not a novice in the service industry and able to start with little training.

"How are you today?" He grinned, handing her a carton of half and half.

She filled the pitcher and began her daily routine which involved frozen cookie dough.

"Why don't you let me bake something real instead of this frozen stuff?"

"I will, I told you we gotta use it up first, I bought too much last time. My budget for desserts this month is spent."

Ann had been hinting at baking something from scratch. Working alongside some talented chefs in Colorado, she gleaned some skills of her own. The way Ben smiled at her when she spoke of some of her ideas gave her confidence; she would soon determine the menu. He told her a change was due. The frozen cookie dough had run its course. Only a few loyal customers left with a cookie and a cup of coffee. Ann knew her smile already had a lot of pull with Ben so she bided her time and would pop something in the oven within the week and that would be it. She would determine the menu going forward. He already let her do most of the ordering. She had changed up some of the décor and rear-ranged the prep area to be more efficient. Complimenting her with every change, Ann kept herself guarded just in case he was impressed with more than her work.

Sarah, of course, would return to her job as soon as she was able. Ann understood that. The latest news was she had not awakened but there was brain activity and her broken bone had been set and was healing. Sarah's father stayed at her side. There were no other relatives; her mother had been gone long enough that there was doubt as to what name she used now. Joe was there for Sarah as he had always been and nothing would keep him from her now. Bingham Country Club would hold his job and neighbors would take care of his home. All of Bingham was pulling for her; there were jars like the one at Level Grounds on every counter and prayers said in every denomination on Sundays.

"Have you been busy?" Ann kept things as platonic as possible. Her instant attraction to Ben surprised her, especially so soon after John. Telling herself it was a child-ish crush; she was close to believing it. Their conversation remained in the area of the mundane, Ann avoiding any personal subjects. Ben must have taken the hint and never pried or offered up a history on himself. It would have been easy for Ann to flirt which was second nature for her especially with someone she liked. Nothing dramatic or overly obvious, just a little fun. If she needed heavy lifting in the past, she could rally a few guys with a smile and a good pasta. Most were just friends, other than Bruno—from high school—and John there had been no serious relationships.

Ben struck her as different from most men she knew. Behind his contagious smile and light attempt at humor, was a serious, solemn side with—what seemed like—wisdom beyond his years. Rachel mentioned a military past and growing up in New York City. Bingham was very different from both. He managed Level Grounds with precision, had a happy clientele, and made a success of the place in a few years. Yet, Ann noticed a brewing restlessness. Between fixing a broken oven and cleaning out the sink drain, Ann caught him deep in thought, staring out the front window onto the street but not really seeing Bingham. His mind elsewhere, Ann took advantage of studying his profile. Undeniably handsome, he had a firm jaw, just the right size nose and waves of brown hair cut short above the collar and ears.

The fact they worked so well together made things easy and at this time Ann needed easy. Her experience in the hospitality industry was a bonus; from the kitchen to the front desk, Ann learned it all. Working under some of the best chefs, always paying attention to detail. Staying for three years in Colorado had not been the original plan. Finishing her education out there had been. It never seemed convenient; interfering with weekend trips, parties, and hanging out. Instead, she waited tables, was a sous chef, and even cleaned rooms. There was also a lot of biking, hiking, rafting, and skiing, never saving a dime, spending what she made on the toys that accompanied these activities. Her friendships were temporary much of the time, Colorado was a transient place. Josie, her employers' daughter, was her constant friend those three years. She left shortly after Ann, taking a job in California. There was nothing left there and the situation with John was reason enough to leave. Regretting no plan B, she was stuck in Bingham for a while.

Sheriff Reynolds appeared for his daily coffee. Ann watched Ben wait on him, double espresso with cream. He would be working the night shift. Ben asked if there were any leads, *No*; the sheriff replied unfazed and to Ann's notion a little unfeeling. Ben pushed, were there any clues found at the scene? *No.* Any witnesses come forward? *No.* Any evidence on her bike? *No.* Ann's frustration mirrored Bens'. He slammed the cash drawer shut a little louder than usual, thanked the sheriff roughly, and walked to the back room. Ann followed.

"He has been sheriff since I was a kid," she offered.

"This town would do better to fire him."

He ran his hand through his hair and held it there a moment. His bicep, noticed by Ann, had a small tattoo she couldn't make out.

"How does someone attack a young girl in a town this size and no one notices?"

Since her return, the crime occupied a good part of Ann's thoughts. Growing up roaming the streets and bluffs around Bingham, it had never occurred to her to be afraid or look over her shoulder. The thought that Bingham, in its cocoon-like rural existence protected from the rest of the world, was becoming vulnerable to outside criminal elements disturbed her. The sheriff's behavior struck her as odd. He had aged since her departure three years ago. There were rumors he and his wife had their share of trouble, but the old Sheriff Reynolds would not have been so indifferent.

"Did you know Quigley lived in the old glass factory?"

Ben looked shocked. "How come he always wondered over to the park when he left here? I always figured he lived over there."

"He used to long ago but he moved up to the factory after they closed the antique mall. Not too many people paid attention to Quigley. But I saw him sneak in the back a few times and knew he lived there. There are people in town who keep track of him, leave baskets at Christmas and Thanksgiving, that kind of stuff. I heard he is missing." Ann, uncomfortable with Ben's look, clarified, "Quigley wouldn't harm anyone, I'm sure of that."

"I didn't think so either, but why leave?"

"Obviously, he saw something and is too afraid to speak to anyone. I would think the sheriff would want to spend time finding Quigley."

"What about his deputy Karl Bruce? Is he good at his job?"

"Mike Reynolds won't let him near a case like this. My dad is a friend of the sheriff's, he said he will handle this himself." Ann, thinking of the factory again asked, "Have you been to the factory since this happened?"

"No, why?"

"Just wondering if there might be any clues left behind."

"You don't think Reynolds already went over the place?"

Ann answered with raised eyebrows, "Oh, I'm sure they went out there but maybe they missed something. You never know."

"Not much confidence in local law enforcement, huh?"

"Just saying, you never know, it's not a crime to snoop around is it?"

"Trespassing comes to mind," he smiled and watched her pull a tray of cookies from the oven.

Ann passed the crime scene several times since being home with a nagging sensation to stop and look around. She had not pursued it but now wondered if there could be something there.

Her morning run took her on the Bluff Trail, starting near the back of Bingham Place. The area where the grandest homes stood, with stately manicured yards overlooking the river. Just beyond their property lines lay the middle of the trail. Ann went south; taking her through the park behind Main Street. The morning sun rose over the river and boasted a breathtaking view. The trail ran behind Main out to the golf course. Ann exited the trail behind JC's, which was near the end of Main and across the street from Level Grounds. Crossing Main and proceeding up Church Street turning left on Seventy-Nine, she experienced a sharp stitch in her side and had to slow down. She was out of shape but determined. The middle and elementary schools were on her left and she glanced to see the kindergarteners were out and Rachel with them; her sister was tending a skinned knee and looked up in time to see Ann go by. The sisters waved. Passing the ball diamonds, she happened to look directly across the street, the factory was barren and empty as usual. Crossing at the Sutter's Grove crosswalk, she ran unnoticed into the overgrown parking lot.

Weeds were thick, the pavement barely visible. No idea where Sarah had been beaten or what she was even looking for, she combed the place near the road believing Sarah may have fallen there. Nothing but trash thrown from passing cars. Venturing further into the lot, she almost stumbled on a rock the size of a baseball. There were no other rocks in the lot and this one was not a typical Missouri rock. It resembled the smooth stones she used to see in Colorado streams. About two feet away there was a dark patch on the ground, it was blood. Ann knew head injuries bled a lot but this seemed excessive. There had been no rain in Bingham since her arrival; the blood was caked to the dry ground. *So, this is the spot,* Ann looked around and then up at the factory windows facing the street.

Quigley could have seen or heard something had he been standing at the window. To the left, Sutter's Grove Road lay on the other side of the trees. The road leads to Sutter's Mobile Home Park where Sarah lived with Joe. Had someone witnessed from there? If so, they probably would have known Sarah, called the police and stayed with her. Ann looked to the right, behind the row of shrubs, and overgrowth was the high school football field. Sarah's attack was on a Friday night; there would have been a game. Surely, the crime happened after everyone had gone home, well after ten.

Walking toward the shrubs, she noticed a worn path, not overly obvious but enough for one person to stoop through. She crouched through herself to the other side. Gym class was in full force and a group of freshmen was panting around the track with Coach yelling at the top of his lungs. Ann looked around on the ground, a few gum and candy wrappers and some empty beer cans. Whoever it was, he possibly could have escaped through the bushes. Sneaking back through, some rocks caught her eye. All the same size as the one she almost tripped on in the parking lot. They appeared to be the sort you would put in a landscaped area. Her gaze traveled the length of the hedgerow, the rocks were dispersed in a straight line for a few yards. Ann remembered coming here with Rachel and their mother when it was an antique mall. The area she crouched in now used to be a neatly landscaped island of shrubs and flowers. The rocks were part of the landscaping.

THE BEATING OF SARAH STRONG

Returning to the place where the rock lay two feet from the blood, she noticed the distance was as they say a 'stone's throw'. Someone could have thrown the rock. Maybe he threw the rock at Sarah to stop her from running. Or maybe it was the weapon used to beat Sarah. It was just a rock, Ann started to walk away, but something made her turn back. She bent to examine it, without touching it; she removed her light jacket, picked up the rock with it, and rolled it inside. Ann debated on whether she should throw it back where she found it; it seemed silly picking up a rock for evidence. Instead, she marked the spot with a discarded soda can and walked back to town.

Imogene Rhymes was entering data on the police computer, one of the monotonous duties of her day. She seldom went on patrol, even though she had been there fifteen years. Looking up at the sound of the door she exclaimed in her high pitched, southern voice, "Lord have mercy child, I heard you were back, Look at you?" Ann braced for the coming hug.

"How are you, Imogene?"

The thirty-something officer backed away to get a good look at Ann. Ann's fondness for Imogene cemented when she sat with her in the back of the patrol car on the Saturday of the flamingos. Sheriff Reynolds spoke with her dad in hushed tones outside the car while Imogene assured her all would be well.

"I'm good as I can be, child," she crooned in her singsong voice. Imogene grew up in the south, moved here after her education in criminology, and had done the most menial police work in Bingham since.

Last week in The Flower Shop Nancy was in a gossipy mood and filled Ann in on Imogene's unfortunate marriage to Baxter Rhymes, a useless man in the eyes of Nancy Fletcher, like all the Rhymes men. Nancy tried to warn her but Imogene was smitten. Not a month after the wedding Imogene caught him with another woman. Her heart broken, she filed for divorce with the proceeds of the refunded wedding gifts and gave him the boot. Ann noticed her name badge still said Rhymes instead of Boudreaux, her family name.

As if Imogene could read her mind she exclaimed, "I guess you heard about my short-lived marriage to Baxter! Your Mama warned me!" she drawled. "I should have listened. Baxter has a way about him, I kept the name, don't know why I want to attach myself to that man, but I just did keep the name. Now what about you, tell me everything you been doin' in Colorado."

Ann filled her in with tales of mountain views, crystal lakes, and white-water adventures until she felt Imogene was satisfied and could get to the question of the investigation. Showing her the rock, she explained her theory. Imogene handled the rock with latex gloves and placed it in an evidence bag. Carefully typing Ann's statement and thoughtfully listening, she answered Ann's questions about the investigation. Ann learned there were no leads or clues as to where Quigley had gone. Sheriff Reynolds had put the word out to all the surrounding counties. In answer to Ann's question about checking the caves, Imogene shook her head explaining there was a witness that saw him getting into a car outside of town.

"He's just gone, to be sure, child." Imogene lowered her head, "Poor Quigs," she whispered.

Ann felt the same. Quigley evoked sadness in the heart of all Bingham, an odd fixture in the landscape of town; he repelled gestures of help and shunned most people. They would help anyway, leaving essentials where they knew he would find them.

"So, you found a rock?" The corners of his mouth slightly raised.

Sensing his derision, she attempted an explanation, "It was in a very odd place, there were no others like it around and it lay near the place Sarah was. It very well could have been thrown from the bushes where more of the same kinds of rock were."

"You think it could have been the weapon?"

"Maybe, I don't know anything about criminal forensics, although, I have watched my share of forensic reality shows," she turned with a smile.

Ben's face was serious, "not sure," he said scratching his chin. "I've seen the x-ray of Sarah's head wound. The doctor believes she was hit with a fist or she may have been kicked. Not sure a rock would be consistent with her wound. And her wrist, the doctor thinks it was broken from a tight grip on her."

Ann cringed. "I guess it could have nothing to do with it, could just be from some random kid goofing around, but in that particular spot there was just the one and I don't know too many kids satisfied with just throwing one rock. I can't help but feel it is tied to Sarah somehow."

"When do the results come from the lab?"

"Possibly a week, Imogene had to wait for the sheriff to sign off on it. In the meantime, I may go snoop around inside the factory."

"You sure that's a good idea? I mean it is private property. Trespassing and all that…"

"I've seen how Quigley gets in; it won't be a problem."


SHERIFF MIKE REYNOLDS LOOKED AT THE BAGGED ROCK, "Fannie brought this in?"

"Yes, she thought it may have something to do with Sarah, maybe the weapon." Imogene continued. "It was in the parking lot, she said she marked the spot with a smashed Coke can she found in the ditch, she can show you where if you want."

"No, I don't want, she had no business going out to a crime scene and snooping around. That girl was always trouble." He shoved the bag aside and turned his attention to his hundred-plus emails.

Imogene, hand on her hip, exclaimed, "You didn't sign."

"I have no intention of signing; I'm not wasting time and taxpayer money on a random rock found in a parking lot. Tell Fannie Fletcher to mind her own business."

Imogene grabbed the bag and shot a look at the sheriff; her patience with this man was running thin.


THE DRESS FIT RACHEL LIKE A DREAM, "IT'S PERFECT," Nancy said with a satisfied look of having something accomplished.

Ann agreed, her sister looked like the cover of a wedding magazine. Glancing at her grandmothers sitting behind Rachel, she caught them each wiping a tear.

"Rachel, you will be the most beautiful bride. Connor is a lucky man." Both ladies glanced at each other, Millie continued, "I have always liked Connor, comes from a real good family."

Nana chimed in, "Very handsome, has the Wellington jaw, very strong. He'll be a very good husband. His mother's family was from Bingham, they moved to the city years ago, but I remember, a very good family."

Rachel rolled her eyes at Ann then looked at the two old ladies sitting side by side on a tufted bench across from the dressing room mirrors; each balanced their complimentary coffee on her lap smiling sweetly. She turned back to the mirror admiring the mostly satin dress with off the shoulder sleeves that stopped at the elbow. It had just enough lace on the bodice and skirt.

"I know what the two of you are trying to do," Rachel glared at them.

"We are sorry Rachel dear; it was a cruel thing to laugh at such a serious and beautiful moment, please forgive your old grandmothers." Nana moaned.

"Things were done differently in our day; we just aren't used to seeing it on display." Millie corrected her tone, "You know shared, as they say." She looked at Nana.

"I have already forgiven you but I hope you watch your words at my wedding. I'm afraid of what you might say to the Wellingtons since you like to speak whatever pops in your head."

Ann, surprised and happy at Rachel's boldness noticed an affronted look, especially in Millie's eyes. Millie started to speak but stopped at the touch of Nana's hand on her arm.

"Whatever you wish, Rachel, it's your day," Nana said with a sparkle in her eye.

Lunch was at a small café on Main in St. Charles. The Patio provided an excellent view of the Missouri River and the breeze was perfect enough to keep them comfortable under the afternoon sun. Ann ordered the fried chicken salad. Next week they would shop for bridesmaid dresses; that would be next week, today she would enjoy. Riding her bike or walking as her only mode of transportation, afforded her some indulgence. Ann heard her mother tell the server she would have a glass of white wine, she looked up in time to see her mother looking her way. Nancy winked and shrugged her shoulders. Nancy never indulged when Rachel and Ann were children and never before dinner. Millie and Nana split a cheeseburger and Rachel ordered the Cobb salad.

The conversation centered on the wedding. It would be the third Saturday in October; they had about five weeks and still no venue. Rachel assured Nancy she had narrowed it down to two places. The Top Floor was available and held a hundred and fifty and offered a great menu, the patio was available if the weather held and they could decorate with their own things. The country club was the second choice, but more expensive and the menu seemed 'stuffy' in Rachel's words. She assured Nancy they would decide by the weekend.

"Invitations should have already been sent," Nancy complained.

Rachel argued they would be out by the following week. Besides they had already sent 'save the dates' to everyone a while ago. Most of the guests were from Bingham. It was no big deal, Rachel persuaded.

Ann marveled at her sister's calm demeanor. Nancy took a large drink and picked at her salad.

Ann changed the subject, turning to Millie, she asked, "Millie, what do you know about Quigley?" Everyone in town knew him to be an eccentric recluse with an aversion to people yet he stayed his whole life, never roaming past the town limits. His sudden leaving would take a lot of courage and was an unlikely scenario. Ann felt there was more to it and could not get it out of her mind.

Millie swallowed and replied, "I believe he has some Wesley in him."

"Bingham," Nana popped a fry in her mouth as she interrupted.

"Wesley!" Millie glared. "I was friends with his oldest sister, we went to school together."

"His mother's people were Bingham," Nana insisted.

"Wesley, his mother's mother was a Wesley. Cotton was her grandfather." Millie looked hard at Nana.

"Cotton was a Bingham! Nana said sternly staring back at Millie. "Was her name Gertrude?" Nana asked with a mouth full of fries.

Millie lit up, "Yes, that was his oldest sister's name." She turned to Ann. "Quigley was always odd and avoided people at all costs. He rarely left the house except to go to school which he didn't do often. Back then they had truant officers who came around. They tried to get him into school but he usually only went the first few weeks and then disappeared. He was the youngest of six and was delivered at a small hospital outside of town; it's closed now. A nurse at his birth said the doctor was drunk and Quigley slipped from his hands. The nurse swore he landed on his head. Quigley's mother, I think her name was Pearl, was out of it. The doctor quickly picked him up, this is all according to the nurse you know, and he threatened her with losing her job. Oh, what was her name?" Millie took another bite, "Well anyway, it was her word against his so nothing ever came of it."

Nana added, "Quigley didn't walk until he was almost two and barely ever spoke a word until he was five; always afraid of people. His family, the Crawford's, were well off. They lived on your street in Bingham Place. That house the Millers live in now, I think."

"I remember once," Millie continued, "I was doing Gertrude's hair in her room; there was a dance that night. Quigley was no more than a toddler. He kept creeping in the room, he would look at me then to Gertrude, back out the door and slam it shut. You could hear him outside in the hall whimpering and crying. After a few times, I asked Gertrude what in the world was wrong with him. She told me; he was afraid, he was always afraid, had cried most of his life and wouldn't tolerate anyone but her mother and Gertrude. I asked if there was anything that helped. Gertrude said the only thing was being alone in the dark. Funny, most children hate the dark but Quigley felt safe in the dark. I'll never forget the terror on his little pale face. He was always pale; he never went outside. Years later, after I was married, I saw him slip down the bluffs behind JC's. He was only about thirteen years old. He started going there during the day. To the caves. Soon after, he just wandered around town and rarely went home. His parents had passed away, Gertrude tried to keep him with her and her husband but Quigley wouldn't have it. He's been on his own, like a ghost ever since." Millie lifted her arms and shrugged.

"Occasionally, Dr. Thomas Bingham, he's retired now, would get him to come in to be checked over. Quigley would go for groceries; which Dr. Thomas Bingham generously gave him." Millie looked at Nana who chimed in.

"Dr. Thomas Bingham was a good Christian man and felt it was his duty to care for all of Bingham."

Millie nodded in agreement.

Nana took over, "Quigley never left town his whole life. He's been a fixture here every day for as long as he's lived. There are people, his family mostly, who keep tabs on him. Did you know the Methodist preacher is his nephew?" Nana glanced at Millie who nodded, "Lowell's son. He brings him blankets and food and if Quigley hasn't been seen around, someone from the family checks on him." Nana plopped another fry in her mouth, "You mark my words, Quigley did not leave Bingham."

Ann had goosebumps. "How can you be sure, Nana?"

"I told you, he never set foot out of Bingham and he never will. He knows how to hide in plain sight and that chuckle headed sheriff will not find him. Not that he cares anyway."

"I have to agree, and Sheriff Reynolds only does his job when it matters to him." Millie said, "Sarah Strong doesn't have a rich daddy and she doesn't have an Uncle in Jeff City. Sheriff Reynolds wants out of Bingham and will do what he can to avoid any real work. His wife has been pressuring him to get a better job."

The conversation drifted back to the wedding and Rachel's assurances that the invitations were ready for printing except for the venue. Ann pictured a sad figure of a man, shuffling through town with his head down in tattered clothing. He always carried a little sack containing any treasure or sustenance he came across that day. How she treated him and looked at him with disdain as a child; it made her ashamed. *"Quigley, Quigley, smells like a pigley."* She chanted along with the rest of her friends. Her mother's voice interrupted her thoughts.

"Sarah is in a hospital not too far from here. Do you think we should order a sandwich and bring it over to Joe?"

As they exited the hospital elevator there was a commotion in the hall, a nurse and doctor ran toward a room.

Nancy stopped and grabbed Nana's arm. "That's Sarah's room."

The group approached cautiously and stopped outside the opened door. The doctor leaned over Sarah, talking so low they could not hear him. Joe stood back in a corner rocking from one foot to the other craning his neck toward his daughter. Ann could barely see through a gap between the nurse and doctor. There was movement. A hand lifted off the bed. Sarah moved. The doctor spoke louder, asking Sarah to move her hand again, she did, next, it was her foot, Sarah obeyed again; next, he asked her if she understood what he was saying, a slow nod confirmed. The exam went on for a long time and no one noticed the small crowd of women outside the door. Two gray heads bowed in murmured prayer; Ann looked on trying to glean every morsel of progress. Rachel and her mother held hands. Finally, Joe noticing them stepped out, tears in his eyes, he fell into a shocked Nancy's arms. She held onto him, they all gathered—arms surrounding him, thanks to God traveling upward.

Rachel texted Connor as they left with the news. Ann knew when they reached home, most of the town would know Sarah Strong was awake.

It was dusk when Ann got to the factory. Rachel went straight to dinner with her future husband and Millie and Nana comfortably sat on the Fletcher couch watching an old *I Love Lucy* episode. Ann tried to sneak out unnoticed.

"Where are you off to?" Nancy poked her head from around the freezer door, a pound of frozen meat in her hand. "I was going to have you take my car and bring those two home. Your Dad and I have plans with the McCombs."

"I won't be long, just a quick run to lose some of that lunch." Ann closed the door behind her, ran up Bingham Place drive to Highway Seventy-Nine, dashed across the street, and went unnoticed to the back of the old factory. Moments later she was squeezing through the unhinged door, flashlight pointed down. If there was anything she hated it was rats. An old abandoned factory might be a haven for them. She glanced around for stairs. Quigley had managed to take the door off the stairwell, she was glad, not wanting to feel a door close behind her in this environment. The stairs creaked under her weight; the handrail pulled from the wall at one end rested on the bottom step and barely hung on at the other. It was the same on each floor. By the time she reached the fourth floor, the shadows of the night made visible a lone figure across the room.

*Could someone be here?* She backed in the stairwell, turned off the flashlight then started again. She moved toward a small room in the corner, keeping an eye on the shadowy figure, it seemed to be moving toward her; she started to turn and run but was now too afraid. Stopping, she waited. *This is ridiculous*, she thought. *I can outrun Quigley if it is him and if not, I'm sure it's just some kid or the sheriff.*

"Who's there?" she croaked. No answer, "Who's there?" Louder this time.

She could see a figure, who was it? Slowly, she walked toward them, holding her flashlight as a weapon. She planned to shine the light in their face, determine who it was, and run. The trespasser remained silent and was only a few feet away, walking toward her. She could feel her heart in her chest, *I should run.*

"Who are you?" she exclaimed in an agitated voice, still no answer. The flashlight felt heavy in her sweaty hands; she raised it to eye level and turned it on. The light glared back at her, she found herself staring into her own eyes.

Relieved, she doubled over and laughed. "You idiot," she said to her reflection.

It was evident that Quigley resided in this place for some time. The room was large, in one corner it appeared to be the remnants of an office—although it was missing a wall. Within it, there was a mattress covered neatly with a blanket—a pillow in the middle. An old table stood next to it. On top, a little statue of a duck with her ducklings, a child's picture book, and a plastic bottle of water. A plastic box filled with clothing and towels neatly folded stood in one corner, in the other, two winter coats were hanging on two old nails in the wall. Next to them, hung a picture of an ocean-scape with a ship sailing into the sunset. It appeared Quigley had been quite domesticated and comfortable.

The light outside was fading; Ann turned the flashlight to a small box beside the bed. It held a deck of cards, some marbles, a JC's Garage keychain with key attached, a Methodist prayer book, a pen, and a small spiral notebook. She examined the notebook; it was a journal of sorts. The handwriting was that of a small child, very elementary, there were scant entries and no dates, just random comments, and happenings. Shoving the notebook in her pocket, she went outside the room. Quigley had organized the remnants of the factory-mall into neat piles at one end of the fourth floor, there was a hole in the middle of the floor that Ann assumed he used as a trash shoot. Ann looked below with disgust; it was the kind of place rats gather. The sun had completely set and the darkness left Ann feeling desolate, she crept back down the stairwell and squeezed out the door. She ran home, glancing at her phone, realizing it had been an hour since she left. Millie and Nana would not be happy.

"Well, it's about time you got back. Your mother left us. We didn't know how we would get home." Millie groaned standing with effort, she held a hand out to Nana, who complained, "It's time for my pills!"

"Sorry Grans, I'll get you home before you know it!"

Ann contemplated pressing the two a little more about Quigley but the entire ride to the retirement home was full of complaints and grumbling about how neglected they were.

"It's so late, my feet are aching," Millie grumbled. "I'm usually in bed by now. And we missed dinner, well it's too late to eat anyway, it wouldn't agree this time of night. Next time Ann, you might think about our age…"

Ann kissed each one goodnight, and that was enough to bring a change in attitude. Nana pulled her close, "Glad you are home, Fannie."

Millie squeezed her face between her hands like she had when Ann was a child and kissed her forehead, "Don't leave us again for a long time."

Each holding Ann's hands, they both said in unison, "so much, so much, so much." It was the Fletcher way of saying 'I love you, followed by so much, three times.' To shorten, they sometimes just said the latter. Ann returned the phrase and blew them each a kiss as she walked out the door.

# CHAPTER 5

The notebook sat unattended while Ann waited on the morning rush customers; they had little patience, in a hurry for their long commute. The lone barista did what she could pouring and mixing espressos, caramel lattes, a tall black, and a few Frappuccinos. It finally settled to a couple in the back, laptops opened and a middle-aged woman reading a book in one of the overstuffed chairs. Ann carefully turned the pages of the notebook. Quigley had no dates to accompany his entries and whatever he wrote seemed very random. The language and writing were both childlike.

"*Tuesday, found a whole sandwich at the park*

*Friday Lowell's boy hollered for me but I didn't answer. He left a box of food*

*He keeps bringin can openers but I got me 4*

*Monday rained.*

*Wednesday that girl passed on her bike.*"

Ann wondered if the girl was Sarah. The journal went on

*T.B. Stoner*

with much the same for several pages and then another entry about Sarah.

*That girl with the bike gave me my coffee at Ben's place. She don't talk. I saw her argue with a man. Ben wasn't there. She didn't know I was watchin cause she left the back door open. He said mean things and raised his fist, a customer came in and he left.*

Arguing with a man? Ann wished there were a timeline. What man? Could he be the—one?

She flipped through the book and found more of the same entries until finally on the last page:

*That poor girl's been beat half to death, I got to go. the sheriff will get me. I got to go but I don't know where.*

This was evidence Quigley had seen something.

"Look at this," she handed Ben the notebook as soon as he walked through the door.

"What's this?"

Ann filled him in on her trip to the factory; telling him what her grandmothers said about Quigley and the sheriff. Working as she talked, her back turned to him most of the time. There was no response. She turned to see Ben standing with his head down studying the notebook.

"Do you see it? Quigley saw something and he felt he had to leave. He also mentioned a strange man. What do you make of it?"

Ben paced the floor without speaking. He scratched his chin and started to speak then looked again at the notebook.

"Have you shown this to anyone else?"

"No, just you. Why? I was going to bring it to Imogene later today."

Ben gripped the notebook a little tighter, "Do you mind not doing that quite yet?"

Ann thought it a strange request and said so. "Isn't that withholding evidence?"

"It is, but this isn't earth-shattering, Ann, most of the town knows Quigley is making himself scarce because he saw something and most likely put the bike in the road." Ben flipped through the notebook again, "I wish he had dates in here." He mumbled to himself.

"What?"

"Nothing," he started to pocket the notebook.

Ann reached to grab it, "Hey, wait a minute, I found this and would like to give it to Imogene." She barely touched it but he was too quick.

"Just wait!" His voice escalated and his gaze was stern.

Ann drew back, this was new and considering her relationship with John, unnerving.

Ben immediately softened and apologized. He moved toward Ann but she backed further away. "Sorry, just think it's a bad idea to turn this over to law enforcement just now. I have a reason; I can't go into it."

Ann stared suspiciously, *what reason and why can't he go into it?* Trust for Ben slipped away, he knew something and obviously was keeping it from her. "Why?"

"Why, what?"

"Can't you go into it?"

"Because right now it's just a hunch and I would like to sort it out before anyone knows about this."

"Does it have to do with the man Sarah was arguing

with?" Ann suddenly had a hunch also.

Ben turned and walked behind the counter, busying himself with the receipts. "It could, but I just can't say now. Would you mind cleaning the restrooms?"

Ann was shocked, since working for him; he had never asked her to do anything. This was his way of saying the conversation was over. Two choices were before her, she could walk down to the Municipal Building and confess all to the sheriff or she could clean the bathroom. If she went to the sheriff, he would accuse her of meddling and probably not believe her due to their past rocky relationship. She chose—for the moment—to trust Ben, there was passion in his eyes, nothing sinister, more like an earnest desire. A desire for the truth, possibly, Ann left it alone, for now.

The afternoon was all business; counters and floors gleamed. The bathroom sparkled like never before. Ann focused on her work to avoid Ben, stepping out to Maggie's Gifts to restock the soap with fancy, scented, foam dispensers. Ben avoided her too; when he was not waiting on a customer he was in the back at his desk. A familiar feeling gnawed at her gut, the same feeling she had with John before his true character revealed itself. It came and went; she now knew her internal alarms were sounding. Had she heeded the warning the last time, she may have escaped John before it was too late. But Ben, he seemed so different, so honest and upstanding. Disappointment weighed her down.

Her shift over, she folded her apron and said goodbye in a sharp tone. He nodded as he finished with a customer. Turning to look one last time as she walked out the door, he avoided her gaze. Closing the door, she suddenly felt very alone and confused about the character of Ben Fontana, someone she had grown to admire. Getting as far as her mother's shop, she sat on the bench in front of the decorated window.

The Apple Festival was right around the corner. Main Street was gearing up. Nancy's display reflected the event in tasteful fall wreaths and bright yellow and orange bouquets in the window. A bowl of red apples a bright contrast to the white background, fall leaves strewn about. Her mother had a knack; Ann's appreciation for her was a surprise. The last weeks working and living with her had opened her eyes to another side of Nancy Fletcher.

Stuart and Nancy bought the old building when Ann was in high school. Restoring it and making it a floral shop had been a family affair. The Fletchers worked side by side painting, building displays, and organizing merchandise. The night before The Flower Shop was to open; they were to meet at the Main Street Grill for dinner. The whole family, Nana and Millie too; a family celebration in honor of her mother. Ann never showed up. Her friends were having a bonfire. The following morning there were angry words between Ann and Nancy.

"What's the big deal," Ann remarked sarcastically, "I helped, didn't I, even when I didn't want to."

Nancy left for her first day in her new business with tears in her eyes. Ann dropped her head in her hands. Her personality had always been strong, stubborn, unfeeling, and impulsive. Never thinking about the feelings of others. Coming home had been different than she had imagined, the former restlessness gone. She found new peace with her family. Strangely, working with Ben and knowing him had changed her too. The look on his face as he gripped the notebook flashed through her mind. It bothered her more than she cared to admit. A chunk of his armor slipped; a side hidden—now exposed.

Ann's eyes traveled down Main. The stores were closing; Maggie was bringing in her signage and sweeping her storefront. The Café's open sign flickered and a few people meandered around the fountain at the Municipal Building. There was a crowd laughing as they walked to Top Floor and JC's beagle, Josephine, trotted down the street as if she owned the whole town. This street and the people, who stroll it every day, were the backdrop to Ann's life. She saw herself, a small child, holding her mother's hand as they came out of the post office one day. Quigley was walking toward them, "Who's that, Mom?"

"That's Quigley." Her Mother's grip tightened. "Don't go near him, okay?"

"Okay, Mom." That was her introduction to Quigley. She watched him from a distance whenever she went to town with her parents. One day with Millie outside the hardware store, Ann watched Quigley dig in the trash across the street while Millie spoke with a neighbor.

Walking away, Ann questioned Millie.

"You must never go too near him."

Six-year-old Ann's face betrayed her confusion and fear.

"He won't hurt you, child," Millie smiled down at her. "He's afraid of you. We do not disturb Quigley, ever. He's very private and we must respect that."

From that time, Ann kept an eye on him. Everyone knew him and everyone left him alone. If someone had an old coat or blanket, it was left on a park bench or behind Lang's Grocery, understood by everyone it was for Quigley. Once when the family picnicked on the bluff, Nancy slipped a sandwich and can of soda out of the basket and left it on a rock near a bench. Ann questioned her. She just smiled and said she saw Quigley earlier walking around. It was Bingham's way of taking care of their own. These memories flashed in her mind almost in a new way; she seemed to understand Quigley a little better. Millie understood Quigley—so did her mother. They were trying to teach Ann that everyone mattered. That lesson was lost to her in the teenage years when she chanted a taunt with the rest of the group behind a sad figure of a man shuffling through the streets of Bingham.

Tears stung her eyes as she thought of Quigley somewhere alone not unlike the toddler Millie described years ago. She thought of her mother, her first day in her shop with the memory of Ann's rejection and selfishness. She thought of Sarah fleeing from a mad man, afraid for her life and she thought of Ben. He had a secret, a secret worth hiding evidence from the police. A lump formed in her throat, disappointment in yet another man, she refused to let it get to her. As she rose to leave, Ben stuck his head out the coffee shop door.

"Will you come back in for a minute?"

They stood in the empty coffee shop. "I'm sorry," his attempt at apologizing seemed sincere; "I can't let you in on what I'm thinking just yet but I need you to trust me. I'm not wrong on this." Ben's eyes pleaded with her.

For some reason, she believed him but stayed guarded. Her expression still showing distrust. "How long do you think you will keep it?"

"Not sure, look, I'm going to the hospital to see Sarah. Will you come with me? I want you to meet her. Keeping this notebook has nothing to do with me and everything to do with her. Will you go?"

The evening was cool despite the almost 90-degree day. Ann was grateful she brought the sweatshirt. Ben, noticing her school logo, made small talk about college. It was neutral territory. His education was sporadic over the eight years he was in the military. Not much to tell, just night classes or online and a lot of homework. He asked her why she never finished.

"Because of Jane Austin," she said with a sly smile. "Do you know her?"

"Hasn't she been dead a few hundred years?"

"We were analyzing," Ann used air quotes, "Pride and Prejudice, in a lit class, by the way, it is one of my favorite books. Instead of discussing the depth of the characters, their personal prejudices of the time, and the incredible story and how it flowed together. How it unfolded, revealing each step of the two main character's revelations of their own flaws and how that affected their relationship, we talked about woman's issues. Well, I should say what is politically correct assumptions regarding women today and historically." Ann took a breath and continued, "How white European men have been oppressors for millennia, requiring women to be dependent on them through laws and cultural mores."

Ben kept silent; she noticed a shocked expression.

"I am not denying men have oppressed women throughout the ages, I take offense at only white men getting the blame. History proves it happened in every nation and race and still happens in China and the Middle East. But I digress; I just got tired of the politics and particularly the politics of my own sex. White man bad, everyone else good! My Dad is a white man and he has never done a thing to oppress me." Ann took another breath, "I went to school to study what I loved, literature, especially the classics. They offer so much," Ann lifted her hands, "life in them. You know?" She looked at Ben, who nodded and smiled. "Do you find all this amusing?"

"No, no, please go on, I just…there is just a lot of passion. It's great, what else?"

Ann checked her enthusiasm and continued, "I left the class and there was some kind of demonstration blocking the door to my statistics class," she looked at him to explain, "A required class, anyway the protest was against a professor who had the gall to fail a student for not following the assignment instructions. The student accused him of being a hater of diversity, racist, sexist, and someone who should be fired immediately. If the professor tried to defend his action, they shouted him down. I missed the class and that got me thinking. I looked around at the causes and ideology of most of my peers and just suddenly felt like I didn't belong. I wanted to learn, not form a new government, which is what they seemed to want." Ann drew a large breath, "TMI?"

Ben grinned at her, "No, not at all, I quite enjoyed it. So, what did your parents say when you told them you wanted to quit?

She cleared her throat, "I, um, actually didn't, tell them I mean, until the day before I took off for Colorado." Saying it aloud really sounded bad. "It was stupid, I know."

"Oh," Ben quiet for a moment continued, "So what does a literature major do in her spare time in Colorado?"

"The usual, skiing in winter, white water in summer, and some camping."

"Life's a party, huh?"

"Not always," Ann felt his glance and put a more responsible spin on it. "I did learn a lot about the hospitality industry. I worked in every capacity and by the end, I was the event and PR person for the resort. Unfortunately, my friend's dad had to sell." Ann looked around the Jeep Cherokee desiring to change the subject. It was an older model, well-worn but in good shape. "I had a Jeep, a Wrangler though."

"I know. I saw you in it."

"What? When?"

"The day you left town, apparently," Ben still grinning. "I was standing in front of Level Grounds with the sheriff, he was giving me the key and you drove by, packed to the gills. Reynolds said, 'There goes trouble'".

"He would," Ann smirked. "So, you moved in the day I moved out?"

"Yep."

"Why? What brought you here?"

"This is our exit, you wanna eat before or after?"

Sarah lay on her back sleeping. Her arm was in a cast, there was a large bandage on one side of her head, her face still slightly swollen with old bruises. She was very different from the girl in the picture on the counter at the coffee shop. Joe and Ben stood in the corner in hushed whispers. Ann stared at the small frame surrounded by stuffed animals and pillows. Half her head shaved under the bandage from surgery to relieve the swelling. There was some movement in Sarah's good arm, it slowly rose from the bed and then dropped from lack of strength. Ann also noticed a pained look on her face, almost a look of fear. Occasionally her head suddenly moved from one side to the next. It was obvious, something was going on in the girl's mind; she was seeing something or someone and possibly reliving her nightmare. Ann reached out and touched her good hand. Sarah jumped a little, reached back, and calmed down with Ann's hand in hers.

Joe stepped over and introduced himself to Ann, who acknowledged knowing him from his lawn care days in her neighborhood and though she did not say so, she remembered it was him, who cleaned up most of her mess on the golf course years ago. They settled in around Sarah's bed and were caught up on her progress.

Joe reported she was alert mostly in the morning and had stood with help twice this week. Every day, someone came to test her reflexes and abilities.

"She passes all the tests," Joe exclaimed with pride. "They did more scans again too and said there ain't hardly any more swellin in her brain. Doc says there's no reason she shouldn't be more alert, says it probably be some days but he thinks she doesn't want to wake up maybe cause o' the pain. She spoke a little yesterday, asked for some ice cream." Joe grinned and looked at his daughter.

Ann continued holding her hand. "Mr. Strong, do you know anyone who could've done this?"

Joe blushed and turned to Ann, "You can call me Joe, nobody ever calls me Mr. Strong. I don't know who coulda done this. I know most of Sarah's friends, not the new ones from the community college, she took a class in the summer and just started her fall classes. She only went twice a week and rode down with Misty, her friend from Bingham school. Sarah doesn't have a car, just that old bike. I rack my brain to think who could do this." Joe's fists were clenched and tears welled in his eyes. "I think I could kill em if I knew, that's why the good Lord don't let me know, I'd kill em for sure." Joe lowered his head and released a sob.

Ben put his arm on his shoulder, the poor man wiped his eyes on his sleeves and looking up at Ann, randomly said, "I sure do thank your Mama for that sandwich the other day. First time I felt like eatin in a long time and here you all come with a sandwich. It was real good." His voice faded and he looked to the ground.

"Has the sheriff been up here, Joe?" Ben asked.

"One time," Joe looked at Ben. "I gave the doctor permission to tell him about her broken bones and stuff. He talked to the doctor and left, that was the next day after it happened. He ain't been back since. One time he called up here and asked after her, a nurse told me."

The three kept a silent vigil for a long while and then Joe asked no one in particular, "Anybody seen Quigley?"

"No," Ben and Ann replied in unison.

"He lives right there where it was, where that man beat my poor Sarah." Joe lowered his head. "I knew she was late coming home. Watched from the porch for a long time, then Karl Bruce came. I knew somethin was wrong."

Ann questioned, "Why do you say that man? Do you not believe it could have been Quigley?"

"No, Quigley, he's harmless. I told sheriff that, old Quigley wouldn't hurt my Sarah. I hoped he saw somethin, but old Quigley won't talk to no one. I've tried. 'Cept Sarah told me he talked to you sometimes, Ben. I couldn't believe it cause old Quigley; he hardly talks. I know if he saw somethin he wouldn't talk but I thought maybe he would talk to you, Ben—if he saw somethin." Joe rung his hands and looked into Ben's eyes pleading.

"Sorry Joe, he hasn't been around, but if he is, I will ask him." Ben glanced at Ann.

She understood the look and didn't mention the notebook. The man was suffering enough, why get his hopes up.

The three sat without speaking for a while. Ann occasionally noticed Ben occupied with something in the corner of the room near the small closet with Sarah's personal items. Joe sat at the foot of Sarah's bed rubbing her left foot. He mentioned something about instructions to keep her circulation going. Ben nonchalantly made his way to the corner. He engaged Joe in small talk as he went, Ann watched from the corner of her eye. He was up to something. Suddenly a hospital worker barged in with linens for the bathroom and all eyes turned in that direction. By the time Ann looked back at Ben he was standing with his hands in his pocket and remarked it was time to go.

A grateful Joe hugged them both as they left. He would sleep on the sofa in the room as he had for the last few weeks. They left with a promise of returning in a few days.

They were the only two in the restaurant. It was late and Ann was sorry she ordered the pasta. Three bites filled her and she pushed the plate away. Ben ate heartily and without thinking scooped up some of hers in the process.

"Sarah seemed agitated when we first got there, did you think?"

"I was just thinking the same thing. Almost as if she was afraid. I believe she remembers something or everything. I feel sure the intention was to kill her and the guy was interrupted, probably by Quigley. The bike standing in the middle of the road proves someone else was there. When a bad guy is chasing you, you don't take the time to get off your bike and put the kickstand down."

Ann watched him attack his burger. "And yet you won't speak about the mystery guy in the notebook…"

Ben stopped chewing and looked up, "There isn't a whole lot to tell. I have no idea who he is." He looked away from her gaze as he said it.

The lie was obvious. "Uh-huh..." she mumbled.

"You're going to have to trust me."

*Trust him?* She wanted to but she trusted John and look how that turned out. Ann picked at her pasta with her fork contemplating another bite. There were some physical similarities between John and Ben. Both tall, dark and handsome, Ben a little more so. His look more refined and cleaner cut, other than that Ben was different than John, in control but not controlling, kind, open and Ann believed until today, transparent.

When she backed away after he raised his voice, it was a reflex. John began with a raised voice and then it escalated to grabbing her arm and squeezing it until bruising surfaced. His fierce contorted face so close to hers she smelled the stale beer on his breath. Ann wondered why Ben would not think this stranger, who was angry at Sarah, was not relevant enough to tell the sheriff. She watched him eat, unaffected by the fact she was losing trust and respect for him by the minute.

There was small talk on the way home with long bouts of silence in between. The events of the day changed things. The car ride down, Ann had forgotten the notebook and his strange behavior, enjoying their conversation. Maybe his questions and indulging her to tell her life story was purposely done to distract her. Whatever it was, the moment was lost now. Ben was someone she had trusted and worked well with from the start. Though they had only known one another a short time, Ann felt there was a secret. It was silly, Ben certainly did not have to tell her everything but she knew there was more to this stranger than he was letting on. When she said goodnight, she caught something in his look. It was as if he wanted to tell her more but couldn't. Sleep escaped her that night, her thoughts raced between the picture of Sarah on the jar in the coffee shop to the Sarah lying bruised and broken in a hospital bed to the blood-stained ground in front of the factory, to a little man hobbling out of town.

IMOGENE RAN OUT OF MAGGIE'S GIFTS AND DOWN THE street after Ann. "The lab lifted prints off the rock." She exclaimed, breathless. "It wasn't easy but they got one good one. Rocks are porous, you know, and don't hold prints."

"They did? Whose?"

"Don't know, it takes so long to look in the database. I sent them Quigley's just in case."

"Quigley? Why? No one believes he could've…"

"I know," Imogene interrupted, "but Quigley could have thrown it to scare off whoever it was."

Ann looked shocked.

"Listen, Quigley has thrown a few rocks in his day and he never misses. Sheriff arrested him once for putting out that light," Imogene said pointing at the street light above their heads, "that's how I got the prints. Quigley used to pitch for the Methodists from time to time when he was a young man when he would show up that is. Some said they never saw anything like it, always in the strike zone. It was the only time Quigley came out around people; mind you he never spoke, went straight to the mound, and pitched. Well, being Quigley, he gave that up after a while. But if Quigley wanted to hit someone or something with a rock he could." Imogene gave her head a downward jerk to emphasize.

"Maybe, what does the sheriff say?"

Imogene glanced over her shoulder at the Municipal Building. "He doesn't know. I haven't told him."

Ann, perplexed, started to ask why.

"He wouldn't sign off on the rock. On a hunch, I sent it without a signature, no one noticed." Imogene smiled. "When he finds out, I'll plead innocent and say I must have absentmindedly stuck it in with some other evidence from another case. We just happened to have one."

Ann wished she was as pleased as Imogene, "What if they are Quigley's prints? Then he'll get blamed."

"I thought about it, there is no blood, hair or anything else on the rock, just prints. I bet my life if they turn out to be Quigley's it was him trying to defend that girl in his own way. He wouldn't stand back and watch a beating. He may not like people but he wouldn't do that." Imogene shook her head.

Maggie, from the gift shop, motioned for Imogene impatiently.

"Have to go, one of the kids bought a ten-dollar gift for his grandmother and paid Maggie with a hundred-dollar bill, Maggie thinks it's suspicious. He told her it was a birthday present from his uncle."

# CHAPTER 6

The dress was a little snug, but Ann convinced it would fit by the wedding, refused to try a larger size. Rachel chose a satin, rich, slate gray gown for her bridesmaids. Ann, the maid of honor, had an off the shoulder, neckline while the three other bridesmaids had capped sleeves. The dresses were form-fitting and while each bridesmaid was a different shape and size, they all wore it well. The day was long and exhausting. Ann knew Marissa, she was Rachel's best friend since grade school. She also knew Zoe, Connor's sister, who had the foresight to duck out when she could. Lauren, Rachel's roommate from college was new to Ann and exuberant and overly enthusiastic about the whole process. Everything was, 'awwwsome,' according to Lauren. From the dresses to the shoes to the little beads for their hair, each discovery met with the long drawn out 'awwwsome,' from Lauren usually followed with, 'oh Rachel, you are going to be so beautiful, I can't wait.'

Lauren's high-pitched enthusiasm ground Ann's nerves to their limit. She ordered a margarita and a plate of nachos at La Pachanga's.

Lauren voiced her warning, "Oh Ann, remember that dress was a little tight."

The server glanced at Ann for confirmation, she mouthed to him to make it a large instead. He nodded understanding. She had not checked her phone all day and wondered if Ben still needed her to work in the morning. There was a message, a number she did not recognize.

*Have been searching for you. I miss you and I WILL FIND YOU!*

Ann slammed her phone face down on the table. Rachel gave her a startled look.

"Have to work bright and early…darn."

The three girls went back to wedding planning. It was John—she knew it. She blocked his number but he must have used a different one. Ann chose the night before he left, to fight fires in California, to break up for good. Harry's Bar was the safest place to do it, crowded with his and her friends; she knew he would not make a scene. Sitting at a corner booth, Josie waiting a few feet away, she told him she never wanted to see him again. Making a quick exit, she escaped to a friend's apartment. It worked out well, she thought at the time. That was over a month ago. She should have changed her cell number. She blocked the number again and drank her margarita.

Ann mindlessly scrubbed the stain on the table for several minutes. Her mind had been on the text all day. It would not be unlike John to come after her. He was well-liked at the firehouse and she knew he had a lot of time off stored up. She could not remember ever mentioning Bingham but she had mentioned Missouri. Ann rarely used social media and after leaving Colorado stopped completely and closed all accounts. Fletcher was a common name, Ann Fletcher even more so. It would take some effort to find her and she was not sure, despite his threat, he would put forth the effort. This was how she reassured herself throughout the morning and afternoon. The morning was busy enough; she worked alone, while Ben ran errands. The afternoon, she spent cleaning and stocking—barely speaking to Ben; reflecting on her life. How she came to be in the situation with John troubled her heart and mind. Abusive boyfriends were for other women, not her.

Sure, she left the nightmare behind in Colorado. Living in anxiety and fear was not her thing. John's change in behavior was gradual, so Ann thought, but looking back there were signs. Like the gnawing in her gut after he drank too much or got too loud. Men like John, popular with friends and co-workers, make it very hard for women to leave them. They are careful to look like a hero in public. He sent flowers, complimented, and flattered her. He would make her feel like the most special woman and then if something irritated him, his voice rose. The escalated voice and swearing were how it began, over little things. Ann forgot to pick up his uniform from the cleaners once, or she overcooked a steak. These few times made her question the relationship, then the evening she had to cancel their date; she was informed that women did not cancel on him. Even though she thought the conversation was odd, she half thought he was joking when she hung up. When he was waiting for her at her apartment that night, she knew they could not go on. The angry words had put her on alert, but waiting for her and subsequently pushing his way in her apartment, swearing, and punching a hole in the wall, she realized she had to get out.

When he calmed down, Ann tried to explain she couldn't see him anymore, he wouldn't hear it. He kept showing up but she would make sure Josie was there with her. He apologized for his outbursts and swore it wouldn't happen again. Ann never trusted him again and could not make him see it was over. Relief came a week later when he left for an assignment and was gone two weeks; Ann communicated as little as possible. Her texts were short answers, avoiding any intimate conversation. He came home angry, refusing to let her go. In the meantime, her jeep had broken down; she was growing dependent on others for rides and acquiesced to let him take her home one night.

It had been a big mistake. He expected to come in, in fact, pushed through the door. Grabbing her arm, he shook her, threw her against the wall, and raised his fist. It came down hard on the edge of the coffee table, her reflexes saved her. Running for the door, he grabbed her again; she stepped hard on his foot, kicked his knee, and made it to the neighbors.

Pounding on the door, she saw him coming after her, in desperation, she screamed and pounded harder. As John reached out for her again, her neighbor, an ex-marine about her dad's age, pulled her in behind him. He made sure John left and understood not to come back. Tears of remorse and apologies were left on her phone. He told her he had to leave town again and would come back a new man. It was the break she was looking for and she took it, breaking up at Harry's for the final time. She told him if he ever came near her again, she would call the police. She stayed away from home for two days, for safe measure—when she returned; her ex-marine neighbor said he called the cops on John because he thought he would break down her door. Ann knew she had no choice but to go home to Bingham.

Ann's vigorous effort on the stain was subconscious. She had not heard Ben ask, *'How'd the dress hunting go?'* from across the room. She had not noticed when he crossed to her and stood over her. He asked again at close range, Ann dropped her spray bottle on the floor and jumped back.

"Whoa, you okay?" He bent to pick it up.

"What?" she almost shouted. "Yes, why? Did you say something?" *Calm down.*

"I asked how the dress hunting went, the other day." Ben looked too closely; his hand extended to her but quickly went to his pocket.

She stared back; something in his face settled her heart and gave her peace. Like coming home and being in her father's arms. *What had he just asked? Something about a dress,* "Fine, Great." Her face relaxed and melted into a smile. "I need to stay away from carbs and run a little more, but I think it will fit by the wedding."

He motioned for her to sit down. "I think you've almost taken the finish off. You wanna talk about it?"

Sometimes when he spoke the New York accent was more prevalent than others. This time the accent was thick.

Ann sat, "Talk about what?"

"What's been on your mind all day; that's what."

She looked down at the stain. "I'm fine."

"It's up to you; I know somethin's been bothering you all day. I'll listen if you want."

Ann shifted; only Josie knew about John. She hadn't told anyone else; she was too embarrassed. Embarrassed at how easily it was to completely trust someone because he said the things you wanted to hear. John was like a dream at first. They met in the mountains on a group camp out. He came with a friend and sat down by her in front of the fire. His long curls touched the top of his collar, he smelled like pine and musk. She was tongue-tied and shy, which was uncommon for her. He mesmerized her when he spoke. Flattered by his attention, she was gone soon after that. What would Ben think if she told him she was worried an old flame may come find her? The kind of old flame that would hurt her, she could not believe, someone like her ended up in a relationship with someone like him. How many times had she judged other women in situations like hers? *The oppressive male! It struck a nerve—a very real problem.* She smiled at him. "I'm that transparent?"

He nodded. "I'm glad to help."

"I know you are, I just can't, not now."

"Understood," Ben got up. "By the way, I bought my outfit too."

"I didn't realize," she stopped herself. "I mean, that's nice."

"Yes, I'm invited too. Connor and I go back. Maybe you'll save me a dance." He winked and disappeared into the back room.

Rachel never mentioned Ben knew Connor but Ann never asked. Since her return home, her thoughts were mostly on herself. With wedding planning, it was easy to avoid any deep conversations so her secret had been safe. She intended to tell Rachel eventually but after the wedding. It wasn't as if Rachel and her mother hadn't suspected something. They whispered a lot, thinking Ann did not notice. The three of them navigated each day with a carefully orchestrated plan of behavior toward one another. Rachel's accusation, her first night home, about how Ann kept them guessing—was never mentioned again. Nancy was almost like a new mother. No picking, criticizing, or helpful suggestions came Ann's way. It was all to keep the peace, Ann suspected. Her mother, probably avoiding anything that would upset family cohesiveness. Secrets from her family were nothing new, sneaking in late and skipping school was commonplace in her past life. What her parents didn't know wouldn't hurt them, the problem was, they always found out somehow. Now she felt very alone, so alone a lump rose in her throat as she stared at the stain on the table unaware of Ben's watching.

He walked her home after closing up, she gave a half-hearted invitation to come in. He declined politely. He must have sensed her hesitation. She could only think of John and his threats. Talking to Rachel was her only answer.

Rachel was in her room wrapping a box. "Don't look!" her back turned to Ann. "I know that's you and I'm wrapping your present."

"My present?"

"Yes, for being in the wedding." She shoved the box in her drawer and cleared away the wrapping paper from the bed. "How are you?" Her look matched Ben's earlier.

"I've been better," Ann fell onto the bed and grabbed a pillow.

Rachel dropped beside her and waited. "I think you'll feel better if you talk about it."

"Ya think?" Admitting this thing with John, even to Rachel made her want to crawl away and hide.

"Yeah, I think," Rachel stared with those same eyes from childhood.

Ann rolled to her back; she did not want to look at her. She attempted to change the subject, "Why didn't you ever tell me Connor and Ben are friends?"

"You're not getting off that easy, you talk first and I'll tell you how they got to be friends."

"I did some pretty careless things the last three years in Colorado, well, my whole life. I met someone last spring and trusted him more than I should have. I thought I was free of the situation, but I'm not."

"It's that John isn't it?"

"How did you know?"

"The last time we talked—when you were away, I could tell someone was with you. I figured it was him. You seemed tense, not yourself. Did he hurt you?" Rachel sat up—the look of a mother bear in her eyes.

Ann kept her eyes on the ceiling. "Nothing earth-shattering as far as physically, a few bruises, I was too fast for him, it only took the once." Ann turned to Rachel for emphasis. She did not want her sister to think of her as Ann thought of others in the same situation. "I broke up with him in front of witnesses before he had to leave town, he fights wildfires, anyway, that's when I decided to come home, called Dad and started shipping stuff." Ann continued to tell her everything from the break up to the neighbor's protection—to the text the night they got their dresses.

"Do you think he'll follow you up here?"

"I don't know I've been racking my brain all day wondering if he would risk it. Bullies like that are really cowards, so if he knows my family is here would he dare come? I thought of changing my number but then Mom and Dad would want to know why I did. I'm so ashamed of myself for falling for such a jerk and for giving him… everything…" Ann's voice caught; her eyes still fixed on the ceiling. Her free spirit had always had its limit, a certain aspect of her life she kept guarded but when John came along her resolve ended. A precept from her upbringing, she had held dear—until John. That idea was soon discarded, her past convictions a distant memory. Her self-sufficiency and determined fortitude were the motivation behind much of what she did. Being in charge of her life, including sex, was her right and privilege. The situation with John now cast doubt on all that; her pride in always taking care of herself faded into humility. Relationships like the one with John happened to other women, not Ann.

There was no judgment and no condemnation from Rachel. She lay flat on her back next to her sister and took her hand. "What are you going to do now?"

"Not sure, keep on the look-out, I guess. I wish there were some way of knowing what he is up to."

"Seriously, Ann," Rachel propped up on an elbow, the crinkle above her nose appeared. "You should tell Mom and Dad."

"Before your wedding, like Mom could handle that stress; no."

"At least let me tell Connor, get a guy's perspective on it. Does he know you live in Bingham?"

"I can't remember if I ever mentioned it, I did tell him I was from around St. Louis. I turned off all my social media accounts before I came home." Ann heard her father's voice as Nancy and he entered. "Please don't mention this to them. I don't want this hanging over your wedding. Tell Connor, see what he has to say about it, but tell him not to tell anyone." Ben came to mind.

Stuart's voice traveled up the stairs with him, he was shouting something about his car. Her parents often communicated by shouting two rooms away. "JC will be back tomorrow; I'll take the car then."

"Are you going to be alright for now?" Rachel held onto

her hand as she stood.

"I am now, thanks for listening." Ann bent to kiss her forehead. "Don't tell anyone but Connor, I really don't want him knowing but since he is your fiancé…"

Rachel nodded and crossed her heart.

Ann crossed the hall to her father's office, "I'll take the car tomorrow if you're busy. I need to ask JC to look out for a clunker for me."

Stuart looked up from the mess on his desk, "A clunker? Are we that desperate Fannie?"

"Getting there," she smiled, "Besides I haven't seen him since I've been home."

"He's been on his annual fishing trip, got home today. It would help a lot if you dropped it off. Bob McComb is driving me to work and your mother has to go to the city, there is a shipment of roses coming from that vendor she likes." He searched his pockets. "Here's the key. Just tell him to check the sound coming from the engine, it's very obvious." His stare seemed to bore a hole in her heart. "Fannie? You okay?"

"Yes," she forced a smile. "I am."

"You're sure? It's just that you seem a little jittery for the last few days and you barely eat anything." Stuart's reading glasses slipped down his nose to the desk, but he kept his eyes on her face.

"Trying to lose a few before the wedding, I'm fine, don't worry." Ann gave him a cheerful smile and backed out of the room. Sharing with Rachel and her father's concern, formed a lump in her throat. They all meant more to her now than ever. Ann was awakening to something that had been an afterthought most of her life. This family, their love, she had taken for granted.

As Ann pulled the car into JC's lot, she noticed Ben slipping around the back of the building. For a moment, she thought he saw her, she raised her hand to wave but he was gone. Odd behavior again, JC was changing the oil on a Suburban when she walked in, "Hey JC."

"Is that Fannie Fletcher I hear?" JC turned with a broad smile; his gray coveralls grimy with grease. "Your daddy said you'd be by. How are you, little girl?"

Fannie climbed on the only clean stool in the shop and sat down, "Pretty good, got home a few weeks ago."

JC continued working, "Heard you're workin for Ben and your mama, how's that goin?"

"Not too bad, trying to save for another vehicle, if you come across a good clunker let me know."

JC laughed and peppered her with questions about the demise of her Jeep, said he could've fixed it, and chastised her for not keeping up on the proper maintenance.

Ann looked at the clock, her shift at Level Grounds started in five minutes. "Did I just see Ben sneak out of here?" She asked casually.

JC kept working, "Ben?"

"Yes, Ben."

"You sure you saw him? Had a battery salesman just leave, he coulda looked a little like Ben but I don't know."

Ann could tell JC was hiding Ben's visit, "Yeah maybe," she played along. "You ready for the festival?"

"Got four new bikes and I'll have a booth closer to the trail this year so that will help. Usually don't have enough bikes to go around but should be okay this year."

Ben was finishing a phone call when she walked in, she caught a 'see you there'. She nodded and went to the back to put on her apron. Sure, it was him leaving JC's, she debated on whether to say something. Before she could speak, he went over some new inventory for the Apple Festival and asked her to create one of her wonderful displays. She eyed him suspiciously as he gave her carte blanche with his credit card for supplies and told her to bake whatever she wanted. Starting to ask him about JC's, he blurted he had an appointment and darted out the door.

# CHAPTER 7

Connor Wellington waited in the back of Rigley's Bar, a dive in the middle of nowhere. He motioned for the server and held up two fingers. By the time she brought the bottles, Ben sat across from him. "So why are we meeting here? I had to drive fifteen minutes out of my way and I'm supposed to meet Rachel for dinner."

"Wanted to talk without Bingham listening."

"I think we're safe," Connor said with sarcasm, "What are we talking about?"

"This whole Sarah thing and Kasov," Ben whispered.

"You still think he had something to do with Sarah getting beat up?" Connor leaned in, "A mission four years ago, halfway across the world; it makes no sense. Why would he do that to Sarah, why not just go after you?"

Ben slid a piece of paper across the table. "It's the name he gave JC when he had his vehicle fixed."

"Davis Tremont. Are you sure this is him?"

"Kasov? Yes. Who else would it be?"

"JC's records show, Davis Tremont had a radiator hose repaired the day I saw Kasov with Sarah outside Level Grounds."

Connor leaned back and scratched his head. "So, you were never actually face to face with him?"

"Close enough, she stood outside with him for a while before they came in. I saw him through the window, they didn't see me. If I hadn't seen the scar under his left eye, I wouldn't have believed it. It was him and I know he was looking for me." Ben took a drink, "They came in, I listened for a while hiding in the back room."

"Do you think he was out for revenge or something?"

"What else, we cost him four years of his life."

"And you gave him a nice scar, how long was he there?"

"They talked for about ten minutes in Level Grounds, he tried to alter his accent. Kept looking around, as if he knew I was there. I'm sure Sarah wondered where I was, but she knows that I walk to the bank sometimes and leave the door unlocked. She yelled for me once but I stayed hidden. He seemed interested in meeting me, asked my name, and how long I had owned the place." Ben sat back and ran his hand through his hair. "He left; I was going to tail him but Sarah found me and started talking, I couldn't get away. When Sarah took a breath, I asked her to watch the place; I searched up and down Main and couldn't find him. He disappeared. It hadn't occurred to me to ask JC if he'd seen anything until later. That's when I found out about the Cadillac Escalade. Said the guy brought it in because it was overheating. He said it looked like the hose had been cut with a knife. It had to have been him, the date matches the day I saw him with Sarah." Ben slid the notebook across the table, "Quigley's."

Connor reading the part about the mystery man said, "You think it was Kasov?"

"Yeah, he came back again, we know now at least twice, I wasn't there, maybe he took it out on Sarah, I don't know."

"So, you think he kept in contact with Sarah after that first meeting?"

"Obviously," Ben held his head in his hand. "She talked about him. Said she met him on the Bluff Trail that day. He told her he was passing through and rented a bike from JC. He charmed her, I'm sure. I tried to act casual, asked if she gave him her number. She denied it. I made a joke about strange men on bikes. That was in June, the first time he showed up. I swear she never talked about him again. I thought he probably gave up on her and left her alone. I was stupid, I blame myself, I should have warned her. I just thought Sarah, I mean—she had no car and stayed close to home. I kept my eyes on her; nothing suspicious…I never thought he would do this…" Ben finished his beer.

"So, when did you tell Barone?" Connor asked.

Agent Linus Barone, served with Connor and Ben in the military. Now employed by the FBI in the St. Louis branch, Ben turned to him with the news of Kasov's being in the area.

"The day I saw Kasov, I reported it to him, he told me he had heard he was in country but didn't know he was in our area. They found an address in St. Louis and word on the street was—he was making money in guns. Barone thought Kasov didn't stick around; the address came up empty. That's why I thought something more important distracted him and he left." Ben pointed to the notebook, "Quigley didn't date anything in that book! It would've helped."

"Did you get her cell phone?"

Ben handed him the phone he lifted from the corner table in Sarah's room, he suspected Ann would have seen him if the housekeeper hadn't been a distraction. "If anyone can do this you can."

"Should be easy," Connor turned it on. "Password protected but that's no big deal. Can't believe you were able to find this; you would think Reynolds would've been on this." He slipped it in his pocket. "You don't want Barone taking a look?"

"Since I basically stole it, I don't think that would be wise, I figured we could find out as much as possible first. I let him in on Sarah's attack when it happened. He confirmed again that there had been no sign of Kasov in the area. I haven't told him anything about the notebook yet, we'll see what her phone turns up. As it is, I couldn't convince him to put protection on Sarah. Joe won't leave her side but we can't leave her alone much longer. If we can come up with something from the phone and with the notebook, maybe the bureau will give her some protection."

"How is she?"

"She recognized me, was sitting up in bed. Talking a little but with effort. With Joe there, I can't ask her anything. Not sure she can remember anyway."

The server caught Ben's eye and he held up two fingers. As he started to nod, Conner interrupted, "No more for me, I promised Rachel."

Ben got it. Sort of. It was a sacrificial kind of thing. Not something he would be willing to do. What was wrong with determining when it was time to stop on your own. Why should the woman in your life do that? The bar was a typical country dive. Supported by a clientele unconcerned with the number of beers they consumed.

He looked at Connor; his work had been indispensable on that mission. It was supposed to have been simple, in and out. Kasov and his cronies were not supposed to have been there, the mission was a rescue. A senator's niece, away at school in Italy, kidnapped. The investigation led deep into an organization widespread throughout Europe. Ben wanted to abort when he found out the targeted house was full of men but orders were to go forward with a rescue only. Just get in and get her out, it backfired, the house was just supposed to have the girls and low-level thugs. But VIP's of the crime cell were there, having a meeting. The mission lasted twenty minutes, during that time Ben found himself face to face with Kasov; he thought his tactical gear would hide his identity. The last shot he fired traveled across the left side of Kasov's face about a half-inch below his eye. Connor, cool as usual under pressure, guided them to the safety of the waiting helicopter. As they took off, Italy's version of SWAT, GIS, showed up. Kasov and company busted; there was enough evidence on sight to put them behind bars for years but there were also warrants in half a dozen countries.

"How'd he escape the Italians? Last I heard they were sending him to Romania."

"Barone's pretty sure he escaped during extradition; the Italians are keeping it hush-hush, embarrassed. He would've been a dead man if he got there—there were some in Romania very disappointed in the loss of income from the bust. That was about a year ago. He worked his way over here somehow, for revenge; I guess…We cost him, not only time in prison but a lucrative business. Most of the cell leadership was in that meeting and they all went to prison. Curia Regis, that was their name, fell into the hands of underlings, thugs that had no head for planning or doing business the old mob way. Barone said it had a ripple effect throughout Europe's underworld, sloppy deals and big mouths caused a lot more arrests." Ben stared out the window, reflecting on the mission, "You have to admit how bizarre the whole thing was, law enforcement collects Intel for months maybe years, goes undercover, solidifies evidence and in one night we bring down a notorious, well-organized group that half the countries in Europe were after."

"Means royal council or kings court," Connor said with authority.

"Huh?"

"Curia Regis, that's what it means, its Latin. We ticked off half of Europe; it should have been their bust. Italian law enforcement got the glory, in the end. It was perfect timing, in my opinion, all the evidence collected, we just did the leg work for them. If it hadn't been for that kidnapping..." Connor mused and then said, "Since we're using Latin, *sic erat in fatis.*"

Ben gave him raised eyebrows.

"Means it was destined or it was fated. My mom made us learn." He shrugged. "Everything happens for a reason."

Ben was doubtful, he could see no reason Sarah should suffer because of him, "I am sure Kasov was able to ID me. We were face to face; he even said something before I shot him. I can't be sure what the whole thing was, his accent was thick then. I did hear, *'this isn't over,'* or something to that effect." Ben sat back, "I blame myself; I could have protected Sarah. I should've finished him then."

"Why didn't you?"

"I had your voice in my ear screaming *'get out now,'* Donovan behind me screaming the same. I had a split second to turn and run or keep fighting, I ran. I could feel his bullets whiz by me. You know the rest, we got there, fought them off in time to lift off and the Italians showed up." The memory left them both wordless for a while, then Ben said, "I should've pried into her life, asked her more questions. She may have given something up."

"Where did you get this?" Connor waved the notebook.

Ben shifted and took a long drink of his beer, "Ann found it, she went snooping in Quigley's place."

"Did she give it to you?"

"I lost her trust taking it. She wanted to give it to Imogene. I wanted you to look at it first, I'm sure the man Quigley referred to was Kasov. I'll give it to Imogene tomorrow for Ann's sake." Ben looked down at a speck on the table. "What will they do? Reynolds will question her friends, they may know about Kasov, or Davis Tremont as she probably knew him. He'll put out some feelers and come up empty. I'll tell them I found it out behind my dumpster, Quigley dropped it on his way out of town."

"Sounds reasonable. He's our only witness and could maybe ID him. Do you agree with Nana and think he's still around?" Connor chuckled.

"I do agree. But from what I understand, if anyone can hide in plain sight, it's Quigley. Eventually, he will get hungry or cold; I'm keeping an eye out."

The two silent, reflecting on the situation and the mission four years ago. Ben could read Connor easily. They often thought alike and were one step ahead of each other. They experienced things civilians could not understand. His time in Bingham was a three-year therapy session. He and Connor up late talking out their memories and drinking coffee at Level Grounds. His engagement to Rachel ended those late-night sessions and about that time Ben's restlessness could no longer be ignored. Leaving Bingham was decided long before Ann Fletcher entered the picture. Now the idea seemed a little harder every day. Connor picked up on Ben's partiality to Ann, Ben knew from a remark and sideways glance last week when the three of them were together at Level Grounds. He had been cool enough not to mention it again but that wouldn't last. It would be just what Connor wanted, something to keep him around.

RACHEL PULLED UP A STOOL BEHIND THE COUNTER AND watched Ann work. "You're a busy bee. I'm starved, what does Ben have to eat around here? Connor texted he's going to be late for dinner."

Ann pulled cookies out of the oven, "I'll be making fresh for the festival but Ben wants to use up this frozen stuff." She made a face, "Frozen cookie dough, can you believe it?"

"Looks good to me," Rachel quickly picked up a hot cookie and placed it on a napkin before her.

"So, you never told me how Connor and Ben know one another." Ann wiped her hands on her apron and pulled up her own stool.

"They were in the military together." Rachel said, taking a bite of her cookie. "They were in the same unit. I didn't know Connor then; you know he's about five years older than I am so I never knew him growing up. I knew his sister a little in school."

Zoe was a year between Ann and Rachel, she was always known as one of the brains. All the Wellingtons were known for their brains. "So, what did he do in there?" Ann asked.

"Ben was in Special Ops or something like that, anyway Connor had some kind of special training—the unit grunt man. He mostly took care of IT problems and things like that. He won't tell me much. He said he had security clearance and was involved in some top-secret stuff, but that's all behind him. He finished his masters when he got out. He still does work for the government on a contract basis."

"So, how did Ben end up here?"

"He's originally from New York City, I told you that, right? Anyway, he said Connor described Bingham as an idyllic, picturesque place that he had to see. He showed up one day for a visit and ended up staying. He bought this from the Tates, remember, it was a donut shop? They still live on Elm." Rachel helped herself to coffee. "You don't mind, do you, I left my purse in the car."

"It's on me. So…New York City; I can't imagine leaving there for here. There has to be something more to it."

"His father worked in Building One at the World Trade Center. He was there when it went down. Ben was twelve, I think. His mother never recovered. She died when he was in high school; he has a sister; her name is Kathryn. He joined the military when he graduated—finished college in there; when he got out, he ended up here. He's very nice but a little mysterious; could be his tours in Iraq and Afghanistan. Who knows what those guys witness? I thought he would be Connor's best man but he didn't ask him to even be in the wedding party. Connor said Ben doesn't go in for that sort of thing. I'm glad he's coming, maybe you'll have someone to dance with besides Eric. Sorry about him," Rachel said with an expression of sympathy.

Ann met Eric, Connor's cousin, recently at a family barbecue; he was a shy, embarrassed individual who found casual conversation painful and awkward. Ann was a little surprised Connor chose him for best man. They were complete opposites.

Ann pictured a twelve-year-old Ben receiving the news of his father that horrible day all those years ago. Her heart ached at the thought of it. Suddenly eager to learn about his past, his present, and those he loved, she asked, "Does he keep in touch with his sister?"

"She's been here twice, I think. Older than him, she's some high roller on Madison Avenue. Followed their father's footsteps in the financial field; and boy does she look the part. Very put together, has that sleek professional look. I'm sure her wardrobe is worth more than my car."

Ann looked down at her t-shirt and worn jeans, she was no slouch but there was a lot of room for improvement, so her mother had mentioned for most of her life. Her thoughts went to Ben and his opinion, which had suddenly become very important to her. She glanced at her reflection in the tall, stainless coffee maker. Her hair was its usual mass of unmanageable curls; her round face stared back at her with disgust. "Do they seem close?"

"Very much so; I got the impression she wants him to move back to New York. We had dinner with them the last time she was here. She mentioned a job that's waiting for him, all he had to do was come home.

"What did Ben say?"

"He mostly laughed at her and tried to change the subject."

There was a twinge in her gut. She didn't like the thought of him leaving. There was absolutely nothing between them. Ben had given her no encouragement in that area and she hadn't given him any and after his suspicious behavior, she was not sure she ever would. They were platonic and may even be friends but nothing more.

"Well, I wonder what keeps him here." She mentioned casually as she put the cookies in the big jar. She did, in fact, wonder it many times. Ben did not seem the type to be running a coffee shop. He seemed misplaced at Level Grounds. Ann had assumed the role of running the place in the last week or so while he mostly went over the books on his laptop.

"Not sure, I've wondered that myself," Rachel replied and then remarked as if she read Ann's mind, "Seems a little out of place here if you ask me. Don't tell Connor I said so, but I think he is really handsome. Have you seen his arms?"

His arms and the rest of him; he was handsome, but the last time she fell for handsome it got her in a whole lot of trouble.

Connor rushed in apologizing and he and Rachel left Ann alone with her thoughts. There hadn't been a customer in half an hour and it didn't look like anyone was on Main Street that time of night. Closing time was in an hour. Walking to the backroom, she opened the laptop on the desk; maybe she could glean some information about Ben. No luck, the laptop was password protected. The desk was neat as a pin. Nothing but the laptop and an old lamp sat on top. No personal photos, mementos, nothing. There was a safe in the corner of the room. Ben had gotten in it a few times. Ann observed every time he got in how careful he was to make sure it locked when he closed it. There was more to Ben Fontana than she knew. Walking over to the safe, to examine it a little more closely, something shiny caught her eye on the floor. She bent to pick it up. It was a bullet, a 9mm if she wasn't mistaken. No stranger to guns, Stuart had seen to her and Rachel's education and many weekends they practiced at the shooting range. It wasn't unusual for a business owner on Main Street to have a safe with a gun in it. Ann discarded it and grabbing a broom, swept up. It was eight when she finished, she was about to lock up when the door swung open.

"What can I do for you, Sheriff?" Ann said with a professional demeanor. "I was just about to lock up, I'm afraid there's no coffee."

"Don't want coffee," he sniffed and looked around.
"Ben's not here."

"Don't want Ben either; it's you I need to talk to."

*Great,* she thought, *now what? Imogene probably told him about the rock.*

Sheriff Reynolds pushed a screen under her nose. There was an email opened addressed to the Sheriff of Bingham. "Can you tell me what this is about?"

It read:

*Person of Interest in a Crime, Coffee County Colorado.*

*Ann Fletcher, about 5'7, eyes blue, hair, curly, brown, weight approx. 140*

*It is believed she is in your area*

*Please advise*

*Coffee County Sheriff's Department*

"I have no idea what this is referring to." It was partially true but her gut told her John was behind it.

"You were in Coffee County Colorado, weren't you?"

"Yes, but I didn't have anything to do with any crimes." Ann thought, "Once the resort had two maids who pulled off a huge robbery, it was a jeweler's convention they got away with tens of thousands of diamonds but I thought they were caught." She looked at the sheriff, worry on her face. "Do you think it could have something to do with that? They did question me at the time. But that was two years ago."

"You seriously have no idea what this is about?"

"No!" Ann felt the blood rise to her cheeks. "You can check with my former employer, he will vouch for me, I never got as much as a speeding ticket while I lived there."

"Calm yourself, I believe you," he scratched his chin and examined the email once more before turning to go. "Besides I checked for warrants before I came over here."

This made Ann indignant. "I'm not eighteen anymore, for your information. I'm a law-abiding citizen."

Sheriff Reynolds laughed, "I know, I'm not out to get you and I had a notion to just ignore this thing, seems fishy to me. Not worded like a normal email pertaining to this subject matter. That's why I came over here to ask." He opened the door and then stopped, "Did you get in any kind of trouble while you were out there? Did anyone pull you into something you didn't understand at the time; something that could have been questionable? As far as the law that is?"

"Nothing." She turned to place the cash in the blue deposit bag. John had friends in the police department. He told her that once when she threatened to call them. "What are you going to do with that?" she motioned toward the tablet.

"I'll ignore it, for now, listen, Fannie, if there is something you need to tell me—you should. I'm not the enemy. I think a lot of your family—your dad and I play golf from time to time. I would hate for anything to throw a wrench in Rachel's wedding plans." Turning toward the door, he added, "Just let me know."

Ann locked the door behind him. John was up to something. What other explanation could there be? He wanted confirmation she came home and thought he would get it. At least the sheriff thought enough of her parents to ask her about it. And to Ann's relief, he would not respond. But no response could be enough to make John think she was in Bingham. She walked to the register to finish the day's receipts.

Ben stood still in the corner of the backroom; having walked in while Ann was talking to the sheriff, he kept his presence quiet. He pondered what he gathered from the conversation. Someone was looking for her and they went through police channels to find her. Reynolds obviously believed her but also knew her enough to figure trouble could follow her without her knowledge. Ben thought he handled it decently. The other night when he walked her home, her look was sad and vulnerable and he wanted to be able to help in some way. His first impression of her was that of strength, independence, and brains. And she was not hard to look at. Something happened to her in the last day or so. Her confidence was slipping; there was fear and uncertainty behind her bright blue eyes. It bothered him and reminded him how little he knew about her.

The back door still stood slightly open. He backed slowly to it and when he got there, he threw it open and yelled, "Hello, Ann you still here?"

Ann jumped. "I'm just finishing up."

"Just thought I'd stop by and let you know Sarah recognized me today. She's making progress, Joe said she can speak a little now and they've started physical and speech therapy."

"That's good news." Ann was careful not to look his way, fearing her face would betray her. "Does she get out of bed?"

"Yep, sat up in the chair for a bit today." Ben moved nearer. "Were we busy tonight?"

"No, not really," Ann felt his breath on the back of her neck.

"Just wondered why you were still here. I thought you would be gone by now." His voice was low and calm. He moved his hand toward her. She took a deep breath. He grabbed the blue bag. "I'll throw this in the safe and walk you home."

"You don't have to walk me home."

"I better, Josephine's out tonight raising hell, Maggie chased her off earlier." He walked to the backroom laughing.

Josephine followed them the length of Main, howling the entire way.

"What's got into her?" Ann mumbled as they reached the Municipal Building.

"JC's let her run wild since he's back from his fishing trip, while he was gone Edger Ditch kept her on the other side of town, now Josephine's home, she can do what she wants. Ain't that right Jojo?" Ben shouted over his shoulder. This set off a barking howl combination that lasted two minutes. Josephine finally caught a scent and lost interest as they rounded the building.

Ann invited him in and this time he accepted. Nancy was reading while Stuart dozed in his recliner. They spoke in hushed tones, Ben updating Nancy on Sarah's progress and his plans for the Apple Festival the following weekend which included his new recipe for apple cider. He waved a hand to Ann and said, "Your daughter will be whipping up some kind of apple tart."

"Scone," Ann corrected.

"Oh," he looked disappointed, "I thought you said tart, my mother made the best apple tarts. I wonder if my sister has the recipe."

"Well if you find it, I'll make those too." Ann couldn't help staring at his profile in the low-lit room as he spoke

THE BEATING OF SARAH STRONG                    101

to her mother. He seemed to enjoy Nancy's comments and observations.

Stuart's sudden jerk interrupted them. Sitting bolt upright in the recliner, he stared at the group wide-eyed.

"Must have dozed off, Ben, how long you been here?"

Ben chuckled and made small talk for a few more minutes. He rose to excuse himself and looked at Ann who followed him to the door. "I've decided to give the notebook to Imogene tomorrow. I'm going to tell her I found it behind my dumpster. I don't want Reynolds to know you went up there, why tell him. It won't matter. Are you good with that?"

Ann was good with that, but she pretended to think about it before she agreed. Why was he protecting her from the wrath of Sheriff Reynolds? She wondered with a little hope that his concern meant something, something more than friendship maybe. She quickly pushed the thought from her head. Not happening, she told herself, just the other day she saw a side that deeply concerned her. "Yes," she said, "I'm good with that."

# CHAPTER 8

S arah Strong was sitting in a chair; her head no longer
throbbed but had a dull ache that never left. Her father
Joe, rummaged through her things in the corner of
the room. Things that were brought by friends and things
in her bike basket the night she was attacked. The phone
was discovered missing when Sheriff Reynolds visited the
day before. He hoped to find some clues on it. Karl Bruce
was supposed to have gotten it weeks ago, but he either
ignored the order or forgot it. And then in his daily duties,
the sheriff must have forgotten himself. Sarah, even in her
weakened state, saw the frustration and disappointment
on his face.

He questioned her and Joe, 'Had she had it the night
of the attack?' She told him she was sure she would have;
she was never without it. Her father confirmed it sat in the
corner for weeks while she recovered. He told the sheriff
it buzzed and dinged for many days with messages from
friends and family. Admitting he paid little attention to it, he
never had a cell phone and wouldn't know what to do with it.

Sarah watched her father do a thorough search of the
floor, her bags, his own pockets. Scratching his head, he
announced with certainty it was just gone. He looked
miserable and disgusted with himself. He confessed to

Sarah; he had not had the wits to search the contents of her phone—something he never would have thought to do under normal circumstances. Sarah could see his frustration and regret in not being able to navigate a cell phone. She knew he would never dream of invading her privacy but now understood he should have tried. He sat down on the bed, head in his hands. Sarah reached over to him. Her speech still sluggish, words were coming back to her quickly now but it was still an effort to speak them.

"Don't worry Dad," she held his hand. "It will turn up," but believing it herself was hard. There was no explanation for where it could have gone. Sarah's distress over it made her progress that day even slower than usual.

The doctors anticipated more from her but she was anxious and nervous most of the time, with little ambition to improve. The eager, helpless look on her father's face was the only driving force to motivate her to obey her therapists. Her memory of the beating was scant, aware she was terrified of the man who came after her and aware he was following her were the last things she remembered. His name, she did not know. Why he wanted to hurt her…she could not think about. His face, a stranger now in her mind but had he always been a stranger? Thinking these things day after day made her tired. Everyone wanted to know the answer and looked at her expecting her to blurt out the events of that night. She could not. It discouraged her and she resented it all at the same time. The Sheriff neglected his duty; her phone sat for weeks, possibly with the answers and now was gone. Why did they not search it earlier?

Sheriff Reynold's interrogation the day before left her exhausted and more afraid. Getting out what description she could, while the sketch artist sat before her, left her unsure and doubting her memory. The scar under his left eye was the only thing she was certain of. It was deep and ugly, about an inch trailing along the side of his face. Everything else seemed ordinary about him. She couldn't remember anything past her first seeing him on Church Street as she rode by on her bike. Looking at his face terrified her and that is why she rode as fast as she could, trying to escape. But why?

This question haunted her. She knew her life to be ordinary; she worked for Ben, went to school, had a few friends, and took care of her father as best she could. How did her ordinary life involve someone who wanted to beat or possibly kill her? The sheriff was suspicious of the missing phone and displayed anger at the whole situation. He had no one to blame but himself as far as Sarah was concerned. They were told her friends had been questioned but none could think of a single person who would do this. The area in front of the factory was searched but there were no clues except one or two footprints they were able to photograph; Sarah's shoes were taken weeks ago and it was confirmed one set was hers and the other belonged to a man who wore a large size, twelve. There was now evidence from a notebook in Quigley's handwriting that he witnessed something—he documented an argument Sarah had with a strange man at Level Grounds. Reynolds believed he could be the culprit. This news upset Sarah more than anything; arguing with a stranger in the coffee shop. She could not imagine such a thing. Quigley had not mentioned any physical appearance or scar but if the man had been from Bingham, Quigley would have used his name, according to the sheriff.

"Quigley knows everyone in town, even if he doesn't speak to them." Sheriff Reynolds told her.

The search for Quigley was still ongoing but so far no one had seen him. The investigation seemed to be getting nowhere and Sheriff Reynolds could not tell them what his next steps would be except to get the sketch out on the streets. As he exited the room, he staunchly ordered them to call immediately if the phone turned up.

Sarah nodded and turned her head to the window. After weeks in the same hospital room, she had almost forgotten normal life. Her memory returning slowly, all but the events preceding her beating were clear to her. Her classes at school, her routine at Level Grounds, life with her father, it was all there. But when it came to that night, she could not think of anything but the scarred face sneering at her as she rode by on her bike. Her legs peddled as fast and hard as they could, she remembered that but anything after was gone.

BEN WATCHED ANN WALK DOWN MAIN. WHEN SHE rounded the Municipal Building, he entered Level Grounds and locked the door behind him. A few minutes later he opened the back door for Connor.

"Here it is." He handed Ben the phone. "I sent you the contents and it's confirmed. She's a deleter; had to retrieve everything via my program. There were multiple texts from 'Davis'. Didn't have time to read everything but am certain he is the one. What now? Will you give this to Barone? We didn't exactly follow protocol in lifting the contents of someone's phone."

"I know. I'll put the phone back tomorrow. Sarah's been up and talking so I'm sure she wonders where it is. Let's look at what you found."

Ben opened the file Connor sent. The two scrutinized emails, photos, and text messages for at least an hour. By the time they finished, they knew Sarah Strong a lot better than they wanted to and they were sure Kasov was Davis Tremont the man who had beaten Sarah. The two communicated by text only and Kasov sent one picture of himself. The texts started with a Fourth of July greeting initiated by Kasov, Sarah answered in kind right away. They were sporadic at first, Kasov was baiting her, taking it slow, pouring on flattery and compliments. He had not stopped thinking of her since that day…remembering her on her bike…the first time he saw her…how beautiful she was and so on.

Ben got hotter by the minute. "Why didn't she tell me about this?"

"What are you? Her dad? You are her boss and old to her. She's not going to confide in you."

Connor was right, he hated to admit it. He thought the relationship was more than employer-employee and his sage advice and warnings about the world were welcome to her. Taking her under his wings, showing her how to run a business, counseling her in her education, all of this was in his thinking, helpful and his way of acting like an older brother. It was now obvious she hadn't wanted him to know about Kasov or Davis as she knew him. It hurt a little but it also increased his guilt over the whole thing. Had he warned her that first day, none of this would have happened. Hiding in the shadows, he felt like a coward.

They read on and discovered, Kasov warned her not to mention him to anyone. After all, he is quite a bit older than she; they should take it slow, see how things go. Her father may not approve at first. The texts continued as casual conversation until he wanted to meet in St. Louis.

Hesitation on Sarah's part, *she had no car...how would she get there...could he not come up to Bingham?*

*No, he could not get away...*he went on about how he had to see her...*talk to her in person...could not get the day they met out of his mind.* Finally, Sarah agreed, she arranged a ride with a friend who would be in St. Louis on August fifth. She agreed to meet and expressed her excitement with emojis and hearts.

Connor taking over the search found texts from a girl named Lacey. Ben remembered Sarah mentioning her, a classmate he thought. Lacey agreed to give her a ride—would pick her up at ten that day. The plan was to meet at the entrance of the museum under the Arch. The next text was from Sarah to Lacey and came as a surprise.

*11:30--August 5; Come back please, it's urgent, where you dropped me off, please hurry, I'm sorry I have to get out of here, please come.*

Lacey's response was immediate; she couldn't have gotten far. The two men went back to Kasov's texts.

*12:10: where are you? Did we get our signals crossed?*

No response.

*12:15 Getting worried.*

No response. This went on for the next hour, finally, Sarah texted back, *couldn't make it, sorry, family emergency, won't be available for a while.*

Connor and Ben looked at one another. "She must have seen something. She was there early from the timeline." Ben said, puzzled.

"But what? It was enough to scare her that's for sure. The Arch isn't a place you would do something illegal out in the open." Connor sat back in the chair and stretched, "No indication of where she was dropped or how far she walked." He continued searching.

"Well, let's give Lacey a call." Ben dialed from his phone. He felt sure Lacey would pick up if he used Sarah's but he didn't want evidence they had it. "Hopefully, she will pick up. It's ringing." A few seconds passed. "Damn! Voicemail." Ben stood and ran his hand through his hair, "Lacey, hi this is Ben Fontana, Sarah's employer at the coffee shop, she asked me to give you a call. Will you give me a call back please?" He finished with his number.

The two men went back to the messages. Kasov was relentless in his pursuit and without any clue as to why Sarah kept avoiding him. She would go days without answering then was brief and sharp in her tone. By the middle of August, she told him she didn't think they should be involved, wished him a good life, and asked him not to communicate with her anymore. There were several unanswered calls and a few more texts which escalated in tone and language. Eventually, she blocked his number because by August twenty-fifth it all stopped. Sarah was found August thirty-first, a Friday night, after the first Bingham football game of the season.

"So, between the twenty-fifth and thirty-first, we know

he was here. Quigley saw him arguing with her in here."
Ben sat back down, running both hands through his thick
black hair. "What was I doing that week? Where the hell
was I, I'm always here?" He stood again, kicked the chair
into the wall, threw the only lamp on the table across the
room, and stormed out the back.

Ben walked to the baseball field and sat down in the
visitors' dugout. He was trained to protect, to serve, to react
coolly under pressure. When he saw Kasov that day in June,
he did what should be done by contacting the Bureau in
St. Louis; they followed up. By the end of June, he was told
Kasov was no longer in the area—vanished, that's what Ben
believed. They dropped the ball; no, he dropped the ball.

He trusted others to do what he should have, now Sarah
lay in a hospital bed. It would never have happened had
he protected her. Ben could barely look at Joe, he felt the
neglect of his duty even more acutely. What was the point
of all his training, the work in his unit, the medals hidden
in his drawer? Medals for being brave, subduing the enemy,
putting his life in danger, they were all meaningless to him
now. Sarah could have died because he had not acted. The
very thing he swore to do. Instead, he hid in the backroom
to avoid being recognized, like a coward. The enemy was in
his territory and he took no action. His gut told him to act,
but his intellect made him follow the protocols made clear
to him in the military. Calling Barone was the right thing
to do, but as Ben mulled it over in his mind, he concluded
there was more than one right thing. Confrontation would
have been the right thing, also. Instead, he hid in the shadows, listening. Ben sunk his head into his hands in despair.

Debating how it should have been handled was eating
him up inside. Looking at it from every angle left him feel-

ing as if he were trying to find a way out for himself. It was a sickening feeling and he hated it. Facing Sarah and Joe would be tough now that he knew the truth. Telling them would be even tougher. But eventually, it would have to be done. Ben stood and walked out to the pitcher's mound on the field. The night was clear and it seemed every star in the universe hung above him. There had only been a few nights in Bingham that he could remember with such magnificent starlight. Something beckoned him standing alone on the field. He felt as helpless as Sarah must have that awful night. His confidence and strength always made him the man he thought he was. That all proved useless the night Sarah was attacked and it seemed, since then.

He was not a man of prayer yet asking for help seemed obvious to him at that moment. The word hypocrite came to mind. He had never given a supreme being much thought but now, the idea pressed on him until he could no longer resist.

In a faint voice, he whispered, "I could really use your help now, so could Sarah." That was it—all he had in him. He made his way back to his business where Connor was looking intently at the screen.

"Look at this email." Connor pushed the laptop over so Ben could see.

*Dear Sar,*

*I'm sorry I won't see you this semester. Enjoyed our summer class together. I have to go home; my mother needs me. Will tell you more later. I plan on being back in the spring. You take care of you in the meantime and stay away from creepy scarface! I bet you no longer find that scar attractive. Still can't believe what you saw him do! What a creep. Glad I was there to rescue you. Will keep in touch girlfriend!*

*Lace*

"She's from Virginia, there now; be great to have a face to face but the phone's going to have to do. Hopefully, she'll call back. She knows what went down, what Sarah saw. It was enough to make them both see him for what he is."

Ben felt Connor's astute eye on him.

"It's not your fault, dude." Connor placed his arm on Ben's shoulder.

Ben would not look up.

"You did the right thing." Connor tried again.

"Yeah. It's late, thanks for going over this with me and retrieving it. I'll see Barone tomorrow and hopefully, he'll put someone on Sarah." Ben looked at the clock; it was midnight. He opened Level Grounds at six. The Apple festivities began in the afternoon. Ann would have to manage without him and she would not like it. Leaving in the morning as soon as she arrived and not coming back till late in the day, he cringed at the fury it would ignite. He was supposed to take care of customers while she baked all day for the festival. It couldn't be helped, he had to meet Barone with the new information and somehow slip Sarah's phone back in her room unnoticed.

Connor rose to leave, "Get some sleep dude, you look like crap."

"Thanks," Ben admired and respected Connor. He had proven himself to Ben repeatedly. *'Con Man can crack it.'* That is what the unit said about him and he could. Ben knew giving him Sarah's phone would be easy. It probably took him five minutes to retrieve the contents of Sarah's life. It was an invasion of privacy. There wasn't much to look at anyway. Kasov gave her what little excitement there was; the hope of a love affair with a strange foreign man with a scar. Ben figured for a nineteen-year-old girl that must have had some appeal. Why hadn't he seen it?

As he did some prep work for the next day, he went over and over the events in his mind. Had Sarah's behavior changed during the summer? Had he missed something? Anything that would have tipped him off? He couldn't think of anything, but he also had his attention diverted during the summer and he suddenly remembered where he was that fateful week; the week of August twenty-fifth when Kasov came back, twice at least. He had flown to New York for an interview with a friend of Kathryn's who had multiple businesses that had contracts with the Department of Defense. They wanted a consultant, someone who was military savvy, and could help them evaluate some DOD opportunities. It was something that interested him, something he knew he could do and told them so. At that time, getting out of Bingham was the obvious next step. With Connor getting married and the coffee shop a success, nothing was keeping him there.

Bingham was the balm he needed after he left the military. He served for eight years and that was enough. Those who knew him were surprised. His tours to Iraq and Afghanistan proved a revelation about the military and what he had been fighting for.

An idealist when he enlisted, he thought he could right the wrong that happened to his father on 9/11. It was taking action. He had grown into manhood without his dad; there wasn't a day that went by he didn't feel that loss. Every ball game, learning to drive, his first job, all of these things his father missed. He needed action, so he joined the Army, trained and excelled in Special Forces, and fought. It wasn't the remedy he thought it would be, and after eight years he wanted out. He wanted more than out, he wanted to go someplace he could get lost; lost from his family and friends in New York. Not that he had much family left, just Kathryn and his Aunt Laura, both of whom tried and still try to plan his life. As soon as he landed in New York, free from military life, they both eagerly told him the plans they had for him. Kathryn had his career mapped out and Laura wanted him to meet a nice girl. When Connor called and invited him to Bingham he jumped at the chance—when he saw the donut shop for sale, he jumped at that too.

Kathryn did not speak to him for six months. But three years later, he needed a change again. So, when Kathryn told him about the opportunity, he was more than willing to make the trip. That was weeks ago, he hadn't heard anything back yet but they told him things were on the back burner for now; he wasn't worried about it. That week his interview had been on Wednesday morning. He remembered leaving Sarah in charge. He flew out after close of business Tuesday and didn't come back until Thursday night, spending in between with his aunt and sister, listening to their new plans for his life. At the time, they hadn't sounded that bad. Bingham had lost its luster and he was getting bored.

He tried to remember if he saw Sarah after he returned... he hadn't. He gave her Friday off. Would he have noticed something? He would never know now, that Friday night was the night. If only he would have spoken to her that day, he may have noticed a change. Level Grounds was left in perfect shape, there was nothing he needed to go over with her so he hadn't spoken to her at all that day. Everything had been in its place; there was not one clue left that Kasov had been there. Nothing at all. He wondered how long he stayed if Sarah had threatened to call the police. To his knowledge, no one had come forward with news of the suspicious stranger. *Was he there on Wednesday or Thursday? Had he known Ben would be gone?* All these questions whirled around Ben's head until he thought he would drop from exhaustion. The couch, with all its pillows, beckoned him. Just a little while, he told himself, and then he would head home to bed.

The keys rattling in the door woke him; he sat up, groggy, wondering why he was on the couch at Level Grounds. His thick, brown hair stood straight up, his shirt discarded over the chair and his shoes strewn across the floor. Before he could get on his feet, Ann was opening the door. His presence was unnoticed by her, she walked across the store and disappeared behind the counter, making a racket like she was looking for something. Scrambling to stand, he stubbed his toe on the table and swore. The next thing he heard was a scream.

"It's me!" he shouted, dodging the hammer Ann had hurled his direction.

"Ben? What the hell? I wondered why the door was locked. Did you spend the night here?"

"What time is it?"

"Six-thirty. I thought you would be open. You're lucky everyone is busy setting up for the festival. I just stopped by to borrow your hammer; I'm helping Mom get her booth ready." Ann's cheeks flushed as she looked at his shirtless chest.

"What time do you come back?" Ben asked with a sudden realization of the plans he had for the day.

"I'm not here until nine, remember? I'm going to start baking then, so I won't be much help with customers."

"About that," Ben walked to pick up his discarded shirt, suddenly aware of his naked top half, "I've got to be out of town for most of the day, it can't be avoided."

"Today! It's the Apple Festival, I told you I would need to bake today if we are going to have anything to sell. What can be so important?" Her hands moved as quickly as her words. There was passion in her voice and her quick reaction to his news brought even more color to her face.

Ben couldn't help but stare at a curl that fell from its place and landed on her cheek. Mesmerized, he could no longer try to deny the attraction. Her figure, that sandy brown crown of curls, the way her nose turned up at the end and those legs. Every day they worked together; the attraction grew. He stood there like an idiot, his hair standing straight up, shirt unbuttoned, no shoes on. How could he ever explain how much he needed her today? Keenly aware of his morning breath, he ignored the desire to kiss her. Now was not the time, he was sure she would leave and not come back. *What was she saying?* Her tirade dying, he realized he should apologize and smooth things over as best as possible.

"I'm truly sorry, Ann but it can't be helped." He softened his voice and moved a little closer to her. He couldn't help himself.

"Well? Where are you going?" She demanded.

"A few places, one of them to the hospital to see Sarah. Joe asked me to bring a few things."

"That shouldn't take long," she reasoned. "So…what? You'll be back around lunchtime, then?" she said it more as a command than a question as she walked to the couch to retrieve the hammer.

Ben followed; he could not seem to help himself. "Not exactly, I have a meeting with an old friend in the city, he only has today." They stood facing one another in silence. He could not tell if Ann was at a loss for words, angry, or the spark he felt was mutual. He took a step closer.

Surprise and suspicion crossed her face. She took a step back. "I don't get it. We agreed, I would do the baking and you would man the store just yesterday. Why is it so important to have this meeting today?"

She was relentless, he moved closer whispering in a low gruff voice, "It can't be helped, I wish I could tell you why but it concerns someone else and it's confidential." He reached to move a curl from her forehead. Her look softened so he inched nearer still.

Ann's eyes widened and she softened her voice, "I really wish you wouldn't go. I'm not sure I can handle it all by myself."

Ben lost the trail of discussion and moved closer still, bending close to her raised face, forgetting his morning breath. As he went in, he felt a hand on his chest, it was not a gentle touch. He landed on the couch and watched her walk to the door.

"Really, Ben?" Ann turned to leave.

"Damn!" Ben bounced upright and ran after her, "Ann, I'll see you at nine? Okay?"

Imogene brushed passed him, eyeing his open shirt and bare feet and let out a deep 'mmmhmmm' while nodding her head in judgment.

"What can I get you, Imogene?"

"The usual," she grinned. "I didn't know you two were…"

"We're not!" Ben snapped. "It will take a minute to brew," he motioned for her to sit. "I'll bring it out." He walked to the back, buttoned his shirt, tucked it in, and found a comb in the drawer.

"Are you ready for today?" Imogene made small talk.

"Ann will take care of most of it," after he said it, he regretted it. Imogene could never pass up an opportunity.

"You sure? From the looks of it, she wanted nothing to do with you this morning," emphasis on 'this morning.'

To Ben's relief, two more people walked in.

"Didn't you have those clothes on yesterday?" Maggie blurted. "Where are your shoes?"

For the next two and a half hours Ben served half the town of Bingham their coffee in 'to-go' cups. The migration went from his store to the booths and tents in the park. The hustle and bustle of preparations for the festival were underway and he was sorry he had to miss the excitement since it could be his last Apple Festival. The thought made him pause; a month ago, he was sure of his plans. Moving on was the natural progression. He had made up his mind to take the job in New York and if they didn't offer, he would go back anyway or somewhere else. After this morning, however, he wasn't so sure. The last weeks, with Ann working around Level Grounds making everything better, had been bittersweet. His guilt over Sarah weighing him down left him temporarily when Ann was there, working by his side. Adding a touch of something here and baking something marvelous, asking him to try, waiting eagerly for his approval.

A few days ago, she slipped a freshly baked scone in his mouth as he was busy fixing the leak under the sink.

He was lying under the drain, she stooped down to feed him, her fingertips barely touched his mouth. When she rose, she put her hand on his knee oblivious to what it did to him. Since that day he was acutely aware of the danger of Ann Fletcher. How much did he know about her? She kept a lot to herself; Connor didn't know much more than he did. The way Connor smiled, when he asked about her told Ben he was being too obvious. The night he walked in on her and Reynolds left him uneasy. The day she scrubbed the table nonstop did too. There was more to Ann than he could make out. Her conversation about the last three years of her life involved her various jobs and activities with friends yet he knew there was something she was holding back. She never mentioned a boyfriend and there was a reason. Ben knew enough to know someone who looked like she did hadn't gone unnoticed in Colorado. The thought made him jealous. Her angry words this morning only made him want her more. Today of all days, he wanted to stay by her side, working to prepare for the fun; joking and laughing. They worked well together, almost as if they read one another's minds. He looked at the clock, almost nine. She would walk through that door, in that skirt, with those legs and he would have to walk out. She would be mad, probably give him the cold shoulder for a while but it couldn't be helped. He would barely have enough time to get to his house, shower, and be on the road.


ANN STOOD ON THE LADDER WAITING FOR NANCY TO hand up the garland. Nailing it in the wood, she thought back to that weird scene earlier. Had she had more time, she would've gotten to the bottom of it. Why did he sleep there last night? He only lives two blocks away. His strange behavior made her mistrust him even more but she couldn't stop thinking about his body next to hers and the way he moved in almost without her knowing what was going on. *Had she been too harsh pushing him away? No*, she determined he was playing mind games. *Who did he think she was? Someone who would fall for that?* She whacked the nail hard and shook the booth.

"What's with you?" Nancy asked as she arranged a wreath on the post.

"Nothing, nothing, why? What do you mean?" Ann flustered and nervous climbed down from the ladder.

"Seem a little jumpy, that's all. Did you see Ben when you got the hammer this morning?"

Her mother knew something. "Yes."

"How did he look?" Nancy smiled.

"Like Ben!" Ann was in no mood to fill her in on the weird scene. "Why do you ask?"

"Oh nothing, Imogene mentioned she saw you leave and Ben wasn't quite ready for customers when she walked in."

Ann turned her attention to a basket of Black-Eyed Susan's. "He slept there last night for some reason, I don't know, can't figure him out. Anyway, he scared me half to death, didn't know he was there, threw the hammer at him."

"Oh, no, did you hit him?"

"No, thankfully, he has good reflexes."

"Must be his military training." Nancy checked her watch. "It's almost nine."

"I better go, since I will be holding down the fort, alone! He said he had to leave town today, couldn't be helped. Can you believe it?"

"I'll send Rachel over later, maybe she can help."

"Thanks, Mom," Ann noticed her mother as she per-fected an arrangement, her hair pinned back—a look of joy on her face. Ann would have never admitted it years ago but her mother was beautiful to her. Appreciation for Nancy had surfaced, Ann saw her in a new light. She kissed her as she left, leaving Nancy with a happy, confused look. Walking to Level Grounds, she determined to get right to work. She wouldn't give Ben the satisfaction of discussing the situation earlier that morning.

She found him in the back slipping his laptop into his backpack. He met her with a big smile. She hung her bag on the peg and noticed a hot pink, bedazzled object in the backpack with the laptop. "What's that?" she couldn't help asking and was mad at herself immediately after.

"What?"

Determined, she reached in the backpack and pulled out the phone.

"It's Sarah's, Joe asked me to pick it up." His tone was casual.

Ann's suspicion surfaced, she glared at him and then the backpack.

"You gonna push me again?" The accent thick and his voice low.

"I should," she held his gaze.

"Ann," he breathed out, "I have to go." He backed away, turned, and walked out the door.

Frustrated, Ann yanked her apron off the peg and went to work peeling apples, chilling butter, measuring and mixing, all the while thinking of Ben, vacillating between outrage and dwelling on his physical closeness that morning. *What had he meant by it all?* She knew she couldn't trust him; he was definitely up to something and it had to do with Sarah. *And her phone, why would she just now want her phone?* It seemed to Ann that the phone should have been examined for clues long ago. *Why hadn't the sheriff taken it?* Her mind raced with questions and feelings; she went through the motions of the day. Greeting customers in between taking things in and out of the oven; around one-thirty she decided to make apple pies. Lang's Grocery happily delivered more apples and flour. By three-thirty, she had the rack in the back room filled with scones, muffins, pies, and cookies all flavored with apples. At that point, she decided they needed an apple cake.

Rachel walked in and surveyed the bounty. "Wow!" She reached for a muffin. "I thought you were just doing scones?"

"Too much?"

"No, it will go like gangbusters. Are you going to bring it to Mom's booth tonight?"

"That was the plan; I would go there, while Ben stayed here. But he has decided to bolt."

"Yeah, I heard. I asked Connor what is up with him. He denied any knowledge, but I know he knows something. I'll help, I can bring some of this to Mom and she can sell them along with her stuff."

"How's it going out there?"

"The mayor made his speech and launched the twentieth annual Apple Festival!" Rachel raised her arms in triumph. "Not too crowded yet. Most people are still at work. Dad is meandering around."

Ann poured a coffee and slid it to her sister. "Did Mom tell you he spent the night here?"

Rachel nodded her mouth full of muffin.

"He wasn't wearing a shirt…" Ann looked at the couch forgetting her sister a moment.

Rachel cleared her throat. "Have you heard from John anymore?"

"No, and hopefully I won't."

"Connor surprised me." Rachel finished her muffin and took a sip of coffee.

"How?"

"He said he had a contact," at this Rachel used hand quotes, "in Colorado. He asked the guy to check John out. Can you believe that? My fiancée has a contact." Again, the air quotes. "What is he a spy or something? I asked him what he meant by having a contact? He just said he knew a guy, as if…"

Ann wasn't sure what Connor meant by having a contact either but he was a man of the world, had been to war, knew people from various places. Ann was glad to hear it. "Did the guy find out anything?"

"Nothing earth-shattering said he followed John for a few days. It was mostly work and hanging out at bars and going to the gym, nothing out of the ordinary."

Ann poured the cake batter into three nine-inch pans. "Good thing the bakery left all these pans." She said absent-mindedly. "It sounds okay, doesn't it? Sounds as if he has gone on, I'm not going to worry too much."

"So far so good," Rachel laughed, "kind of nice—having our very own spy…" she slipped on a Level Grounds apron. "Do you have a basket?"

Ann dug around in the drawers and found the perfect size. She lined it with a blue checkered cloth; she purchased a few days ago from Maggie's. Layering the day's labor inside, made her proud of her product. She quickly made a price label and taped it to the handle.

"There, I doubt you make it to the booth. Just drop the cash in your apron pocket."

She watched Rachel wind through the now crowded park.


BEN MET AGENT BARONE AT HIS COUNTRY CLUB WHERE
they had lunch and drinks, something Ben hoped to avoid.
Getting back to Bingham and Ann occupied his mind a lot
during the conversation. It was agreed Barone would put an
agent outside Sarah's door but she would be undercover. He
didn't want to step on local law enforcement's toes. Barone
said he would come up with a subpoena for the phone by
Monday and to let him know when Lacey calls back. She
was a key witness. As for Kasov, everyone was on alert, if
he were still in town, they couldn't find him, he was laying
low. The bureau had learned, during his short time here
he managed to do business trafficking guns. They also got
word that local police picked up a thug with an arsenal
in the trunk of his car; after hours in his cell, he bragged
about doing business with a guy with an accent and a scar
under his left eye. That was over a month ago before he got
to Sarah. Since then there has been no evidence he stayed.

"It's not like him to leave things undone. Sarah could
make him and that's not good for her." Barone said.

Ben left the meeting with Barone's words ringing in
his ears. By the time he reached Sarah's room, it was three
o'clock.

"Ben!" Joe looked surprised to see him. "Why aren't you
at the Festival?"

Ben took Joe's extended hand. "I was driving by on my
way there and thought I would stop by. How is she?" Ben
looked at her empty bed.

"She's doin real well, they got her down at physical
therapy. She talks real good now. Been askin for her phone,

we can't tell what happened to it, used to sit in that corner but now we can't find it. Sheriff Reynolds was askin for it and was good and mad it wasn't here."

Ben moved his fingers over the phone in his pocket. He glanced around the room, sure they had checked the corner thoroughly, he would put it somewhere else. Joe motioned for him to sit, but he remained standing with an explanation he had a long drive.

"When will she be finished?" he hoped the distraction of getting her back in bed would give him an opportunity to drop the phone.

"She's been gone a long time; I was watching *The Price is Right* and it's over now. I think she'll be along soon. Sure you won't sit?"

"No thanks, Joe." Ben changed the subject to the festival and filled Joe in while they waited. It was easy and comfortable to talk about Ann and her culinary efforts, how well she was doing, and how business was booming until he noticed silence and a somber look on Joe's face. He quickly recovered, "Of course, Ann is just filling in for Sarah. I'm sure, she'll be back sooner than you think."

The physical therapist knocked on the door and said hello as she pushed Sarah through. "We did so well today. Didn't we Sarah?"

Sarah nodded weakly but brightened when she saw Ben. She was able to say, 'Hello Ben' with little effort. She asked a few questions about Bingham and then looked at the bed longingly.

"Okay, Sarah, let's show them how we get into bed." The physical therapist gave instructions to Sarah as Joe anxiously looked on.

Ben took advantage of the situation and stashed the

phone on the nightstand under a magazine by Sarah's bed. He lingered a few minutes more and made his excuse to get back to Bingham and the festival.

# CHAPTER 9

The icing was perfect, one of Ann's best. Cream cheese, cinnamon, and a lot of powdered sugar with a little cream; it looked luscious on the three-tiered cake. Level Grounds was empty, the festivities in the park were in full swing. Looking out the front door, she could just glimpse the ride with the swings that spin in a circle and all those little feet going around. It had been her favorite ride as a child and she hoped to get on sometime tonight. Sitting down in an overstuffed chair with a cup of coffee and the icing bowl, she kicked her feet up and scraped the leavings with a wooden spoon. An eighties tune about coming home was playing on the radio. Her father used to listen to this song a lot when she was a child; it was still one of her favorites. Her feet moved to the music and occasionally her head, too. As she spooned up the icing, the music spoke to her about coming home.

Her homecoming had been a pleasant surprise. Her relationships with her family and the creative freedom Ben gave her at Level Grounds gave her a simple, unexpected joy. Despite the disappointment in Ben's leaving for the day, her baking proved a welcome distraction and pleasure—being alone to work with her hands and make something for the happiness of others.

The music moved her to stand and begin dancing, spoon in the air, beating the bowl with it as the artist sang. She danced to the kitchen sink and dropped the bowl in; she circled Level Grounds with her broom, stopped to fluff the couch pillows, picked up some empty cups, and danced back to the sink. Caught up in the moment, she did not notice someone looking in from the sidewalk.

He hadn't meant to watch. As he reached for the door handle, the music caught his attention. She was having such a good time and her dancing moved him. He turned to go once, feeling like a creep, but decided against it. Looking in from the outside gave him a glimpse of Ann with her hair down. The Fannie everyone remembered but he had yet to meet. Driving home, he could not stop thinking of her. The speedometer reached illegal levels most of the way. Feeling this way was new to him; his focus had always been on survival and success. His father's death propelled his internal drive to succeed.

He was a twelve-year-old boy who had to look out for his mother, who could not grasp the fact her husband would never come back. After she died, he moved on, building a career in the military, fighting battles in foreign countries and within his own soul, never stopping to think about long term relationships. The kind Connor now had. This thing made no sense really, he couldn't stay in Bingham, he would go crazy. The time here had healed some of his wounds, kept him grounded and balanced but now he needed a challenge. As he indulged himself in watching her, he contemplated the risk factor in getting involved with someone from Bingham. He convinced himself there was a spark earlier that morning or it could have been wishful thinking. Either way, he was determined to find out; and for him, there was no time like the present. The song ended and she disappeared in the back. He swung the door open and shouted, "I'm back."

Ann appeared arms folded. "Hello," she said coldly.

The aroma of baked goods reminded him of what she had been doing all day. Walking to the back he couldn't believe his eyes. "You did all this?" He looked at her with a broad smile. "This is amazing, you're amazing."

"Rachel has already taken two basketfuls to Mom's booth. They are selling, like hotcakes." She pushed passed him to the sink behind the counter and began doing dishes. "How's Sarah?"

"She was just coming back from physical therapy, said hello to me very plain sounded like her old self." He picked up a scone.

Ann continued tidying up her mess. She glanced his way.

Elevating his eyebrows, he nodded approval.

"I have to tell you," he said swallowing the last crumb. "That was amazing, I've never tasted anything so good, and I'm not much of a dessert person." He moved nearer.

"I'm glad you like it, your bill from Lang's Grocery will be a little higher this month."

"It will be worth it." Standing next to her he spoke in a low tone. "I'll finish up here if you want. You can go to the festival." He thought he should offer, the last thing he wanted was for her to leave.

"I think I will," she said but stayed rinsing a dish for much longer than necessary.

He moved closer still, putting his hand under the running water, he took the dish and placed it in the rinse rack. They stood, awkward and silent. Ben weighed the options in his mind. Time and place were important, he was her employer, after all, he left the ball in her court.

Ann was very still for a long time, he stood so near her he could feel the warmth of her body. She moved closer still and thinking this could be the moment, he lowered his face to the back of her neck.

"Excuse me," she pushed past him suddenly. "I will go to the festival if you don't mind." Walking to the back room, she tossed her apron on the hook then reappeared.

He stood arms folded, leaning on the sink, dejected and brooding. For a moment, he thought he glimpsed a change of heart but that was a false hope. She walked by and out the door leaving him alone with an empty feeling.

Rachel and Connor were in line at one of the game booths when Ann found them. Rachel held the empty basket in her hand. "We sold out; I was just going back to refill. Is Ben back?"

"He is, I didn't think it would be empty so quick, I just left." She looked at Connor. "You wouldn't mind would you? I may need some sister time."

Connor grabbed the basket and kissed Rachel's cheek. He walked toward the coffee shop. Rachel shouted after him to re-attach the sign and make sure the pretty cloth hung over the sides. When he arrived, Ben was standing in front of the baker's rack surveying the abundance. He hadn't heard Connor come in.

"Wow, what's all this? I thought she was just doing scones."

Without turning, Ben motioned toward the counter, "Look at that cake."

Connor breathed out another wow, "I think we need to taste test this." He grabbed a knife from the drawer. Ben clutched his wrist just in time.

"Sorry, Bro! Can't let you do that. It's too perfect."

"Like her?" Connor laughed.

"She's not interested, made that clear about five minutes ago." Ben started washing dishes and wiping down counters.

Connor snuck around the counter and scraped his finger along the bottom of the cake, "Well I just saw her, said she needed some sister time with Rachel. That's why I'm here with the basket." He licked his finger and raised his eyebrows in approval. Throwing the basket at Ben, he ordered, "You're supposed to fill this with nice layers or something and stick the sign back on. I'm sure they're talking about you, that's what they do, women I mean, they have to talk everything out with one another before they can commit to anything. You try something or what?"

Ben ignored the question and carefully placed muffins, scones, cookies one on top the other until the basket heaped with goodies. "How's this?"

"I think that checkered cloth is supposed to hang over the sides." Connor took the basket and tried to arrange the cloth, spilling two muffins in the process. "I'll eat those, just set them aside, we don't want to waste."

Ben threw them at him. "Can't figure her out, something's up." Ben dropped the dishtowel on the counter and pushed his hand through his hair.

Connor looked away.

"What?"

"What?"

"You know something."

"Why do you say that?" Connor headed toward the door, "Just because a woman doesn't fall all over you, doesn't mean something's wrong with her."

"You have a tell, do you know how many times we've played poker? You look down and to the left when you're hiding something."

"I didn't do that...I don't do that. Do I?" He started for the door again.

Ben jumped in front of him, "I don't think so, Bro."

"Rachel made me swear, don't make me tell, I'm marrying her." Connor tried to push past, more muffins tumbled to the ground. "Look what you made me do."

Ben slid his arm around Connor's neck and grabbed the basket with the other hand. A crowd outside the coffee shop looked in amused as Connor reached with no success for the basket. The whole thing resulted in a dance that looked ridiculous, the pair holding each other in a strong grip pushing around in a circle, as goodies dropped to the floor. Ben finally glimpsed the crowd and released his grip. Connor fell to the floor and looked up embarrassed, he waved to the crowd.

"Now we have to re-do it."

"You can get it ready but you aren't getting out of here until I hear what you're keeping from me."

Connor took his time arranging and rearranging until Ben snatched the basket again.

"I really can't say," Connor started.

Ben glared.

"I can sit here all night but if we don't get that basket out there, they'll come back and wonder what's up." Connor looked determined.

"I don't care."

Connor hesitated, looked over his shoulder to the crowd in the park, and then began, "She was in a bad relationship. She got out, came home. He texted her a week or so ago. Rachel told me, said she wanted a man's perspective, I said the guy's an ass, the only perspective I have is to have him followed. Remember Scotty? He checked him out. Said he was up to regular stuff, working, drinking, going to the gym. I think it'll be all right. She's embarrassed by it and doesn't want anyone to know, her parents don't know and now I feel like a jerk for telling you."

Ben listened intently; his stomach turned at the thought of it. "What else did Scotty get?"

"One arrest two years ago in Denver, beat another girl-friend up pretty bad. Nothing after that."

"So, what did he say in the text? Is he coming after her?" Ben suddenly thought of the conversation with Reynolds. "Reynolds was in here the other night; someone out there is looking for her. He had sense enough to keep quiet." Ben paced the floor. "I don't think this guy is going to give up."

"Rachel didn't tell me about Reynolds." Connor took his phone out. "Let me text Scotty again and see if he has anything else on the guy."

"What's his name?"

"Grossman. John." He typed out a message to Scotty. "I haven't heard from him for a few days. Maybe he has some more news."

Ben had his laptop out tracking John Grossman on social media. It didn't take long. He scrolled through the guy's feed and instantly disliked him. He was one of those unshaven, longish hair, square jaw types that all women like. So that was the attraction. When he got to the picture with him and Ann, he audibly gasped. Connor looked up from his phone. Ben turned the computer toward him.

"Good lookin guy…I guess, except that stupid man bun."

Ben could only look at Ann, she looked happy, her hair a shade lighter and down around her shoulders, she wore cut off shorts and a white blouse. Her feet were bare. John had his arm around her neck with his fingers wrapped in her curls. There were a few more shots, Ann's expression changed as time went on. The last picture was dated early August. John's arm again around her but Ann was visibly tense and had a look of fear in her eyes. Ben turned the laptop toward Connor without saying a word. Both were trained to read a person's body language. Connor gave an understanding look. His phone buzzed.

"Rachel calls." He grabbed the basket and left Ben looking at his computer.

Ann let her feet dangle and closed her eyes. It was her third time on the swing. Just what she needed, she felt free—almost as if she was flying. The buzzing phone in her pocket went unnoticed. Rachel was in the swing in front of her, whooping and yelling. The little children giggled as they watched their kindergarten teacher. As the swing slowed, Connor stood below waving—a full basket in his hand. They walked to Nancy's booth together.

"That cake was tempting, Fannie." Connor had taken up the nickname and Ann didn't mind. He was to be her brother after all.

"Thanks, you could have had a piece."

"Ben wouldn't let me." He walked ahead of the two of them and placed the basket on the counter.

Nancy peeked inside and informed them there had been a demand for scones.

"There's a bunch more at Level Grounds," Ann replied.

"Good, I was afraid you may have to get up in the morning and make more." Nancy looked at her tired daughter and brushed her curls back from her face.

Ann didn't fuss as she would have three years ago; she just gave her mother a weak smile. About that time Sheriff

Reynolds walked up with his wife Paula. While she browsed Nancy's arrangements, Mike bought two scones.

"Heard about these," he said as he took a bite. "Not bad. You make these, Fannie?" Before Ann could answer a loud ding came from his pocket. He pulled his phone out. "Paula, I have to go."

"What is it?" Ann inquired, "Something about Sarah's case?"

He looked up, annoyed with her inquiry, "Yeah, it's from Sarah, they found her phone. Now we can see if there are any clues on it." Reynolds seemed pleased with himself.

Ann questioned again, "Found her phone? Was it lost?"

"I went to pick it up last week." The sheriff stuffed the last of the scone in his mouth, "Couldn't find it." A crumb fell on his shirt, "Joe said it had been there the whole time, corner of the room. Said he knew because it buzzed and rang a few times. Went missing," he swallowed the last of the crumbs, "turned up today. Gotta go. Paula!" he motioned for Paula to come.

"Of course, it showed up today. Because he brought it back," Ann mumbled under her breath. Ann thought back to their first visit to Sarah. Ben seemed fixated on the corner of the room. He must have taken it then, but why? Was there something he wanted removed from it, a message he didn't want anyone to see? Her heart beat faster. She turned toward Level Grounds and walked that way.

He was still there, wiping the counter, saying goodbye to JC who came out with a large cider. "JC," she rushed past him. JC nodded and went on his way.

Ben looked pleased to see her. He wouldn't be for long. She wanted answers, had a right, or so she thought, she worked for him. If she was working for a criminal, she wanted to know.

"Just talked to Mike Reynolds," she walked fast toward him, "He had some interesting news." She was in front of him now, looking up, eyes locked on his. "Seems Sarah's phone was missing from her room, that's what I said, her room at the hospital. Seems Joe verified it was there, heard it ring, and then poof it was gone."

Ben backed up and sat on a stool. He folded his hands over his chest.

She stood over him, "Reynolds went looking for it last week, Joe told him the phone had been there. You know what I think?" Ann pressed her finger to his chest, "I think you took it. That's what. That night we went up there, the night you mysteriously didn't want to show anyone the notebook, the night you kept looking in the corner of the room as if you knew it was there." Ann began pacing the floor, "Question is…why you wanted her phone?" The possibility of answers to that question made her heart beat faster. Was Ben involved in Sarah's beating? Had he wanted to erase something on the phone? Only a few minutes ago she could've been in his arms kissing him, now she wondered what kind of violence he was capable of. She backed away to the door, her voice was shaky, "Why did you take it, Ben? Why? What are you hiding? What did you do to Sarah?" Tears formed in her eyes. She debated on running but he just sat on the stool staring at her.

Forgetting what Connor had just told him and with that forgetting what she must have experienced with someone volatile, he only thought of himself. Her accusations cut deep. He was no longer amused with her flare-ups. "You done?" He slowly rose from the stool.

Ann nodded; she hit a nerve. He walked to the door and locked it. She moved away from him, unsure. She should have run, "Why did you lock the door?"

"I need to tell you what's going on, I don't want anyone coming in. Sit," he motioned toward the couch. They sat side by side on the couch he had slept on the night before. "I took the phone the night we visited Sarah; you are right. I had to; after I saw the notebook I had to be sure." He ran his hand through his hair in the usual way. Hesitating, he began again, "I know who did this, her texts confirmed it. The sheriff will do his work, he won't find him, won't even figure out his real name. The FBI is on it. They'll have a guard on her by morning."

Ann was stunned, she finally asked, "Who, who could have done this? And how do you know him?"

"It had something to do with a mission from years ago. He came here looking for me. I was informed he left the area; I didn't know he was in communication with her. I still don't know the reason, why her? Why he didn't bide his time and get me?" He looked away, "It's my fault this happened. I didn't protect her." Ben filled her in with scant details, never revealing Connor's role in the whole thing or Lacey, her friend who may be the only witness they had besides the missing Quigley. Ben, hesitant in going into too many details, mumbled something about security clearance.

Ann understood. They sat in awkward silence. Ann thinking how little she knew this man, yet how drawn to him she was. A few minutes earlier, she imagined him capable of unspeakable things, now she felt foolish and paranoid. Once again, her passion and reactionary disposition got her in trouble. Mumbling an apology, she met his eyes with sympathy. Their hands were inches apart on the couch; she moved her fingers toward his, barely touching the tips. He inched his over the top of hers then seemed to change his mind. Ann, embarrassed, pulled her hand away and rose to leave.

"I'll walk you home," Ben said standing with her.

"It's okay, really," confused by the mixed signals of the day, she wanted to walk home alone and think.

He insisted. They walked in silence.

The first evening of the festival was dying down. The rides were still and quiet. Edgar Ditch was picking up trash in the park, vendors were loading their vehicles and heading home, a few people lingered on Main Street greeting them as they passed. Josephine wobbled down the street, drunk from overindulgence; she passed them without looking up. Ann once again invited him in, he declined. Ann figured he had little sleep the night before. When she closed the door behind him her phone buzzed in her pocket, she hadn't looked at it all day. Rachel and Connor were dozing on the couch. She went to her father's recliner, took her phone out, and discovered she had two voicemails and a half dozen text messages. She went through the texts in order:

From her friend Josie:
*You Ok? John called me demanding me to tell him where you are.*
From John:
*I'm tired of this, we have unfinished business.*
From Josie:
*I've had to block his number, he's crazy, please let me know you are fine.*
From John:
*I'll find you*
From John:
*Soon*
From John:
*You shouldn't have left it like you did, I'll find you.*

The two voicemails were from John, he was drunk and barely audible. She made out the words Missouri and St. Louis. The second voicemail was him declaring his love for her and swearing he would never hurt her again. As she finished listening, she noticed her rapid heartbeat. Fear, she hated fear and she hated John for making her afraid. Rachel and Connor continued sleeping soundly and peacefully. Waking them crossed her mind but why bother, John was not anywhere near her tonight. She put a blanket over the two of them and went to bed anticipating a restless night.

Ben slept like the dead. He hadn't heard the first two knocks and barely heard the third. He staggered, shirtless and in his pajama bottoms to the door. Whoever it was, they were impatient. He opened the door and groaned.

Connor pushed his way in, "You still in bed? I thought you'd be heading to work."

"Is there a reason for this?" Ben motioned toward Connor in disgust.

"We need to talk. I saw Ann hot and bothered going toward the coffee shop last night, I have a feeling you let her in on some of this stuff with Sarah, I trust you didn't mention my name."

Ben looked annoyed which answered Connor's question. "I have my integrity, unlike some people." Ben was referring to Connor letting him in on Ann's secret; he was glad he did but felt he should rub it in a little.

"Yeah well, you forced me and if we hadn't been through so much together, I wouldn't have told you and I know that you liiike herr, you waaaannaa kissss herr," Connor mocked in a sing-song voice.

Ben threw a pillow at his head, "Did you hear any more from Scotty?"

"I'll check; my phone has been on silent." Connor's face went from a smile to a serious look in a second. He handed Ben the phone.

*Sorry dude, lost him, he didn't show up for work yesterday, checked out his house, it's locked up tight and the dog is gone. Not sure if he's gone for a day or longer. I'll check tomorrow and let you know.*

"So, I guess we wait and keep our eyes open, do you think we should talk to Reynolds?"

"I do," Ben said, "But it will have to be you since I know nothing about it. Print his picture off the social media account. It's on my laptop, I'm going to shower. Let yourself out and get that picture over there as soon as you can."

Ben showered quickly. He texted Ann as he walked to work. No answer. He texted her again pretending he couldn't find the vanilla-flavored syrup, no answer. Barely able to concentrate, he thought of calling Scotty himself. As he picked up the phone, he saw a call coming in, an area code he didn't recognize. It was Lacey. He debated on letting it go to voicemail; he wasn't prepared to ask questions. It buzzed for the third time, "Hello."

The voice on the other end was from a young woman, "Hi, this is Lacey, are you Ben?"

"Yes. Thanks for calling back, I have a few questions." Ben had to think about how to ask them without letting on he went through Sarah's private correspondences.

"Sure, is Sarah okay? I haven't heard from her in weeks."

Ben hesitated, debating how much he should tell, "She's much better now, she was a victim of a crime, beaten up pretty bad but she'll be okay." He heard the gasp and exclamations as he spoke.

"Who did this? I can't imagine anyone wanting to hurt her. Are you sure she's okay?"

"I believe she will be okay; she is up now and doing her physical therapy, it was mostly her head, but a broken bone, too. As for who, I was hoping you could shed some light on the whole thing." There, he said it, now he would wait.

"Me? I don't know, I can't think of anyone at school, we only just met this summer, wait…" She gasped, "wait…oh, that guy, that guy with the scar, Davis, or something."

Ben spoke little, encouraging her to remember.

"She asked me for a ride to St. Louis, he was there, supposed to meet her at the Arch. I dropped her off at City Park and told her she could walk through City Park, then Peabody Park and Kiener Plaza, then cut through the Old Court House and it would take her right there." Lacey paused for a breath.

Ben asked, "Who was this guy?"

"I don't know, she said he came to Bingham one day and they hit it off, rode bikes or something, he was a lot older than her, ugly if you ask me, she had a picture on her phone."

Ben had seen the picture; he was uglier than he remembered the day he shot him.

"Anyway, I dropped her off; she was excited to walk through the parks. Her dad never took her to the city before, so she wanted to walk. I drove away not expecting to hear from her for at least a few hours but it hadn't been an hour, she texted and told me to come get her where I dropped her off. I did, when she got in the car she was crying and telling me to get her as far away as I could."

"What happened?"

"Well, it took her awhile to calm down. She said she walked through the parks like I told her, then crossed Broadway in front of the old courthouse and walked toward the Arch. But she noticed a little alcove off to the side, she's like that, always interested in the out of the way space. Anyway, she said it was like a miniature park within a park, a cleared circle with concrete benches. Fairly hidden from the sidewalk traffic. So, like Sarah, she ducked in there to take a closer look." Lacey let out a sigh and then continued.

"That's when she heard his voice, Davis, I mean. He has an accent; did I tell you that? Anyway, she peaked through the bushes and saw him talking to some creepy guy. So they started walking toward the entrance to the alcove—she ducked behind the bench and crouched in the bushes. She didn't know why, but she felt like she should hide, which she did and I'm so thankful. There were no other people around and the alcove hid them from the street on one side and the sidewalk on the other. They sat on the bench she was hiding behind." Lacey's voice rose to a higher pitch, "she said she could have reached out and touched them. She was terrified. The other man, she said, was huge, with like a shaved head and tattoos. She listened but couldn't understand all of what they were saying but heard enough to know she couldn't meet Scarface or Davis." Lacey popped her gum and went on, "There was something about a delivery of guns and she saw the bald guy open a backpack and take out a handgun and several bundles of money. Well let me tell ya, she shook so much when she told me this, she could barely get it out. The bald guy shoved them at Scar..., I mean Davis. Davis put the gun in his back pocket or back of his pants or whatever they do in the movies…and pocketed the bundles in several different places. Sarah was frozen and praying they wouldn't see her. Whatever business they were doing, ended, Davis got up and left. The bald guy stayed and smoked a cigarette on the bench. Sarah said she closed her eyes tight and prayed, he turned and looked in her direction, then stood up and was about to separate the branches when a group of teenagers ran into the alcove. These kids saved her life. Baldy left. Well, she sat there for what seemed like an eternity debating on whether she should pop out of the bushes and scare these kids or wait. That's when she texted me." Lacey drew a deep breath, "As soon as the teenagers left, she got up and ran as fast as she could through the city until she was at our meeting place. I wasn't close, so she had to wait about ten minutes. By the time I got to her she was crying and shaking."

Ben asked if she said anything else.

"Ummmm, yeah, she said she never really trusted Davis, but wanted to know what it was like to go on a date, she'd never been on one. She did mention you warned her about him. Anyway, tell her I'll call her soon. Are you sure she's okay? I bet it was Scar…Davis, whatever his name is. She told me he wouldn't stop texting and she felt creepy, finally blocked his number. Oh, I'm so sorry about this, poor Sarah, please give her my love. If I need to talk to the police, I will. I'm just sure it was that creep."

Ben gave her all the assurances she needed yet Lacey rambled a few more minutes about what a good friend Sarah had been to her. JC entering for his morning coffee was his excuse to hang up. Absentmindedly, he gave him the usual and said goodbye. He would have to tell all now—to Mike Reynolds, Ann, Sarah, and Joe. That stung the most, knowing now for certain it was Kasov and Ben was the reason he came to town. Had he been more proactive he might have prevented it. Joe may never forgive him; he doubted he would if the situation were reversed.

He looked at the time, nine-thirty and still no answer from Ann. He texted Connor, he knew he and Rachel were spending the day at the festival. Rachel's kindergarteners had a song they were performing sometime and he knew Ann wouldn't miss that. Connor answered he hadn't seen her that morning but Rachel said she was at breakfast. Connor told him she was probably showering or something and to chill out. The basket sat empty on the counter; he began filling it again to occupy his mind. He would walk it over to Nancy's booth and maybe Ann would be there by then. When he got there, Nancy was thrilled, people had been asking. No, she hadn't seen Ann since this morning. She thought she was going on a run, usually went for about forty-five minutes or so, then she'll shower and come to the festival.

Ben walked back, eyes scanning the crowd, as his training demanded. No one suspicious and no one who looked like John Grossman. He tried to shake the uneasy feeling he had. Calculating the hours it took to drive from Colorado to Missouri he convinced himself he would not be here yet unless he flew. When he got back to Level Grounds, little James Johnson was waiting for him.

"I came to buy some of Fannie's apple cookies."

"Well, come on in little dude," Ben held the door for him, "How many?"

James seemed deep in thought about the matter; he pulled a bill from his pocket. "How many will this buy?"

Ben had to look twice, "Where did you get that?"

James, with a look of guilt, stuttered out, that his rich uncle usually sends him a hundred dollars every couple of months as a sort of allowance. He looked away from Ben's gaze and settled for ten cookies if Ben could spare them.

Ben packed up an even dozen and discovered he had no change. "I'll tell you what, you take the cookies and when you get change, you come back and give me six bucks, deal?"

James wholeheartedly agreed, sticking his hand out for Ben to shake and ran out with a sack of cookies.

Several more customers followed ordering coffee, apple cider, muffins and a few enquired about the cake, which he said wasn't for sale just yet; sitting under a glass dome and looking like something from a magazine. It was close to ten; he had texted over two hours ago. That was as long as he could wait; he would lock up and search for her. As he closed the cash drawer and watched Karl Bruce leave with a box of muffins and two coffees, he had made up his mind. Untying his apron and throwing it over the counter, he headed to the front door, Ann burst in at that moment with two large bags of groceries.

Relief flooded his body, he tried to remain casual, "I thought you weren't here till noon."

"I thought I would make some apple tarts. I found a recipe."

"Sounds great," he restrained himself from picking her up in an embrace, instead he took the bags. "What are you going to do with that cake?"

"I was going to put it in the silent auction for Sarah. But I may have to touch up the base here…looks like someone's finger stumbled upon it." She gave a mean look as she circled the cake.

Ben raised his hands, "That would be your future brother-in-law."

"I found some tart pans back here somewhere yesterday," she was in the back making a lot of noise, then reappeared, "Only ten, but aren't they a cute size? We can get three servings out of them. You'll have to get out from behind here."

"What do I do if someone comes in?" He grinned; suddenly he was hungry and grabbed a muffin from under a glass dome. Biting into it, he sighed, "Everything you make is delicious." Why did everything seem right now that she was here? The conversation with Lacey crossed his mind. He chose not to bring it up, Connor should be filled in first. "What have you been doing this morning; you didn't answer my texts."

Ann silenced her phone last night and hadn't looked at it all morning, afraid of what she might see; she pulled it from her pocket. The latest texts she had kept to herself, Rachel was leaving the house as she got up this morning so she never mentioned it. Pulling her phone out, she was relieved there were only two texts both from Ben. "Did you find it?"

"What?" he said with a full mouth.

"The vanilla syrup," She looked at him suspiciously.

"It's over there, isn't it?" forgotten he'd asked in a text.

She glanced at the table with the flavored syrups, "Why yes, it is, isn't that something?"

"I just needed an excuse to text," he said casually, "But you didn't text back so…"

Tossing him an apple she demanded with a smile, "Start peeling."

As he peeled, he mentioned his odd encounter with James Johnson.

Ann remembered Imogene saying something about one of the kids buying something with a hundred at Maggie's. It was an odd coincidence. She joked about James' sudden fortune.

The tarts, ready for the oven, would take an hour to bake. Ann mentioned to Ben that she would go to the kindergarten concert when they finished baking—if he did not mind. He surprised her by asking if he could join her.

After replenishing the basket at Nancy's booth, they left Imogene in charge and the Fletcher family walked to the gazebo. There were twenty-five kindergarteners dressed as apples, glasses of cider, and slices of pie prepared to sing and dance as Rachel taught them. The play consisted of the usual delayed entrances, forgotten lines, and a wardrobe malfunction when the felt apple slices fell from the piece of pie. The audience roared with laughter, Rachel scurried around giving orders and picking up apple pieces. Overall it was a success and the town of Bingham was pleased with the new kindergarten teacher. Millie and Nana beamed with pride and told everyone Rachel was their granddaughter.

Connor and Ben walked ahead on the way back to Nancy's booth; Ann knew they were talking about something intense. Connor kept looking back. Ben seemed to be trying to convince him of something. Rachel was oblivious as she had a pack of five-year-olds vying for her attention. Finally, she gave in and went to ride the merry-go-round with them. Ann kept a close eye on the conversation in front of her; they stopped and stepped away from the crowd by the old tree near JC's Garage. Her mother was saying something, but Ann paid no attention. They reached the booth; Ann could no longer see the two of them as a group of bikers just returned from the trail and were putting their bikes on the racks in front of them.

"Ann!"

"Hmm?" she looked around.

"Imogene sold almost everything."

"Girl," Imogene crooned, "who would've thought, you're going to put us all to shame, I'm never going to bake again after tasting these scones. How'd you learn to do this?"

Ann looked at the basket in disbelief; it had not been more than thirty minutes. Passersby inquired about the scones; asking if there were more.

"I'll go get some and the tarts," Ann said, grabbing the basket. The popularity of the scones was unexpected. While at the resort, she learned about baking from Clair St. John. Clair was the pastry chef for about a year and Ann assisted her, picking up baking tips along the way. The last Ann heard she opened a restaurant in the east somewhere. She made a mental note to look her up. As she walked, there were shouts asking when there would be more scones. Ann smiled and waved; it made her giddy. She could not remember the last time she felt this way. Where was Ben? She scanned the crowds, it occurred to her she wanted to share her success. Yet, she had not looked for Rachel or her father. It was Ben she wanted near her. *Strange*, she thought.

Climbing the step to Level Grounds she noticed the door slightly ajar. Ben hadn't locked it but she could have sworn he pulled it closed. The tarts would be cool enough to sell, contemplating how she would transport them, she reached for one and found the pan empty. Looking down she noticed coffee spilled on the floor. Ann froze, she faced the counter so most of the room was behind her; she listened. There was a faint snore and rustling noise from the other end of Level Grounds. Grabbing a spatula, she slowly turned.

Someone was on the couch and it was obvious, whoever it was they did not notice Ann. She stood still, unable to move—all was quiet except for the sound of steady snoring. The intruder was sound asleep. Tiptoeing to the door, she kept her eye on the couch. Her heart raced the closer she got. As she reached to turn the handle, the door swung open. A loud gasp escaped her lips and she put her hand to her heart. Ben started to speak but she stopped with a raised finger to her mouth. She took his hand and walked him to the couch.

"It's Quigley," he whispered.

# CHAPTER 10

The two stood over the intruder. He was much thinner and had a scraggly beard. Ann pulled her shirt up over her nose. It was apparent, he had not bathed in some time. They decided to let him sleep but agreed to stay with him just in case he decided to disappear again.

Ann packed up the rest of her baked goods and brought them to the booth in a hurry. Handing them off to her mother, she explained she had to get back to Level Grounds.

Nancy shouted after her, "I thought you would help. What are these? Tarts? How much should I sell them for?"

"Ten dollars apiece or $3.50 a slice," Ann shouted back.

"A slice, I don't even have knives or plates." Nancy looked after her daughter, disgusted.

Stuart appeared and was enlisted to help.

"What's got into her?" Millie asked. She and Nana sat on stools making daisy chains for Rachel's students.

Ben locked the door behind her after placing a closed sign with a note that said all baked goods were at The Flower Shop booth. He dimmed the lights and pulled the shades down. Both looked down at the sleeping Quigley.

"Where do you think he's been?" Ann asked.

"I would bet he's been here all the time."

"Do you think we should get Mike Reynolds?"

"I've been debating; he came here because he trusts me; if we get Reynolds he may not talk."

Quigley grunted and rolled over. Ann motioned for Ben to follow her to the back. "We should let him sleep as long as he can. Who knows where he has been trying to sleep all these weeks."

They stationed themselves near the front window and spoke in whispers. Ben told her Lacey's story; Ann's curiosity was piqued and she pressed for more information about his mission and why Scarface had it out for him.

"Because I gave him the scar and he was locked up in an Italian prison for three years, I guess he blames me."

"How did you give him the scar?"

"I shot him, it was him or me."

Ann shifted uncomfortably; "Was Connor on this mission?"

"He was a part of it."

"Did he shoot someone or get shot at?"

"No, Ann, I can honestly say, his role kept him out of harm's way. That's why I'm sure Kasov was looking for me and me alone."

Ann was relieved for her sister. The two sat quietly for a while, listening to the snores coming from the couch. It had been over an hour since Ann discovered Quigley. He couldn't have been there too much longer before that, enough time to eat a tart and drink a cup of coffee.

"Did you bring all those tarts over to your mom?" Ben asked.

Ann nodded and took the hint. There was a brick of cream cheese, some eggs, and milk. She made them each an omelet with cream cheese. Despite Ann's whisking in a metal bowl, Quigley hadn't stirred; she had a feeling he would not wake up soon. Ben devoured his and half of hers. "Who would've thought, cream cheese in an omelet, you're a genius."

"You never know until you try," Ann said, clearing the plates.

Her phone lit up with a message from Rachel wondering if they were going to come to the concert. They decided it would look suspicious if she didn't go. Ben would stay behind with Quigley. He watched Ann as she wove her way through the crowd and reached her sister.

In front of the gazebo, Rachel had put down a large quilt furnished with a cooler full of wine and cheese. "Where is Ben?"

"He's working. Why? Should he be here with me?" Ann asked with a defensive tone. Her feelings for Ben were obvious; taking it out on Rachel was easier than dealing with the truth of the matter. Every day she felt more attached than the day before and because of John she struggled against it with all her resolve.

"No, I just thought he may want to come to the concert. Wine?" Rachel passed her a glass while looking through her with those same eyes from childhood.

Ann accepted too willingly. Since coming home, she had limited her alcohol intake but a few glasses of wine were what she needed to keep her thoughts from Level Grounds and its current inhabitants. Lying back on a pillow, she enjoyed the bands warm up. It was a mild fall evening, sweater weather. Evie Camden would be singing tonight with some locals—some of whom Ann knew.

Evie and Ann had a history, Ann considered her one of her best friends in high school and Evie was her first-year roommate in college. Evie transferred the following year and they lost touch. The few conversations they had since Ann's homecoming confirmed, Evie had changed. Not something Ann could put her finger on exactly but different. Partners in crime long ago, Evie followed where Ann led, singing as they went. Evie's voice was always strong and smooth. Ann used to call her the soundtrack to their adventures. If there was a gathering, Evie would sing...especially if it involved karaoke. Ann might have been jealous at one time but now she admired her more than anything, Evie's confidence, and contentment. Evie had grown from an anxious, follower seeking attention to maturity and poise. Evie prepared, testing the microphone, and joking with the band. Tossing her long brown hair behind her. Ann would recognize her laugh out of any crowd. How they laughed together throughout high school, it made her smile.

The concert began as the sun set. It consisted of the more popular tunes from every genre in the past fifty years even some old hymns to re-purposed music. Ann recognized most of them, after all, she and Evie sang them together in the church choir on those occasions they showed up. Evie and another woman closed with *The Old Rugged Cross* acapella and in perfect harmony. Even though it got standing applause, especially from the over fifty crowd, Ann thought it an odd way to end the show even though it had moved her. It was around eleven; Ann, a little woozy from the wine, stumbled trying to stand. Connor helped her and offered to drive her and Rachel home. Thanking him, she started back to Level Grounds.

"Ann," Rachel followed. "It's after eleven, what do you need to go back there for?"

Ann hesitated and looked around; Connor was talking to the drummer. There was no one near. "Can you keep a secret?"

Rachel looked worried, "What kind of a secret?"

"Quigley is back. He's asleep on the couch at Level Grounds; he snuck in today when we were at the festival. Don't tell anyone, it will be out soon enough. We're going to talk to him about what he saw the night Sarah was attacked." Ann still feeling the effects of the wine, looked around concerned about the volume of her voice.

"Why didn't you call the sheriff? He will want to speak with him."

"He trusts Ben; we thought it would be easier for him to tell Ben whatever he has to say."

"I guess that makes sense, but why do you need to be there. I think you should come home with me; you've had a little too much to drink."

Ann knew the look, the crinkle at the top of her nose. "Oh please! Quigley's in there and probably awake right now; I want to see what he has to say. You don't have to be my conscience anymore!" Ann turned, crossed the street, and headed for Level Grounds. "You never did!" she shouted back.

She used her key to get in; the door squeaked, stirring Ben from a light sleep. "Concert over?"

"Yes, did he ever wake up?

"No." Ben looked at her, his gaze intense.

"Where are Connor and Rachel? Maybe you should go home, I'm not sure he will wake up tonight." Ben peaked out the window.

"I'm sure they've gone; Connor has his car. He offered to take me home but I wanted to see if Quigley woke up." Ann suddenly felt like a child up past her bedtime, first Rachel and now Ben. "You're probably right, he looks pretty out of it, I'll go." She turned to leave. "I'll see you tomorrow."

"Wait." He looked at Quigley and then her. "It looks like everyone has gone home out there."

"So?"

"Well, I guess I can leave Quigley and walk you home."

"I'm a big girl; I think I can handle it. I've walked home on Main Street later than this…" she opened the door and mumbled, "and drunker."

Ben caught the comment. He grabbed his keys from the counter. Quigley stirred on the couch. Ann was out the door. Keeping his eye on Quigley, he kept as still as possible. "Please don't wake up now…" he whispered. Putting his head out the door, he could still see her and hear her, she was humming a slow, mournful song. It sounded familiar to him, like a church song. He glanced back at Quigley; who stopped moving and settled into a snore. Pulling the door quietly shut and locking it, he jogged down Main.

Ann hearing running footsteps behind her walked faster. John being in Bingham crossed her mind. The day had been so packed with things to do, she forgot all about him. Pulling her phone from her pocket, she glanced for any texts. Nothing, she turned the flashlight on. The footsteps were closer and louder. In her condition, she knew she could not out-run anyone, let alone John, with his firefighter training. She regretted not carrying a purse. One good swing would give her a chance at getting away; she decided her fist would have to do. Stopping in her tracks, she waited for the opportune time and swung around with a right hook only to have it stopped in mid-flight. The grip on her hand was strong.

"Ann!" Ben loosened his grip, "It's me."

"You scared me. Why were you running up the street?"

Ben looked around and shrugged, "I didn't think you should walk home alone."

Ann laughed, "This is Bingham, Missouri, not New York. Aren't you worried Quigley will wake up and escape? I can manage getting home. Go back, he may get spooked and leave again."

Ben started walking, "You coming or not?"

"Why are you intent on being a knight in shining armor? I'm not afraid to walk home."

"I never said you were."

It crossed her mind to just keep her mouth shut and appreciate the gesture, however that would not do. He had walked her home before but that was for company and possibly because he was interested, this was different. He was playing the role of protector for some reason. They both knew Quigley should not be left alone. She stopped, he kept walking. "Hey, what's going on?"

Turning to face her he gestured with his hand, "Let's go. I need to get back to the shop."

"So, go, I can manage the rest of the way by myself." Ann stood stubbornly in the middle of the road.

"Why are you doing this? I just want to make sure you get home safe."

"Why would you think I wouldn't be safe?"

"Have you read the news lately?" He tried a jocular approach.

"I'm not moving until you tell me the truth." She sensed he knew something and she was pretty sure Connor told him about John. "You've lived in Bingham for three years, I've lived here most of my life, no one has ever been attacked but Sarah. All the sudden you don't think the streets are safe. Why?"

"Just a hunch," he moved toward her. "Now, are you coming or not?"

"Not until you tell me what you're really thinking."

He moved closer still, "I can't if I did, I'd have to shoot you."

"It will just be easier to explain yourself, then we can go. As it is, Quigley is probably awake and planning his escape." He was directly in front of her now.

"Explain myself, huh? Or I could just sweep you off your feet and carry you home; somehow I think that would be easier than trying to reason with you." He made a motion to pick her up.

Ann backed away playfully, "You wouldn't."

"Why wouldn't I?"

"I'll scream, that's why."

"I'll take my chances," he ran for her, wrapped his arms around her, and swept her off her feet. He carried her around the Municipal Building and down Bingham Place Street to her front door. She did not protest. "That wasn't so hard, was it?" he said as he set her down in front of her door.

"Not for me. If you are going to walk me home all the time, it will have to be like that. After a few times, you'll get tired of it and won't be so concerned about me."

Her eyes shone; it could've been the wine. He leaned in close, his arm above her head against the door, and whispered, "That's not likely. Quigley...I better..."

"Yes, go, I'll see you tomorrow." She slipped inside backward.

Ann woke to an empty house. Sunday, they were all at church. There had been no discussion about her going since her homecoming. Pouring her coffee, she glimpsed the blue sky; it would be a beautiful day. She finished her coffee and changed into her running clothes, heading out the door her phone rang. It was Ben, she had been wondering what happened with Quigley.

"Hey," she answered.

"Hey, so Quigley's in the hospital."

"What happened?"

"When I got back last night, I thought it was weird how long he had slept, so I felt his forehead—he was on fire. I had no choice but to call Reynolds and an ambulance. They took him to St. Joe's in St. Charles. He has pneumonia. I'll head out there later."

"Poor Quigley, I guess I should have known something was up. He slept so sound."

"What are you doing?" Ben had a text this morning that John was still MIA.

"Getting ready to go for a run, I'll mind the store when I'm finished if you want to go to the hospital."

"I'll join you…all your baking…"

Suspicion crept over Ann again, "If you want. Meet me here in ten, I haven't got all day."

"Okay, okay, be there in a few."

She kept pace with him—in spite of—her headache. Her left side ached but she refused to slow down. They spoke only a little, she noticed Ben looking from side to side from time to time. They pushed for thirty minutes but she could go no more. Collapsing on a bench along the trail, Ben seemed relieved and joined her. The Mississippi sparkled in the bright sun above the farms in Illinois. The view was amazing. They both sat with unspoken awe.

"We should stretch," Ben said, standing.

Ann reluctantly joined him. Ben bent over in front of her, hands gripping his calves. It was hard to figure him out. So much potential wasted here in Bingham. Level Grounds did well, it was one of the most prosperous businesses in town; he was well-liked and respected. It may not be long before he would be gone. Reminded of Rachel's words about his sister, Kathryn, and her job connection, Ann's insides twitched.

As she stretched her calves, she debated confiding in him about John. It was obvious he was in full military protection mode, so he probably already knew. The attention both flattered and provoked panic. Her well-being shouldn't be his concern. Forgoing her shame and embarrassment, she debated telling all. *Her shame; what did she have to be ashamed of? Falling for an abusive man? Is it too much to assume that a man would act like a man and not be a bully in all aspects?* She had wrestled with these questions for months. Her confidence and self-worth were wounded more than any physical bruising he caused. Ben stood, lifting his arms above his head. She mirrored him, scrutinizing his face.

"What?" Ben asked uneasily.

"You know about John, don't you?"

He dropped his arms, surprise in his expression, "Don't blame Connor, I forced it out of him."

"So much for all his security clearance, he can't even keep a family secret. So, are you assigned to be my bodyguard or what?"

"Self-appointed and at your service," he bowed in front of her.

"I'm not really all that worried about it," she lied and plopped down on the bench.

"Uh-huh, no sense worrying about it," he sat next to her and examined her profile.

"Well, you may as well see the latest," she handed her phone to him.

"Did you block this number?"

"Yes, but he seems to come up with another one, every time I do."

"It's not hard to do; you should change your number. What about social media that tracks your location, are you on any of that?"

"I closed all accounts; the only person who can track me is Rachel."

"Do you mind if I look at your settings?"

She nodded approval.

He was in her settings pushing and sliding. "I blocked any number, not in your contacts."

"So, what now, we get married?" As soon as she said it, she wanted to die, "I mean you can't be by my side constantly, you have to give me some credit, I am aware of my surroundings and I do know a few moves; I lived alone, I took a self-defense class." She didn't mention that's how she avoided the worst of John when she stomped his foot.

"It's not realistic, for you to never be alone. We can go over what you already know and I may be able to give you some more pointers. Connor gave Reynolds John's picture and updated him, I'm sure John had something to do with the email he got."

"You knew that, too?"

"Guilty, heard him speaking to you that night."

"Lurking in the corners, listening to my conversations, what else have you spied on?"

His thoughts went to her dancing around Level Grounds with a bowl and wooden spoon. "Not a thing."

"Stand up," he held out his hand. "Here are some simple tricks. The eyes, ears, nose, throat, and chest are the most vulnerable parts of the upper body. The lower body you want to go for the ankles, knee, and obviously the groin."

They spent the next ten minutes in an impromptu self-defense class, Ben advising her on what to do if grabbed from different angles, how to turn her wrist if she were in someone's grip, how to use her head as a weapon and how to be aware of her surroundings. Some of it she knew but was grateful for any new information. They walked home in silence, Ben thought of all he could have taught Sarah if he had only known. The day was getting away from him, he wanted to question Quigley, visit Sarah, and stay with Ann all at the same time. The coffee shop opened at ten on Sundays and it was nine-thirty by the time he brought her home.

"If you can trust me alone, I will shower and go open for you and you can get going," Ann sensed his hesitancy in leaving. He reluctantly agreed but went into the house and looked around anyway.


QUIGLEY, STILL SLEEPING IN A HOSPITAL BED, IV's IN HIS arms, had no idea what transpired the night before. When Ben arrived, Lowell Crawford, Jr. was at his bedside. Ben introduced himself and explained how he found Quigley on the couch at the coffee shop the night before.

"I'm his nephew, Lowell. He and my dad were brothers."

Ben shook his hand.

"We have tried for years to get Uncle Quigley to let us take care of him but he wouldn't allow it, Aunt Gertrude made me promise to keep an eye on him when she was dying. He's one of the reasons I came back to Bingham." Lowell ran the back of his hand over Quigley's forehead. "Thank you for getting him here."

Ben felt he should have done more and sooner but only nodded. He stayed only a short time. Quigley would not wake soon and on a good day, it was difficult to get him to speak. On his way out, he ran into the sheriff; they made small talk. Ben could sense Reynold's mistrust. He came clean the night before about the phone, Kasov, and his involvement with the FBI. He sent Reynolds the picture from Sarah's phone that morning. The sheriff barely made eye contact. He had been insulted professionally. Ben tried to explain his position but Reynolds looked on skeptically. He knew he had more confessing to do. He said goodbye to the sheriff and headed to Sarah who was now in a rehab facility. When he arrived, he recognized an undercover agent dressed as a housekeeper mopping the floor in front of Sarah's room. Sarah was sitting up with a book reading aloud with some difficulty. Joe looked on proudly. Ben learned from Joe her progress was slow and difficult, doctors and staff thought she should be further along. Depression was proving to be another obstacle. Ben asked Joe to step out in the hall. He told him everything from the stranger named Davis Tremont who was Kasov who was after Ben, to taking Sarah's phone to returning it—to the contents they discovered. He finished with Lacey's account of the day in St. Louis.

Joe sat down in a nearby chair, speechless. Ben waited in expectation of an angry outburst. A man whom he respected and sympathized with—may now hate him. He attempted an awkward apology; no response came from Joe. They sat in silence, therapists and nurses went back and forth about their business. Joe finally spoke,

"You knew 'bout this guy when he first came to Bingham? And you didn't do nothin' to stop him?"

"I called someone to have him followed. I was told he most likely left town, I believed them." Ben didn't tell him Sarah never spoke of the relationship; he couldn't defend himself on that point in his own mind. He should have known. "Believe me, Joe, I wish I had acted differently, you have no idea how many times I have gone over this in my mind. I can't say how sorry I am."

No response.

"I would do anything to trade places with her."

Joe looked at him for the first time since they sat down. "I don't know, Ben, I can't help but be a little mad at you for keeping this secret but I don't see how you should go blamin' yourself. Sarah's always been a good girl; I don't know why she'd go off to meet a man I never met. I'da thought she told me everything, my poor girl." His head dropped to his hands again. "No one, knows where this man is now?"

"No, hopefully, he is gone for good but we can't be sure until he surfaces somewhere else. He's wanted in three countries so he'll play it safe and keep a low profile." Ben hated to say what was on his mind, that he may never be brought to justice for what he did to Sarah. "My friend at the FBI has people looking for the tall, bald man Lacey described. He may know something. They have also spoken with her and taken her statement." Ben had been updated by Barone on the phone earlier while driving to the hospital. "Do you mind if I speak to Sarah? Ben hated to ask but knew Reynolds would be there soon, and for some reason, he wanted to stay ahead of him. Joe acquiesced.

Sarah was reading *Charlotte's Web*.

Ben sat down by the bed and asked, "How's Wilbur?"

"He's terrific." She smiled her old smile, "My favorite as a child."

"I saw the sketch of the guy that attacked you. Do you remember anything else?"

"Did he have a scar under his eye?"

"Yes."

Leaning back, "I remember giving his description to the sheriff, I don't know why his face sticks out in my mind, I saw him that night." She hesitated. "I don't know what is right and wrong."

"What do you mean?"

"His face is so real to me; I saw him standing on Church Street. I thought he was chasing me, but I can only see him standing there; he was bigger." She seemed to be looking at something in front of her.

"Who was bigger?"

She looked at Ben as if he should know, "The guy."

"The guy with the scar?"

"No, the other one; he was bigger than the guy with the scar; bald too."

Ben confused, asked, "Did he have tattoos?"

"It was dark, but somehow I know he did. Why do you think that is?" Sarah picked at the blanket on her bed, "I'm sure I gave the wrong description to the sheriff. I mean, the man with the scar, he was there but he isn't the one." She hit the bed with her good arm. "Why didn't I remember the other one, the bald one?"

Ben placed his hand on hers. "Don't worry; we'll get to the bottom of it."


ANN TOOK SOME FRESH SCONES OUT OF THE OVEN AS James Johnson walked in with a fist full of one-dollar bills. "Where's Ben?"

"Hello, what do you have there?"

"Money for Ben, where is he?"

"Not here, I can give it to him if you want."

James looked at his fist and then to Ann, "We shook hands and everything."

"I understand, how 'bout a warm scone, fresh from the oven." She handed him a plate with a glass of milk. "So, I heard you have recently come into some money, a rich uncle or something."

James's mouth was full; he looked at her untrustingly and nodded a yes.

"Wish I had a rich uncle," she joked.

He looked at Ann as if he wanted to say something but drank the milk instead.

Ann poured some more, "A hundred-dollar bill is a lot of money. What did you buy with all that money?"

"Not much," he looked away from Ann.

Ann remembered Imogene and Maggie that day on Main Street, "Maggie has some nice things at her shop, doesn't she?"

James squirmed, "Uh-huh," he started to get up, but glanced at the glass-covered plate containing a mound of scones. "Those blueberry?"

"Uh-huh." Handing him the scone she busied herself, occasionally glancing his direction. Aware that James came across his money by less than ethical means, she contemplated her next question. His grandmother, Denise used to work at the school cafeteria. She was a generous, kind woman; Ann knew James' mother ran off years ago, wandering in and out of his life only when it benefitted her. Denise did her best to care for him. He now sat with his head down, scone untouched. Ann continued clearing cups from previous customers. Whatever was on his mind, it seemed a heavy load for such a small boy.

"Did you go to church today?"

"No," Ann said with no explanation. The question caught her off guard; she turned to see him standing right behind her, his big brown eyes staring up. Why her answer bothered her was a mystery. She hadn't been in a church in over three years and it had not bothered her in all that time, but those brown eyes seemed to search right into her soul.

"I did, we go to the Bingham Baptist, Gran takes me every week. I go to Sunday school, too."

"That's nice," Ann placed the cups in the sink; the eyes still looking deep into her soul. "What did you learn today?" Not knowing what else to say, he did look as if he wanted to get something off his chest.

"We learned that a lie can be somethin' you know about and should tell someone but you don't, it's called de…dece… decention or somethin' like that."

"Deception," Ann helped him out. "Yes, I suppose that's true."

"You think so?"

Those eyes! "Yes, I do."

His little head went down. He moved his foot over a crack in the concrete floor. When he looked up again, his eyes were brimming with tears.

Ann stooped to his level, "What is it, James?"

He reached in his pocket and pulled out a plastic bag that looked like it had seen better days. It contained a gold money clip with a hundred-dollar bill still trapped inside.

"I found this," was all he managed to get out.

Imogene took his statement as Ann held his hand. There were many tears and apologies and promises to pay back the money he spent. Denise, his grandmother, rushed in and started to scold but when she saw his face, she wrapped her arms around him. He was able to let loose in the safety of his grandmother's arms and had a good, hard cry. After multiple assurances to James, he would not go to jail, they left with a promise of pizza for dinner from Denise.

"Well, can you beat that?" Imogene said examining the clip in the bag, "Sheriff is off visiting Quigley and Sarah, we'll send this to the lab and see if they can manage to get any prints besides James Johnsons' from this thing. It could have something to do with Sarah."

"It certainly isn't Quigley's" Ann blurted. Imogene reached in the cabinet for evidence bags. Ann noticed Imogene's tailored suit, like her family, she had attended church that morning. Presbyterian, also like the Fletchers. The suit flattered; Imogene kept herself in shape, jogging and going to the gym, with the goal, Ann presumed of eventually doing more than desk work. Ann believed Imogene to be the smartest of the three Bingham officers and resented—for Imogene—her minimized role.

"You look nice."

Imogene looking down at her clothing replied, "Thanks, bought this a few weeks ago, thought I would wear it to the wedding, but do you think it's too businessy?"

"It's fine, you look very smart."

"Smart wasn't what I was going for but I'll take it. I probably won't wear it to the wedding since I've already worn it to church. I think I'll get something more feminine. You never know who will be there." She said with a twinkle in her eye.

Ann laughed and turned to leave.

Imogene stopped her, "I'm sorry about this," she held up the picture of John.

"Yeah, I was hoping to leave that behind in Colorado." Her skin crawled at the sight of him.

"Despite what you think, Sheriff Reynolds is discreet. We all three met about it and we understand it stays here. He really doesn't want anything to upset Rachel's wedding."

Ann expressed gratitude for that discretion. They parted and she jogged back to Level Grounds. Zoe, Connor's sister, and Marissa the other bridesmaid, were waiting for her when she arrived. She had forgotten they agreed to meet and plan the shower. Apologizing as she opened the door, Ann quickly recovered the situation with coffee and scones. It was decided the shower would be in a week at Level Grounds; Ann assured them it wouldn't be a problem—at least she was pretty sure. It was supposed to be a surprise, which was old fashioned, as Marissa put it, but Ann and Zoe liked the idea. Since the engagement was one of the shortest any of them had ever heard of, there was hardly time to plan a shower. Rachel had only registered a few days ago. They divided the guest list and agreed on electronic invitations.

"Do you think Lauren will be upset with us for meeting without her?" Zoe asked.

Marissa rolled her eyes, "I'll call her and explain. I'll put her in charge of the cake and have her bring some decorations—that should smooth things over."

"She'll think it's aaawwwsome…" Ann said tongue in cheek.

The three parted as an afternoon crowd entered. By five-thirty Ann still had not heard from Ben. Business died down and she decided to tidy up. If he wasn't back by six, she would close and go home. She checked her phone for messages, none. It surprised her, he was very concerned for her last night and that morning, now, crickets. She wondered if Quigley had awakened and if he was able to get any information. She decided to text him. By six there was still no answer. She locked up and started home. It was still daylight and Main had a few people on it.

"I guess I'll be okay." She laughed to herself. Josephine caught up to her and trotted beside her, she was glad for the company. As she walked through the kitchen door, Josephine snuck in behind her.

"Ugh," Nancy cried, "get her out of my house!"

"First, a treat," Ann reached in the fridge for a piece of her father's salami. Josephine gratefully took it and left reluctantly when Nancy showed her the door.

Ann filled her mother in on the shower plans and they discussed the family invitations. Ann also told her about James' secret and how Imogene would have it checked for prints. Nancy asked what Ben thought about it which prompted Ann to check her phone again; nothing. Casually mentioning she hadn't heard from him all day; Ann turned her attention to a bag of chips on the counter. Nancy looked sympathetic. *What was she thinking?* Ann wondered.

"Let's go get something to eat at Top Floor." Her mother said cheerfully, putting the chips away in the pantry. "If we are going to have the reception there, I would like to at least taste the food."

Sara heard Ben curse his phone. The battery was dead and he forgot a charger. There was one in the drawer next to her bed but she wouldn't offer it to him. The constant calls and texts to Agent Barone dried it up. The afternoon unfolded with more progress than in the last several weeks for her. After a few hours to wrap her mind around Ben's confession, she began remembering the contents of her phone. Forgiving Ben for taking it and viewing her private conversations proved a bit harder. She was working on it but had not reached that point yet. Her charger would stay hidden in the drawer for now.

The texts with Davis Tremont, as she knew him, triggered her memory and the excitement in meeting him that fateful day. Her stomach now turned at the thought of it. Agent Barone sent a file with some photos of men fitting the description of the bald man with tattoos; Sarah studied each one on an FBI computer as she sat in a chair by the bed. No one seemed familiar. An FBI agent stood in the corner conferring with Sheriff Reynolds. Ben kept glancing their way but would not approach them. He also glanced at Sarah's phone sitting on a table nearby. She decided if he asked, she would let him use it. As it was, she wouldn't offer it. Her head ached and she felt her heart rate increase with every mug shot she viewed. Now certain her attacker and Davis Tremont was not the same person, she believed him to be the man speaking with Davis that day in the park. *But why?* She could only imagine it was because the men thought she heard too much. It all made her head swim. She glanced up to see Ben pacing the floor.

"Do you mind, Sarah?" Ben said pointing to her phone.

Sarah reluctantly gave him permission. Whoever he was calling did not answer. She suspected it was Ann. There was a spark every time he spoke about her. Sarah doubted his promise to give her old job back when she recovered. Another reason to resent him. She nodded and smiled as he put the phone back.

Ben, frustrated he could not reach Ann, was about to make an excuse to leave when Sheriff Reynolds, looking his direction, mentioned checking in with Imogene. Ben asked to speak with her when he finished. Reynolds eyed him with suspicion.

Apparently, Imogene had much to tell the sheriff. "Uh-huh, yes, what else did he say? Uh-huh, and Fannie brought him in? He confessed to her? This morning, yes, a sermon about lies? Well I guess that's good, she picked him up, crying, yes, you didn't lock him up?" At this he chuckled a little but looking over at Ben he suddenly stopped, remembering Ben's request.

Ben hearing 'Fannie' became more anxious by the minute. *What could all that possibly be about; could it have something to do with John?*

Reynolds went on. "Let me tell the agent here and we'll see how they want to handle it; it will be faster in their lab. Yeah, okay, okay. Yeah, you can go home, wait Ben wants to speak with you."

"Imogene, yeah, hi, yeah I'm okay, no I don't know what that was all about. Is Ann okay? My phone is dead and I can't reach her." *Relief!* Imogene informed him she saw her and Nancy going to Top Floor a few minutes ago.

"If you see her tell her my phone is dead, I'll be home later tonight. Yes, Sarah is better, yes, I'll tell her; goodbye, yes, you too, bye." Ben handed the phone back to Reynolds and caught the end of what he was saying about James Johnson and the money clip he found.

"I'm sure it's evidence!" Reynolds was speaking with a raised voice to the agent.

"Too bad it was found by a nine-year-old," was the sarcastic response.

Reynolds left the room in a huff. Ben questioned the agent and learned the details of Ann's discovery. James was a man of his word; he smiled thinking of him bringing the six dollars as he promised with a handshake. Ann probably worked her magic with a scone or something. He knew she wouldn't let it go; a nine-year-old walking around town with a couple of hundreds in his pocket would be too much for her curiosity. Suddenly, he wanted to be back in Bingham. Sarah still puzzling over the photos on the verge of tears; Joe sitting in a corner wringing his hands nervously, Ben knew it was time to break this up. A nurse walked in at that moment. Surveying the situation she strongly recommended rest and quiet for Sarah. Ben was relieved. He kissed her forehead, shook Joe's hand, and left without a word to Reynolds who was still brooding out in the hall.

It was nine when the front doorbell rang; Ann peeked through the peephole and considered letting him stand there a while but couldn't resist. Opening the door, she stood with folded arms and remarked, "Where have you been?" Turning from him, she crossed the room and sat down, "I broke the James Johnson mystery wide open."

He followed her in, closing the door behind him

# CHAPTER 11

A nn put the finishing touch on the arrangement for the nursing home, "Who this week?"

"Mabel Wesley." Nancy slipped the list back under the cash register in her usual sly manner.

"I'll bring it now when I get back let's figure out the arrangements for the shower? I would like to brighten Level Grounds; it's a little too brown for me."

Her mother nodded agreement.

Ann had not had the pleasure of bringing the nursing home arrangement for a few weeks and was looking forward to delivering this one. Mabel Wesley taught her fifth-grade class and she remembered her as one of the few teachers who understood her.

Mabel sat by a window in the dining room. She brightened at Ann's approach.

"Fannie?" she asked, struggling to stand, "Is that you?"

"Yes, Mrs. Wesley, don't get up." Ann placed the flowers on a nearby table.

"Did you arrange this?"

"Yes."

"Aren't they gorgeous?"

"There is no signature on the card," Ann said apologetically.

"No,"

*T.B. Stoner*

"You don't seem surprised."

"I love the colors, last time I got daisies, they were beautiful too. You have your mother's talent."

Evidently, the mystery of the bouquet giver was no mystery to Mabel. Ann suspected her mother for a few weeks. She opened her mouth to question Mabel but was interrupted.

"You were always more creative than you let on. And smart, remember the spelling bee? You surprised everyone, but not me. When you put your mind to something, you stuck to it."

Winning the fifth-grade spelling bee was a gem in her mother's crown. By the time Nancy told the third person, Ann decided against any future spelling bees. She knew now, it was to get to her mother. Nana used to call it kicking against the goad. Any time Nancy showed approval or encouragement, Ann would do something to disappoint her mother. It was as if she couldn't be consistent in anything but disappointment. Any approval or compliment put tremendous pressure on Ann to keep it going. The solution was to sink back into mediocrity and less than stellar behavior. Coming home brought fresh reminders of childhood and its struggles. Both young and old women stared at the arrangement lost in their own memories.

Mabel, remembering herself inquired after Ann and her family wishing the best for Rachel's upcoming wedding.

"Rachel was always a good student and very kind…" Mabel paused for a moment, "she will always be content, I think, because of her nature. You know, none of us are good in the sense we should be. Our selfish nature takes care of that. Rachel is one of those rare people that make kindness look easy. I saw it on the playground early on. I'm sure she has it tough with some people, she's a sinner like the rest of us but she has that gift of making one feel cared for."

Ann could not argue with that.

"The two of you are very different. You're like your mother."

Ann laughed out-loud before she could stop. "I'm nothing like my mother."

Mabel smiled, "Did you know, in Bingham, there is a silent code that passes from one generation to the next?"

"I don't know what you're talking about."

"Well, we all grow up doing things we regret. If anyone denies it, they are a liar. In this town, one generation to the next sticks around. We know everything of significance about one another. We grow up and have our children. So, all our folly goes into the closet so the next generation knows nothing about it. For instance, in nineteen-sixty-nine, Harold Bowman burned the old general store on Seventy-Nine to the ground. You probably never knew it existed. I tell you as an example. We never speak of one another's mistakes. Its code. So, now I will just tell you. I watched your mother grow up and I watched you grow up—and you are a lot like her. That's all I'll say about it."

"Then why do I feel nothing like her?"

Mabel shrugged, "that's always the way with parents and children. As a parent, we see our sins and folly in the children we have. That drives us to purge it from the child. Most of the time it backfires. That's my theory anyway."

Ann stared at the arrangement. It was her own style but there was something in it that belonged to Nancy too.

"Each generation, especially at your age, believes their parents were never young." Mabel took Ann's hand, "Contentment, doesn't come easy for you, does it, Ann?"

Ann shrugged.

"No, it never has," Mable answered for her. "Restlessness has always been your companion. You were, and probably still are, impatient. Impatient with the nonsense of other people, quick to speak and ready for action. I heard you have been gone these three years."

"Yes, why do you call me restless?" The accusation hit a nerve.

Mabel laughingly replied, "You were not content with the status quo but in your haste to change things and move on, you sometimes took two steps forward and one step back. Do you remember Billy Garrett?"

She nodded; Bingham was small enough you knew everyone that you went to school with. Billy Garrett was a thorn in her side, but she couldn't remember why.

"You were a torment to that poor boy! But what he never realized—he was a torment to you just by being in your presence. He was so meticulous and always had to be the best: the best handwriting, the best at the math quiz, the best on the playground. Why Ann, you could not stand him!" Mabel leaned back in her chair, laughter on her lips. "Oh, my! Remember the time you tripped him as he was carrying his science project to the back of the classroom?"

Ann shifted in her chair. The project had to do with ball bearings which scattered across the floor and sprung twenty fifth graders into action. Evie Camden tripped and fell on them. She suddenly felt the need to explain.

"I have no idea why I did that, I'm sorry Mrs. Wesley, what a nuisance I was."

Mabel still laughing, "You truly don't know why?"

"No, it was a cruel thing to do."

"I'll tell you why…deadlines were a curse to you, couldn't stand them. Any other time I could trick you into getting things done on time and I had no problem with letting things slide too. But the science fair was different, everyone had to turn it in step by step and the deadlines were absolute. You never liked details and it was a detailed project, requiring documented information every step of the way. I had sent you back to your desk for the third time that day, you were of course behind. When Billy chose to go down that row, the row you were sitting in, I knew, I knew by the look on your face. I stood to say something but Evie walked up and distracted me. The next thing I knew, ball bearings, everywhere." At this Mabel was laughing so hard her eyes held tears.

"You were as shocked as Billy; I could tell by your reaction; you didn't know how bad it would be. Well…fortunately, it was only a matter of picking up the pieces and putting it back together, which all the kids helped with. I didn't have the heart to send you to the office. I made you sit by me for the rest of the day." Mabel sat up, pulling a tissue from her sleeve, "Don't you see, Ann? You have always wanted to succeed but were too impatient to go the usual route. I don't know why I told you that, seeing you again, and I don't mean to pick at you, seeing you again reminds me of that little girl, so anxious to grow up and do her own thing. And here you are, grown up and I suppose doing your own thing." Mabel squeezed Ann's hand, "Sometimes our own way isn't the best way." She turned to the arrangement in admiration, "Very good Ann, beautiful. I have no doubt, there is much more beauty where that came from."

The walk back to The Flower Shop proved to be a time of soul searching. Ann thought Mabel was in the early stages of dementia or something to believe she was anything like her mother. Nancy always wanted Ann to be different if she were like her mother, why the pressure to make her something else? The question of how well she knew her mother popped in her head. All she knew about her was that she was her mother. She wanted a picture-perfect, happy family and to create bouquets for the town of Bingham. That was her mother. As far as Ann thought, there was not much more. She loved her God and went to church. Ann had no reason to doubt her love for Stuart. If Ann were the daughter she wished for—Nancy Fletcher's life would be perfect. She stopped in front of The Flower Shop. Nancy was finishing a funeral arrangement. Her father would come by to pick it up and deliver it to the funeral home. He always did that on Saturdays for his wife. In fact, Stuart did anything Nancy wanted, it seemed to Ann. He had also delivered the nursing home arrangements the few times Ann could not. Ann went inside.

"Why do you do it?" she asked her mother when she returned.

"Do what?" Nancy put some clippings of roses and lilies in front of her. "What about these?"

Ann pointed to the burgundy lilies and pulled some dipped carnations from the cooler. "Send those flowers every week?"

"How do you know it's me?" Nancy turned to pull out some vases.

"Who else would it be? What if we did the tall square vase instead?"

Nancy nodded approval. "I do it because I am able and there is no reason not to and the best reason to."

Ann turned to the baby's breath and added it to the collection. She knew the best reason. Selflessness and serving. They came naturally to Rachel but for her, the interest of others historically held no interest. The two worked putting some simple arrangements together. Ann watched her mother closely. Since her homecoming, Nancy's self-restraint in spiritual commentary surprised her. In the past, Nancy tried persuasion, cajoling, and guilt—the result was Ann ran away from it, instead of to it. How could Mabel possibly think she was like her mother?

"Do you want to hear something funny?" Ann would test the accusation.

"What?"

"Mabel Wesley said I take after you."

Nancy smiled and kept working.

"Well, really," Ann laughed, "is that the most ridiculous thing or what?"

"We both hate broccoli."

"That doesn't mean anything, most of the world hates it—they just won't admit it."

"Well, you're getting pretty good at this," Nancy nodded toward Ann's arrangement.

Exasperated, Ann said, "She meant our personalities or something. Said she watched us both grow up and we acted alike. Then she had the nerve to say I wasn't content and restless. I mean, maybe that's true about me but you…"

Nancy didn't answer.

"Since when have you ever wanted out of Bingham and wanted adventure?"

"I may have at one time," Nancy said affronted.

"You grew up, went away to college, came home, married Dad, and never looked back. How is that adventure?"

"Raising children is adventure enough for anyone."

Nancy's phone buzzed for the third time. She continued working.

"Aren't you going to see who that is?"

"It's Nana. She's learned to text."

"Well, aren't you going to answer her?"

"She's been after me all morning to pick up her order from Lang's. I told her I would when we've finished." The phone buzzed again; Nancy turned it off. "When I'm working, I don't bother with it."

Ann was surprised. Her mother ignoring her mother. It was something Ann would do. Nancy and Nana always seemed to get along. Could there have been a time when the relationship was strained?

Ann decided to try to understand her mother a little more.

"So, when you went to college, were you dating Dad?"

"No, we knew each other and were friends but we didn't start dating until we were sophomores. There were six of us from Bingham that went to the same college. We made a pact before we left."

"What?"

"It was silly really, my idea in fact. I was disgusted that I wasn't going on my own, away from everyone I knew. It was your dad, me, two girls and two other guys. We agreed to live in separate dorms, avoid one another, if possible. I said we had to make new friends."

"How did that work out?" Ann had enjoyed Evie's company her first year away. But Ann and Evie were 'thick-as-thieves' as they say.

"It was okay that first year. We were busy enough with classes and clubs but by the spring semester of our sopho-

more year, we were inseparable again. Small town relationships never die. I married your dad and the Compton's
married. You remember them. They were two of the group."

"So, what about that summer? After your freshman year?
Did you pay any attention to Dad then?"

Nancy looked down at a bow she was tying, "I didn't
come home that summer."

"Where did you go?"

"I've told you I'm sure. I stayed with Nana's cousin in
Indiana." Nancy cleared her throat and turned away from
Ann.

"Well, what did you do there?"

"Just helped on the farm. I'm sure I've told you this."

"What? The whole summer? "

"Yes, and a little after. I went back to school that spring."

"You skipped a semester?" Ann tried to read her mother.
She had never heard this part of Nancy's life before.

"Not really skipped, I arranged to do some correspon-
dence courses. We didn't have the internet then. I was still
able to graduate in time."

"But why did you have to go out there?"

"They needed my help, with the farm." Nancy kept her
answers short.

"Why did you have to go?" Ann pushed, "Why not
Uncle Peter?"

"Ann, he's younger than I. Still in high school. I went
because they are family and needed help with the farm."

Ann knew Nana's extended family was large and wasn't
satisfied with her mother's vague answers. There was more
to the story. "Why?"

"Because of the baby." Nancy again turned so Ann
couldn't see her face. "They were in the process of adopt-

ing, they needed help with chores going through that. I was around to do anything they needed doing."

"Oh, they adopted from overseas?" Ann felt like she was the inquisition but none of this added up.

"Well, no they never left the country but there was a lot to it." Nancy finished her bouquet and placed it in a box where they had put the others. "There, I think that's good. I'll put these in the cooler for tomorrow. Don't you need to be at work next door?"

"I have a few minutes. What brought you and Dad together?"

Nancy seemed relieved Ann changed the subject, "you know that story. It was our faith. Your dad was in a faith fraternity, he was one of the founders. They had a dance. He asked me. I didn't want anything to do with him, I didn't believe then. Or I thought I did but not like him. Thought he was a fanatic."

Ann shocked by this, said, "You thought he was a fanatic?"

"Yep. He told me he was praying for me. I laughed at him. But his prayers worked and I'm so happy they did. Anyway, I went to the dance because Ellen Compton was going, she was dating Mr. Compton by then. She talked me into going. I had a wonderful time. Your dad was different. Growing up he could be pretty obnoxious and there were times I just could not stand him and told him so. Once a group of us got ice cream cones at the drugstore. Stuart came out carrying two, one for Sue Bingham—couldn't stand her either, so I tripped him. He fell flat on his face losing both cones. Now, isn't that terrible?" Nancy shook her head. "What made me do that? I could be obnoxious myself."

Ann's thoughts flashed to Billy Garrett. At that time, Stuart came in to collect the funeral flowers.

"How are my girls?" He kissed his wife.

"You came just in time. I have been telling Ann things I shouldn't."

"Like what?"

"Like the time I tripped you with the ice cream cones."

"Ahh, I loved her then and still do." Stuart smiled at his wife.

Ann, puzzled by new revelations of her parents, grabbed her bag and headed to Level Grounds. She had never heard her mother say she, 'couldn't stand', anyone. It was something Ann was reprimanded for her whole life. In fact, ashamed to admit it, she said it about Rachel a few times. Rachel, whom she had grown to love even more since being home—experienced Ann's old resentment the night of the concert. Ashamed, she apologized the next day and Rachel forgave with her usual grace. Apologizing came easy—being so used to it. This time though, Ann meant the apology, more than any other time in her life.

Rachel had always tried to be her protector. A few times she succeeded in convincing Ann of thinking things through before charging headlong into trouble. Mostly, Ann chased her home and went off with her friends doing what teenagers in small towns do. Getting into trouble, disappointing her mother, and ignoring the precepts by which she was raised.

If someone told her two months ago she and her mother would be working together in The Flower Shop, creating floral arrangements for her sister's wedding she would have laughed. In fact, she had laughed many times as she and Nancy joked impiously about people and circumstances in the town of Bingham. If Ann were being honest with herself she would have to admit, at this juncture, she was happy. Most of her life she had been concerned with what made her happy in the moment. Mabel's accusation was true. Ann found contentment hard to obtain so she rashly sought to be happy. Reflecting on her past, Ann saw a pattern. Impulsive behavior had been her answer to boredom and many other problems. The parties, the drinking, and her last big mistake, John, plagued her thoughts. At least since Ben blocked calls, not in her contacts, she hadn't heard from him. It felt as if things were improving and she was settling into life in Bingham. It had been a good productive week and not only for Ann.

Her interest in Sarah's case increased and the week brought good news on that front. Fingerprints found on the money clip belonged to a felon who lived in St. Louis. There was an active search. Sarah was improving and as an incentive to reach her physical therapy goals, Rachel invited her to the wedding. Her doctor said she could go if she passed a few stamina tests. Nancy bought her a dress and some shoes. Another generosity Ann couldn't ignore. The invitation, Joe informed them, seemed to cause her to turn a corner. He excitedly told Ann, he believed he would have his Sarah back soon.

Ann reached Level Grounds; Ben was inside. Determined to focus on preparations for tomorrow's menu, she would make a conscious effort to avoid small talk. Ben agreed to close early for the shower, it hadn't been difficult. Ann smiled and looked into his eyes and that was it. She knew he would. It made her feel a little guilty but it had to be done. At times, she believed there wouldn't be much Ben would refuse her—yet she still tried to maintain a professional relationship. Most of her planning she would do today—tomorrow morning she would cook.

Her family would be at church. Since James Johnsons' question about church, Ann had contemplated going with her parents. She made a mental checklist of reasons not to. Her relationship with God's people was not something she remembered fondly. A series of events that included: smoking pot with Reverend Todd's son and kissing Bruno behind the vestry. Both didn't bode well with the congregation. It didn't seem to matter that Matthew Todd supplied half the high school with their weekend dope. His father, the good Reverend Todd made himself oblivious to the fact. Ann remembered how he sat smugly in the Fletcher living room shaking his head in disapproval, offering parenting advice which Nancy took graciously but Stuart reminded him to look to his own household. God's people made sure to keep their daughters at a distance and soon invitations to sleepovers and picnics stopped coming. Except for Evie— she stayed faithful—following Ann into adventure and trouble. Like the time they stole Reverend Todd's car and parked it in front of the bar on Seventy-Nine. It sat an entire night and day before the sheriff noticed it on his rounds. To this day, no one knew who did it. The revenge was sweet. Reverend Todd and family had long left Bingham; had he still been around, that would have sealed it. But since he was gone, Ann considered going back. It would have to wait. She entered Level Grounds. Ben was not in front.

# CHAPTER 12

Ben finished the email from Kathryn informing him he would be getting a call next week from Joel Brandon of Brandon, Brandon, and Stump. He had almost put the interview out of his mind, the offer so long in coming. A month ago, he would have accepted, no question. In fact, job or no job, if Ann hadn't shown up—there would be a 'For Sale' sign on the door now. One month ago, leaving Bingham was the obvious thing to do if he ever wanted to do something worthwhile. This position offered a chance to do just that. Using what he learned in the military and putting it to use helping firms negotiate contracts with the government. And he missed New York a month ago; Bingham had lost its charm. Being there with Kathryn, in the city that never sleeps, gave him longing for home, a Mets game, and some real pizza.

"Now what," he said aloud to himself. While there was technically nothing between himself and Ann, she occupied his thoughts almost constantly. Always watching the clock, anticipating when she would walk through the door. She was due now. He closed the laptop intent on finding something to do in the coffee shop. There would be a lot of women there tomorrow night; maybe he should clean the bathroom.

He hadn't heard the bell when the door opened over the noise of the toilet flushing. He turned, with toilet brush in one hand and bucket in the other, she was there smiling.

"That's a good look for you." She nodded at the gloves.

"Didn't hear you come in. I'm almost done."

"I need to order food for the shower tomorrow, is there anything you want me to order for here?"

"I don't think so, what's on the menu?" following her to a table he turned a chair backward and straddled it.

"I'm thinking a small plate thing, definitely something with bacon and pears, possibly together but maybe not. Some kind of slider or finger sandwich involving chicken, pasta salad with artichoke and goat cheese and maybe some bacon mixed in, I'm not completely sure but I'm getting there."

"It does sound like you are making it up as you go along. But it also makes me sorry I'll miss it."

"No boys allowed, but thanks for letting us have it here."

"No problem, the couch has been replaced." He swept his hand in that direction. Quigley made the old one unusable. They discovered the source of the odor a few days ago. "And it's a darn shame, that couch was comfortable. Since you're having the shower, Eric and I plan on doing a little impromptu bachelor party."

Ann raised her eyebrows, "It's a small town, not New York or Vegas. So, keep in mind what happens in Bingham will be all over Bingham by morning."

He laughed; she seemed to make him laugh a lot lately. "It'll be tame, don't worry. You know Connor and his faith."

Looking up from her computer, their eyes meet. "I do and I'm glad for it. For Rachel's sake, I mean. Her faith is strong and it wouldn't work for her to marry outside of it."

He noticed a look of conviction.

"Why don't you believe what your family does?"

"Who said I didn't?"

"Sorry, it's just, you don't go to church. I thought that was in the rule book."

She looked back at her computer. "I grew up in church, I guess I can make a lot of excuses for not going, but if I'm honest I would have to say, I just don't want to."

Ben leaned in and with honest interest asked her why.

"Why don't I want to?"

"Yes."

"A lot of reasons, I guess."

He stared, expecting more. She continued staring at the computer screen.

"God's people," she used air quotes, "aren't exactly the most understanding group. What about you? Have you ever been?"

"Weddings and funerals. My mother started going after my father was killed in the towers." Saying it aloud still triggered emotion. He cleared his throat, "My sister Kathryn went for a while but quit after we lost Mom. I never really believed God could exist after what happened to my dad and all those other people that day. It was done, in the first place, for some god apparently, but either they are way off or that god is cruel. And who is to say which one is real or not? I knew a few guys like Connor in the military; they tried to talk to me a few times. Connor and I have sat in this very spot till the wee hours discussing it. And I have to admit, a few times, I wanted to believe. I just couldn't for some reason. It's easier to believe my dad was in the wrong place at the wrong time and things just happen because people are crazy and don't care about human life. You can blame the tornado—that destroys one half of town and leaves the other untouched—on wind directions and gusts and atmospheric pressure. Too bad, my house is obliterated while yours stands. My dad is killed at work because someone blew up his office with an airplane while your dad came home that day." Ben pushed back from the table, "You want some coffee?"

"No, thanks," Her eyes looked directly into his, they were sad. It was if she could see right through him. "I'm sorry about your parents…" It came out almost in a whisper.

"You and me both," he kept his back turned. Her look made him uncomfortable. "Mom died about four years after Dad. She was diagnosed in March, died by August. Kathryn and I didn't know what hit us. I had just graduated high school and her undergrad. She went on to graduate school in the fall and I went to basic. Kathryn said I abandoned her. I guess I did, she has never quite forgiven me, then when I came here instead of staying in New York, she didn't speak to me for months. I guess I have neglected her. It's easier to keep in touch now with smartphones." Now was as good a time as any to let Ann know about the interview. He may be able to gauge her feelings. He turned to look at her, "She wants me back home."

"Oh." Her eyes held steady.

"A month ago, I was ready and willing…"

"And now?"

"I was ready for a change," he waved a hand around Level Grounds. "I lost interest about a year ago, building it, making it profitable, it was easy, I have to move on." His eyes searched hers. "A month ago," he repeated, "it was easy…"

"It's not easy anymore?"

"No…"

A group of young people entered. Ben greeted them, served them, and made small talk while keeping an eye on Ann. She appeared to be making little progress with her menu, staring at the computer lost in thought. He hoped the distraction may have to do with the possibility of him leaving. He wouldn't find out; the remainder of the day was busy with customers coming and going. The young people stayed long after they paid for their small coffees—taking advantage of the new couch. Their laughter distracted him and Ann, she repositioned herself in the office until it was time for him to leave.

"I'm off," he put his head in the office.

"Oh, I'll come out. The kids still here?"

"They left after they finished their third cup of water," he said laughing. He watched as she put her apron on and rebound her thick curls into a ponytail. There always seemed to be a strand that never made it. The urge to brush it away was overwhelming.

"Well, have a good day. Hope your friend Barone has some good news." She stood still with expectation on her face.

There was an awkward moment until he realized he was blocking the door. They did a sort of dance trying to arrange her exit. The blush on her cheek was obvious. Finally, he gently took hold of her shoulders and reversed their positions as if they were dancing. She smiled that smile and turned to greet an entering customer.

Driving to the city, his mind was on Ann alone. He would not see her again until tomorrow and then they would have little time to talk. Reading her proved difficult because of his own emotions. If she were not interested, she might have encouraged him to follow his dreams, so to speak. Asking why he didn't find leaving easy anymore gave him some hope. But what hope? Building a future with one woman for the rest of your life, like Connor believed, never made sense to Ben. Sure, his parents got along okay from what he remembered but they didn't have time to go the long hall. Everyone Ben knew growing up that married was now divorced. Kathryn had a different boyfriend every time he talked to her. Why did he think Ann Fletcher was any different from any other woman and why did he think of her constantly? And could he possibly spend the rest of his life with one woman? Driving south on The Avenue of the Saints, he realized he could—if that woman were Ann Fletcher. Laughing at the idea of it—he hadn't even kissed her; how could he decide to devote his life to a woman he hadn't kissed. The idea of it increasingly appealed to him. By the time he reached Barone, he had almost convinced himself of turning down the job.

Barone, wearing khaki slacks, an argyle sweater, and sunglasses, was fresh off the golf course. "Thanks for meeting me here at the club." Barone got immediately down to business, "The prints on the money clip belong to Estaban Ramos Freeman, thirty years of age, wanted for assault with a deadly weapon, armed robbery, illegal possession of a firearm and a laundry list of misdemeanors. We think Kasov hired him to kill Sarah. The three hundred was half upfront. Question is, Estaban is a gun dealer, been selling guns on the street for years, why wouldn't he have just shot her, why go through the trouble of beating her and then running after a rock is thrown his direction?"

"Sick and ruthless," Ben puzzled by the method himself continued, "Did Kasov want it that way?"

"Possibly, but a hired hit is supposed to be a get-in-and-get-out kind of thing. Don't draw attention in any way. The job isn't finished, Freeman is out the three hundred and might want to finish the job to collect the rest." Barone flagging a waiter ordered two beers. "That local cop, Reynolds, says he and his lackey went over the crime scene but I'm sending two guys out there Monday just in case. It's possible the weapon never left his pocket but it won't hurt to go over the lot again, I know it's been almost two months and it's rained but it should be done. Hell, when you have a nine-year-old find evidence placing Freeman at the scene that's pretty bad."

Ben agreed, "What about Kasov, anything on him?"

"As far as we know, he's gone. If Freeman finishes the job and gets paid it won't be by him. Sarah has positively ID'd Freeman as the man with Kasov that day in the park; we sent his mug shots over yesterday. She can't swear he beat her because she swears Kasov was on Church Street that night. That's why she ran or peddled faster; she was convinced he was after her but she can't place his face as the man who attacked her. That's where Quigley comes in if they ever let us near him. As of yesterday, he was still on oxygen in ICU."

"If Freeman finishes the job?" Ben stopped listening after that statement, "You still have someone on her, don't you?"

"Yes, don't worry, she's got someone there twenty-four hours. You blame yourself, don't you?"

Ben, peeling the label on his beer shook his head, "Why wouldn't I? Kasov was there looking for me, can't understand why he would risk it but he was."

"Maybe, but he's gone now. It's not your fault, Ben, it just happened. Happens all the time, bad men doing bad things.

I know you think if it weren't for you Sarah wouldn't have been caught in the crossfire but things happen for a reason." Barone held Ben's gaze as he said this. "Stop questioning yourself and your motives, it doesn't do anyone any good. We'll get this guy and eventually Kasov will be caught by someone, I'm confident of that."

"How can you be?"

"The bad guy never wins really," Barone said smiling, "Hey by the way, what is Connor up to? Got a call from Scotty in Colorado, said Connor called in a favor and he was tailing a guy."

Ben, sure color rose to his face at the mention of the situation, replied, "His fiancé's sister, she got mixed up with someone out there, dirtbag, made threats. Local is aware and has a picture. Probably won't follow her but Connor's being diligent." Silent alarms going off in his brain, he asked, "Why, what did Scotty tell you?"

"The dirtbag was arrested out there, bar fight or something, he made bail and then left town. I'm sure Scotty's updated Connor but I wouldn't be too sure he'll keep away, sounds unhinged to me."

Ben finished his beer, thanked Barone and left in a hurry. Texting Ann from his car, he debated on whether to see Sarah as planned or head back to Bingham. His text, a simple *'Hey'*, was responded to with *'hey yourself.'* It was close to eight, she would have to lock up soon and walk home alone. Thinking of something else to text so he didn't look like an idiot, he sent, *'did I leave my blue jacket in the back room?'* He called Connor and filled him in on Barone's intel. Connor assured him; he spoke with Scotty yesterday and had been keeping an eye out. Ben made him promise to walk Ann home. With that promise, he went ahead with his visit to Sarah.

# CHAPTER 13

Ann glanced at the time as she walked to the back room; seven-forty-five. She would close early; it was slow and she would have to be back early in the morning to do prep work for the shower. No blue jacket. The front door opened, so much for closing early.

"Be right there," she yelled as she took one last look around. Backing out of the room, she sensed someone behind her. Turning slowly, she saw him out of the corner of her eye. It was John. Her heart raced. Backing away, she felt his hand grip her arm. He pulled her to the front. The lights were off and it was dark.

"Lock the door," he demanded.

Ann obeyed. She searched the street as she turned the lock, hoping she could catch someone's eye. As was usual at this time, Main was deserted. Remembering her self-defense lessons, she gauged the nearness of John's head behind her own, jerking her head back with all her might. Amazingly, his grip disappeared as he grabbed his nose. As she reached for the lock again, she felt a blow to the back of her head.

She awoke in pitch black, a gag on her mouth, and her hands bound in front of her. The dank, damp smell surrounding her was familiar. Confused, she tried to sit up, her head throbbed. Sensing she was on a mattress or large couch she shifted her legs to the side and tried to stand.

"Whoa, don't get up."

"*John*," Ann panicked, her breathing grew rapid. She suddenly remembered seeing him show up at the coffee shop. Straining to make out the room, she glimpsed moonlight coming in through a window. A broken window. There were dots of light up and down the wall, indicating more windows hastily covered with cardboard. A realization that she was in Quigley's factory apartment added more confusion and fear.

"A head injury is a pretty serious thing. I think I hit a good spot though, just enough to knock you out. I knew you wouldn't want to come with me so I had to do it, Ann. You've just been so unreasonable, blocking my calls, ignoring me. I mean, what's a guy to do? And the head butt, I have to admit was pretty quick thinking. Had no choice but to incapacitate you." John was now next to her on the mattress stroking her hair.

Ann, eyes wide with fear, assessed her situation the best she could. Except for the moonlight, it was pitch dark. Her heart pounded in her chest; *where is my phone?*

"I just want to talk, Ann," John assured her. "I don't know why you have to be so stubborn, why you left the way you did? We had a good thing, a good thing." An adamant declaration, he grasped Ann's bound hands in his. "I told my mother about you; told her you were the girl I was going to marry. She wants to meet you." His smile was sickening and she could smell the alcohol on his breath. He continued talking as if they were meeting for coffee.

Her head pounded with pain but she tried to think. He was drunk and impaired, but so was she. She couldn't

THE BEATING OF SARAH STRONG

scream, the gag on her mouth was so tight she wanted to vomit. Her feet were free, could she run? Possibly, but even drunk he would probably catch her and that would make him angrier. He continued with his rambling, she tried to look in his eyes as if interested, it might buy time. If she showed interest and sympathy maybe he would untie her, she kept her eyes on his and debated tearing up. Would crying make him angry or something else? As it was, the pain was so bad she wanted to cry but held back.

"Everyone thinks we're still together, told them you needed space. It was hard tracking you at first but old records pop up; misdemeanor, from your senior year in high school, something to do with destruction of private property and theft of flamingos." He laughed. "Good thing you were eighteen at the time or the records would have been untraceable. So, here I am. I bet you thought you would get away with it, that I would just forget about you and leave you alone. But we were meant to be together, you and me." Leaning in close he began kissing her. "Now what? I bet that's what you're thinking. I found this abandoned place on my way into town, watched it for a few days then came up here to see what's up. I do have a plan but thought it best to let you in on it first so there would be no surprises. From either of us, that is, if you understand me correctly." A phone buzzing in his pocket distracted him. "That isn't mine, must be yours." Pulling it out, "From Ben; says, '*did you find it?*' Find what? Let's scroll up and see." John scrolled through her phone, reading every text he could from Ben. "I think he wants to be your boyfriend." Anger was in his eyes. Ann shook her head no. "Maybe we should answer him."

Ann tried to think, it was the worst possible scenario. If he answered the text Ben would think she was okay.

Ann tried to speak with the gag; she had to give Ben a message somehow in a short text. But how and what could she tell him.

John annoyed, "It's a yes or no question just shake your head."

Ann dropped her head, refusing to answer.

"Okay, I'll tell him no."

Ann nodded in agreement. If John told Ben no, it would make no difference to Ben; but Ann would lead John to believe otherwise. John hesitated.

"If I say yes, he may ask for details." John tapped her phone against his head. He looked at her with disgust. Ripping the gag from around her mouth he asked, "Who is this guy anyway?"

Ann could see the jealous rage in his eyes. "No one."

His hand went hard across her mouth. She could feel blood trickle down.

"I work for him. That's all."

"It better be." He handed her the phone. "Answer him one word, to get him off our back, no more than one word. Do you understand?"

His sickly, fermented breath caught in her nostrils. Shaking, she desperately tried to think. What word would give them away, it was obvious. She quickly typed it and hit send. Another slap to her head.

"I wanted to see it before you sent it!" Grabbing the phone, "What is this? Quigley's?"

"A friend. The other side of town. It will take him an hour to drive there." Ann was desperate.

John paced the floor mumbling aloud the fact that he hadn't thought this whole thing through. He hadn't considered her cell phone as a link to all she knew. They would be looking for her soon. In frustration, he threw it against the wall.

"Well, we can't stay here. Anyway, the plan." He came back to the bed. "I scored some fake passports. We're going to Alaska via Canada. Isn't that great?"

Ann, wide-eyed, vacillated between fear and amazement. He was obviously insane. Her instinct to run was turning to something more practical. What if she played along? She would bide her time.

"I can see you're surprised. I thought you would be, but I've thought this through. You are good at roughing it; I mean we did meet on a camping trip...I'll never forget those pancakes you made over an open fire. Remember? We were so happy those first weeks. I knew then that we were made for one another. I think you knew it too." He moved his arm around her and leaned in.

"John!" she surprised herself. "What if we," she hesitated, "I mean, Alaska, I've always wanted to go. What if we sort of started over?"

He looked at her suspiciously.

"I think you should meet my family; I mean you want me to meet your mother. Why don't we meet my parents? We can tell them in person." Ann held her breath. Would he possibly buy this?

"What do you mean?"

"Well, I don't live far from here, we could stop by there before we leave."

John stared at her. His eyes seemed to look right through her. The animation in those eyes at the idea of going to Alaska transformed into a sinister, disgusted look. He ran his fingers through the back of her ponytail and forced her head nearer to his.

"I don't trust you." He whispered.

Ann swallowed hard. The plan backfired. The grip on her hair tightened making her scalp tingle and then searing pain. Pulling her down on the bed, he pressed his body against hers making her feel as if she would suffocate.

"I'm not an idiot." He sneered. "We will do things my way and only my way. I gave you your chance and you blew it." The things he whispered in her ear made her sick. Tears welled in her eyes and she began to choke. Pinned to the bed, helpless, his rough hands tore her clothing and violated her making her cry out. Dizzy with pain and gasping for breath, she knew she had to think. His strength felt like ten times her own. There had to be something but nothing came to mind. Nothing but a name, a name as familiar to her as her own. A name she was taught to call upon but ignored for most of her life.

*Help me, Jesus, please.* About that time, John raised himself on his knees, both hands went to his belt to work it loose. She only had a second, sliding her foot out from between his legs, she drew her leg back and kicked with all her might. Her aim high, landed on his stomach.

He doubled over, coughing and cursing. Rolling to the floor, she sprung up but he was behind her, clutching her ponytail again. Ben's lessons ran through her mind, she was in fight mode and knew this would be her only chance. Her hands still bound, she only had her feet and legs, her right foot went down hard on his ankle, she knew she couldn't stop there. Turning, her tied hands grabbed his ear and she pulled and twisted with all her might. His left hand went to his ear but his right still had her hair firm in his hand, she was facing him, her knee went up with as much force as possible.

She was free! Sprinting for the stairs she stumbled down the first flight. It was difficult to get back up with her bound hands. She managed and flew down to the third-floor landing. He was close behind her. By the time she reached the bottom, he had her by the hair again.

Whirling her around, he pinned her shoulders against the wall, breathing obscenities in her ear, anger, and hatred with each word, pushing against her. There was no help, the force of him against her was so strong that she couldn't move. Crying and choking trying to make noise, his hand closed around her neck, she felt herself losing consciousness.

BEN LEFT SARAH AND JOE AFTER A SHORT VISIT, MAKING an excuse about work he had at Level Grounds. Sitting there making small talk, he couldn't shake the uneasy feeling. On the way to the car, he texted again about his jacket. That was about twenty minutes ago. As he waited for an answer he called Connor.

"Hey, what's up?"

"So, did you get Ann from the shop? She's not answering my text."

"I went by but she was already gone, locked up. I'm at the house now. Nancy said she was in her room."

Ben started to speak but heard Rachel in the background. Rachel was practically perfect in every way but one. If you were on the phone, she wanted to share in the conversation. Now Ben heard her saying something about Ann.

"What's she saying?"

"Just a minute. What do you mean she's not here?"

Rachel's voice was as loud as if she had the phone to her mouth.

"Ann's not in her room, Mom must have heard me. I went to her room to get my jacket back. Who is that? What's going on?"

"You hear that? Maybe she stopped somewhere on the way home."

The pit of Ben's stomach felt heavy; his mouth was dry. A text buzzed in his ear.

"I have to go; I think she's texting."

*"Quigley's"* That was it. *What the hell?* Somethings wrong. He accelerated. About thirty minutes from Bingham he would make it in twenty. Dialing Connor back, he got no answer. He tried Rachel. No answer, then her parents.

"Where is everyone?" He kept trying as he flew down the highway.

As he turned from the Avenue of the Saints onto Highway Seventy-Nine, Connor called back.

"What's wrong? You've called me three times."

"Get to the old factory now, I'm almost there. Just go. And call Reynolds."

Connor tried to get an explanation but Ben threw his phone in disgust.

Slamming the car in park, he ran to Quigley's door and kicked with all his strength. The chain broke away from the wall. He ran, screaming Ann's name as he went. Frantically searching the first floor, he found no one. He climbed to the second floor. Nothing. He was losing his head. His training kicked in. Standing silently, he listened. It seemed an eternity. If John had her, he would've heard his entrance. *"C'mon Ann, give me something."* He waited. Slowly, he started up the stairs to the third floor, stopping from time to time to listen. By the fourth step, he heard it, a faint whimper. What followed was an angry voice, Ben could not make out the words but a dull thud echoed off the walls.

Ben rushed in the darkness up the steps; he heard the bitter, foul words of a man.

"John Grossman," he yelled into the blackness.

"Who the hell are you?"

"Where's Ann? Is she there with you?" His heart beat against his chest. Why can't he hear her voice? All was still and his eyes searched in the darkness for anything.

A cynical laugh came from above Ben.

"So you're the new boyfriend, Ben? I knew she tipped you off. We were just leaving but we had a little lover's spat. Ann is indisposed…at the moment."

Panic and adrenalin coursed through every nerve ending, he let Sarah down and now Ann. Remaining calm, he struggled to see at what angle he should approach the enemy. John had the advantage, he was above, Ben below. Ben bided his time, his ears and eyes on high alert. In an instant, he saw it. The familiar glow of a cell phone receiving a call, giving away John's location. Ben sprinted up the stairs. The two struggled and rolled down a flight of stairs.

John recovering first, landed his right fist across Ben's face. As John laughed and mocked, Ben charged him, knocked him down and began punching. Overcome with rage, his fists were relentless. John's hands reached Ben's neck and held on in a death's grip. Ben was able to maneuver his arms in between John's and push them apart. He fell back and John was on top of him. Ben overpowered him and stood, pulling John up with him. He forced him against the wall, knocking his head against it. John struggled; Ben continued to punch until resistance from John ended. He dropped him to the floor and yelled for Ann.

Groping his way up the stairs, he felt frantically along as he climbed. He remembered the flashlight on his phone and searched. She lay against the wall, her body descending the stairs, clothes torn apart. Her head was bleeding, he felt for a pulse, whispering her name. At that moment, he heard sirens and shouts. As if a bystander, he heard his own voice shouting desperately for help. Connor was first, then Stuart and the sheriff—the EMT's soon followed.

# CHAPTER 14

Her father's voice echoed in her throbbing head. There was a bright light above her; it was hard to lift her eyelids. The voices were low and hushed. "Dad…"

"She's awake, I'm here Ann, can you hear me?"

"Dad," it came out in a whisper. Her eyes closed again.

Reynolds looked over at Ben; he was holding the towel against his nose. "Has it stopped bleeding?" No answer. "She'll be alright, don't worry."

The patrol car was right behind the ambulance; Ben willed them both to go faster. They wouldn't let him close to Ann. Stuart knelt over her until they came. Connor held him back and tried to talk to him. It took awhile for the rage to subside. Now Ben was left with grief, remorse, regret. He'd failed again, failed to protect Ann, he should never have gone to see Sarah. He should have gone back to the coffee shop as soon as Barone told him the news John was missing from Colorado. This was his fault, his alone.

At the hospital, a team of doctors and nurses waited for the ambulance. Ann was wheeled behind two big doors; Ben stood alone in the waiting room. An alarmed aid rushed to him with a wheelchair and commanded him to sit. He ignored her and stared at the doors where Ann had gone—hidden from him. Blood dripped from his head and nose without his knowledge. The nurse gently pushed him into the wheelchair and asked his name. Connor, Rachel, and Nancy rushed past him behind the doors, he tried to move to go with them but hands were holding him down. There were questions about insurance, where he lived, did he want them to call a relative. Frustrated, Ben threw his wallet on the receptionist's desk as she was requesting his insurance card.

"Just find it in there. I don't need a doctor; let me go back with my friends."

Reynolds came in from parking the car, he took over and Ben was finally wheeled back and put in a room. They wouldn't tell him anything about Ann; he tried texting Connor but got no answer. His nose and face felt like he was hit by a truck. The nurse persuaded him to lie down by promising to see what she could find out.

Nancy stood next to the bed holding her daughter's hand. Ann's eyes had not opened nor had she spoken since the ambulance ride over. Doctors and nurses moved about the room; the words rape kit were trapped in her mind. The ripped t-shirt, jeans, and Ann's underthings were quickly placed in a bag and taken from the room. Nancy was sick to her stomach; surely this was all a nightmare. Who was this monster that tracked her daughter to Bingham and would do this? And why did no one tell her? Rachel cried nonstop in the car while Connor kept apologizing. They sat in the hall now, while the doctor examined her, Nancy wouldn't leave her, not while they did such things. What if she woke up again? The doctor remarked he believed there had been no sexual assault but they would wait for labs to be sure, Nancy was relieved. They would do some scans on her head, there were no broken bones. Her neck was bruised and her wrist and hands were cut and beginning to swell from the zip tie her assailant used. The doctor left and Stuart entered, his eyes red from crying. Nancy would not cry, not yet, she knew if she did, she would not stop. Ann needed her now; she had to keep it together.

The nurse insisted Ben keep the ice pack on his face. The bruising and swelling were getting worse, they would take him to x-ray soon. She told him nothing about Ann, just that the doctor had seen her and they would do imaging on her too. She examined his right hand; the knuckles were bruised and bleeding. Applying salve and gauze she asked what the other guy looked like. Ben said nothing, he knew he hadn't killed him, he was conscious when they took him away. Reynolds assured him there would be an officer present when he reached the other hospital. He would be taken into custody when he was released and sent back to Colorado where he would go to jail for violating his parole; then he would be sent back to Missouri to face charges here.

Connor entered, his head down. "Sorry, man, I dropped the ball. How did you know?"

Ben handed him his cell phone and told him to read the texts. "She sent me a cryptic message." He lay back on the bed, his head now splitting, "You thought she was home."

Connor again apologized, "I didn't see her, took her mom's word for it. Rachel went to her room for something and we all assumed..." His voice trailed.

"Is she still out?"

"Yes, her head is pretty bad. She woke up in the ambulance for a second, so that's hopeful."

"What else?" Ben asked dreading, "Did he?"

"They don't think so. It would've been a lot worse if you hadn't gotten there when you did." Connor's attempt at comfort fell flat. "You going to be okay? You want me to call Kathryn or something?"

"No! Not Kathryn, she'll only worry, I'll be fine."

"You look like crap."

"Part of it was the fall down the stairs, my head hit hard. That's why I didn't see it coming, I was still down." Both men were silent, thinking of Ann and the blows she must have taken.

The imaging on Ann's head showed no swelling, just a severe concussion. The doctor believed she would wake up soon. They put her in a room for the night. Nancy sat beside the bed, while Stuart dosed in a recliner and Rachel and Connor occupied a couch in the waiting room. The clock said three in the morning. Ann had not stirred. Nancy holding her hand prayed continually. The door opened slowly, Ben crept in, Nancy motioned for him to take the chair beside her.

"How is she?" The words came out thick and hoarse.

"A bad concussion they say, no broken bones, just a lot of bruises." Nancy kept her eye on Ann, "Thank you for what you did."

Ben could not respond; he was too late as far as he was concerned. "May I stay with you guys?"

"Of course," Nancy turning his way saw his injuries for the first time. The left side of his face was bandaged and he had two black eyes. "How are you?"

"I'm fine." Ben murmured.

They kept vigil in silence until the sun came up. Nancy fell asleep with her head on the bed next to Ann's arm. Stuart also slept. Ben studied Ann's face, searching for signs of consciousness. He considered praying several times but could not find the words. What did people say when they prayed? It was a common phrase, "I'm praying for you." After his father died, it seemed to be the thing people would say to them. His mother would nod and say thank you. Ben wondered at the time what these people were asking God for. His father was already dead, it seemed to him there was nothing else to say or do. Prayer was wishful thinking, a human gut response to cry out for help to the unknown. Some people call it the universe as if the universe had a mind and will of its own. Something inside nagged him, it couldn't hurt. There was nothing else for him to do. He was helpless. Maybe that was the point, being helpless. When you cannot help yourself or the ones you love you ask for help. So he did, very simply, raising his head, he whispered, "help." The clock said six-thirty; he had been sitting there for over three hours willing movement from Ann.

Stuart stirring from his chair in the corner asked if she had awakened. Ben slowly shook his head. Walking to her side, Stuart bent to kiss her forehead; he moved her hair from her face. A massive pile of curls. He took her small hand in his, it was warm and swollen, there were abrasions across her wrists. Bringing her hand to his lips he kissed it, tears ran down his cheeks.

Ben felt he should leave the room but couldn't bring himself to move, still watching with angst for her to open her eyes. An hour passed as the three sat in silence. Rachel and Connor persuaded Nancy and Stuart to take a walk for coffee. Nancy left with hesitation and told Ben she would be back in five minutes. Ben's eyes were heavy, lowering his head to the place where Ann's hand lay, he took it in his own and gave in to his weak eyelids.

Ann's eyes, wild with fear, flew open. The room was unfamiliar. She lay in a strange bed. Her body ached and her head throbbed. She turned to the light coming in the window, she could only remember darkness and terror. Someone held her hand, she instinctively pulled it away. Looking down, she saw a dark head of hair; the side of the face was bandaged. Her mind raced, *who is it*? Terror gripped her again, *John, John was here*, repulsed by the person at her side she screamed but barely a sound came out, her voice was gone. It was like a bad dream. Pushing the head away, she attempted a scream again. He was up, saying her name, she screamed again and fought.

Trying to calm her, he stepped back, "It's me, it's me," he said, "It's Ben."

She stared in disbelief, she knew him but why was he here and why was she here? She looked to the door, where was her family? At that moment Nancy walked in, seeing her daughter she dropped her coffee and ran to her. Ann sobbed in her mother's arms as her family gathered around her.

Ben backed into the hall, sliding down the wall in exhaustion—he wept alone.

A flurry of doctors and nurses entered and exited the room throughout the morning. He heard Ann from the hall, insisting on going home. More tests were ordered and by the afternoon a neurologist spoke in low tones with Ann and her family.

Ben waited outside the room, keeping his distance. Afraid to face her. Holding his pounding head in his hands, he had yet to take the pain pills prescribed. He deserved the pain, he told himself. Connor and Stuart appeared looking relieved to have something to do. They would be releasing

Ann late that afternoon, another car was needed to get them all home. Ben declined the invitation to go with them.

Connor looked at him with pity, "Are you hungry? We can bring you something."

"No thanks, I'm good." He watched them walk down the hall.

Nancy put her head out the door and waved for him to come into the room. Ann was sitting up, her eyes black and her neck bruised. She spoke in a whisper, thanking him for all he did. It was undeserved thanks but he smiled instead of arguing. She extended her hand and he took it too willingly. There were few words. Ann could barely speak—her vocal cords injured. The four sat in quiet relief, Nancy and Rachel giving silent thanks to their God.

When Ann woke Monday morning, Millie and Nana sat perched at the end of her bed.

"She's awake." Millie nudged Nana who had been gazing out the window.

"Well aren't you a sight, child! How do you feel?" Nana reached up and patted her hand.

"I've been better," Ann rubbed the back of her head. There was a knot. She looked at her wrists, bruised and cut.

"We brought you some soup."

"Thanks," her voice seemed better. She touched her hand to her throat.

Millie, as if reading her mind, pulled a compact from her purse.

Taking it, Ann hesitated.

Nana nodded and patted her hand again.

She lifted the mirror slowly. The two old women glanced at one another. Ann brushed the hair from her face. One eye was black, her lip cut and swollen, there was bruising on her neck. A lump formed in her throat, her hand shook. She handed the mirror back to Millie.

"It will heal," Millie said, "give it time."

Her mother appeared in the doorway behind a large bouquet. "This is from Ben. I no longer have any inventory."

Nana cleared a space on the nightstand and handed Ann a card.

"*Sorry...Ben.*" Ann discreetly tucked it under the bed-sheet.

"Mike Reynolds is downstairs. I can tell him to leave if you aren't ready."

"No, I would just as soon get it over."

The interrogation lasted longer than Ann anticipated. By the time Reynolds left she wanted nothing but to go back to her room and crawl in bed. A new phone was on her pillow when she returned. Her father had retrieved the old one, but it was beyond fixing.

*"How are you?"*
A text from Ben.

She typed in 'fine' and sent. She was tired of the question—not even sure she knew the answer. Lying back on the bed she gazed around the room. Books lined the walls, classic literature, books on theology, given by her parents, novels, and cookbooks. She had only taken her favorites to Colorado, the Brontë sisters, all of Jane Austin, and The Joy of Cooking. These books shaped her life, formed her worldview, and taught her things she could never learn in a classroom.

"I wonder if there are any on the subject of stalking, crazy, abusive ex-boyfriends?" She said to no one in particular. She had always tried to find the answer in a book. The one book, the Bible was between Dickens and Lewis. It sat as if it were as ordinary as any other. Ann retrieved it and brought it back to bed. It was a two-tone leather, lavender, and deep purple. Her father gave it to her when she went to high school. It was virtually untouched. When she opened it a few papers fell out, a youth Bible study questionnaire, an old church program, and a peeled label from a bottle of beer. These slipped from the page to the floor. There was something highlighted: *Turn to me and be gracious to me, for I am lonely and afflicted. The troubles of my heart are enlarged; bring me out of my distresses.* Ann knew she had never highlighted anything in this purple Bible. She had barely ever opened it. By the time it was given to her, she had left its teaching behind like a Sunday school picnic. Yet, here were these highlighted words staring her in the face. She closed it, held it to her chest, and lay down and slept.

The following morning, she felt amazingly refreshed. Nancy took her to breakfast at the café where they met with well-wishers and breakfast on the house for Ann. The attention was overwhelming and a bit unwelcome. After breakfast, they walked in the park. The leaves were magnificent, every color imaginable against a blue sky. The river danced in the sunlight and a barge slowly drifted past as they sat quietly on the bench her and Ben occupied several weeks ago. Nancy clasped her hand and Ann allowed it. There had been few words between them since she got home, Nancy had not demanded any explanation about John and Ann was not willing to speak of him anyway. Both sat content with the silence between them. The wedding was in eleven days and Ann felt terrible about the shower. Nancy suggested they try again this Sunday, persuading her she would just have the café cater and Ann could relax and enjoy. Ann argued—her menu—already planned, it wouldn't be difficult to resume where she left off and it would be the distraction she needed. They agreed to go forward, hoping there would be guests on such short notice.

Ben got the job offer Monday morning. Joel Brandon made a generous offer. Ben requested a few days. The job was exactly what he had been looking for. Kathryn had called twice since the offer; he hadn't picked up, her message of congratulations filled with excitement and anticipation of having him home. He knew something was going on in Kathryn's life that she wasn't telling him, he had sensed it since he was in New York the last time. Kathryn had always wanted him around; they were all they had left of their family. But now she seemed almost desperate to have him there. Afraid to ask too much, he had avoided her since Ann came into his life. He was willing to go home and care for his sister in any way she needed him, but now…Ann. His phone buzzed again as a customer left, there was no reason not to answer.

"Hey Kathryn, how are you?"

"Never mind me, I heard about the offer, so when do you start?"

"Still working all that out," there was a catch in his throat.

"What's wrong?"

She knew him too well.

"Nothing, why do you ask?"

"There was hesitation in your voice, that's why. Is it the money?"

"No, the money is great, more than I expected. It's nothing, don't worry. How are you?"

"Never mind about me, I can get you a studio in my building—it's pricey but in a great location. You need to respond by tomorrow morning or it's gone, I've emailed you the lease and contact information."

"Sounds good," tomorrow morning, that soon, Ben pressed again, he knew Kathryn's voice like she knew his. "So, what's going on with you?"

"Why do you keep asking me that, I'm just happy you're finally coming home. It will be better…" Kathryn quickly recovered, "Do you need anything, a bed, a couch, surely you'll buy new and leave that old stuff."

"Better, how? Is Aunt Laura okay?"

"Yes, she's fine. Don't worry we are all fine." Her voice rose at that last statement.

"Uh-huh." There was silence between them. "You know, I don't like surprises." More silence.

Finally, "It's nothing; I don't want you to worry."

"Well now I am, so you may as well tell me."

Silence.

"Kat," he thought the old nickname would help.

"It was just a small lump," her voice cracked, "no big deal…but it is cancer."

"What?" Ben's heart dropped; it was their mother all over again. "Where, what did they tell you?"

"I found it on my breast before your last visit, they removed the lump and all the lymph nodes around it, a few more chemo treatments and I should be fine. The scans came up negative. It's fine Ben, I didn't want you to worry."

"Didn't want me to worry, I wish you would've told me; have you been doing this all alone?"

"No, Aunt Laura has been with me all the time, she's nursed me through the first few treatments, but it is wear-

ing on her a little."

Ben knew the last comment meant she needed to lean on someone else now. He knew now he had to go home. Kathryn was alone but for him.

"I'll sign the lease and nail down a start date. Do you need me home in the meantime? I mean I have to figure out what to do here but I can do that from New York."

"No, you get your affairs in order; I have a friend going with me to my next treatment. I don't want you coming home with unfinished business in Bingham, Missouri, that's for sure. I hope that chapter in your life is closed."

Far from it, Ben thought, "I'll let you know when I can get back, please call me if you need anything. I love you, sis."

The call ended and Ben felt sad and empty. Duty to his sister had solidified his decision. There was no turning back. Kathryn needed him; he hadn't been there for her since their mother died. Looking around Level Grounds a lump formed in his throat. In his military career, he had seen unmentionable atrocities humans committed against one another. Hardening his heart had been a defense against the erupting emotional reaction of those scenes. Loss and sadness had not been familiar to him for a long time. It was like someone hit refresh on his feelings. It was as if he was receiving news that his father was never coming home for the second time. A deep ache in the middle of his chest sat like a bowling ball, heaviness, and loss. It was not the coffee shop—he knew that; it was the loss of something he never even had. She would come back to work tomorrow but he needed to tell her before; for some reason, he needed to talk all of this over with her. What to do with Level Grounds, his house, even his car, he wanted to give it all to her. He trusted no one else with the care of it. She ran the place better than he ever did and his profits had gone up since she started baking. His mind was made up—this way he would have to stay connected with her too.

Ann applied a thin layer of concealer around her eyes, covering the green bruising. She looked at the various shades of lipstick on her dresser; she chose a subtle gloss, hoping it would draw his eyes away from hers. He should be there soon. The last few times he came, there were well-wishers and family around. They had only spoken alone briefly. His attentiveness and care had been constantly on her mind. Ann felt strongly something was developing and she had made up her mind to let it take its natural course. Examining herself in the mirror she was satisfied, the blue sweater with ankle jeans presented a casual, not too eager look. She put her hair loosely on her head with a few strands left framing her face. Rachel passed as she finished.

"You look pretty, what's the occasion?"

"Nothing," she said too quickly, "Ben's just stopping by, wants to talk business, I guess. I go back to work tomorrow."

"I think you like him," Rachel smiled, "I approve, he saved your life after all."

Ann smiled and said nothing. She did like him and expected to hear the same from him. Her heart was set on it, she was sure it would happen. She rubbed on some more gloss.

They sat on the back patio, a fire glowed in the fire pit and Nancy had strung some Christmas lights around. The night was cool and the rustle of falling leaves broke the strange silence between them. Ben stared intently at the fire. Ann began to think there was more on his mind than what was between the two of them. For some reason, she said, "How's your sister?" It was a strange question and she was not sure why she asked, she had never asked before.

Ben sat up in his chair surprised. "I don't know, I spoke with her today."

Ann sensed her evening would not be what she had hoped, "What about?"

Ben turned to face her and reached for her hand, "I was offered a job," he hesitated, "in New York, she called about that. I haven't accepted yet, a few hours ago, I was leaning against it." His hand held hers a little tighter. "Kathryn told me she has been fighting breast cancer for the last month." Ben's head dropped; he ran his free hand through his hair.

Ann tried to hide her disappointment, she knew he would leave, his sister needed him. She was drawn even more to him, "I'm sorry," she managed. "You'll take the job then," it was more of a statement than a question.

"Yes," he dropped her hand and sat back. "She needs me there, my aunt has been helping her but they both need me, I guess." Ben stared at the fire.

Ann, knowing how quickly his mother went, understood he didn't trust this disease and must be with his sister. She did not feel angry, but sadness and loss—loss of what? There had been no commitment between them, they had not even kissed.

"When will you leave?"

"I'm thinking shortly after the wedding."

"So, soon…," Ann turned her face from his. "What about Level Grounds?" She stood, anxious to be moving, and put another log on the fire.

He made her an offer. She would manage Level Grounds, drawing an agreed-upon salary, his jeep would be her company car and he would throw in the use of his house if she chose to live there. He owned both the house and the building Level Grounds occupied. His confidence in her was flattering, believing she could keep it running at a profit.

"I'll have an attorney write up a contract if you want."

"You don't want to sell?"

"Why should I? I own the real estate, Bingham is growing, so it's an investment. We'll keep in touch." He held Ann's hand again, "I mean if you want."

The evening turned out very different than Ann had imagined. She watched him drive off; there was no kiss goodnight, no embrace, a handshake, and Ann's agreement to think it over. Whether to cry or not was the only immediate decision she faced.

# CHAPTER 15

S arah packed her things with the help of the occu-
pational therapist. She would leave today. All were
amazed at the progress she made in rehab. Fear and
anxiety had been slowly fading into the background. Working with the police to find Estaban Ramos Freeman had
been both therapeutic and empowering. She knew now that
he must have seen her cowering in the bushes that day in
the alcove, he told Kasov and they plotted to kill her. They
failed. Sarah assured they would soon find Freeman and
with the FBI agent outside her room, she found no reason
to be afraid. Agent Barone told her that Kasov had left the
country and likely had given up on his pursuit of Ben and
her. She was satisfied.

Quigley recovering from pneumonia was able to
describe Freeman; the money clip with his fingerprint
proved he was there and likely the three-hundred dollars
was upfront payment for her death. The idea that someone
wanted to kill her had sunk in. All because of a stranger, a
stranger she understood was no stranger to Ben. He likely
would've killed him too if her assassination wasn't stopped
by Quigley, her unlikely hero.

Sarah's job at Level Grounds waited for her and she
would be back in school spring semester. Level Grounds

would be different, she knew she would work for Ann, not Ben. Unsure of how she felt about working for Ann, she barely knew her and at one point felt threatened she would take her job. Ben was a wonderful boss; she liked working for him and was sorry he would be leaving but Ann seemed nice and knew she added baked goods and atmosphere to the place. Lacey was coming to take her home and stay a few days. Sarah looked forward to the visit. Joe, her father, had gone back to work, he never wanted to leave her but she insisted. Now she waited for Lacey and would be back in Bingham by evening. It was Thursday, Rachel's wedding shower would be Sunday, she had been invited. Things were looking much better for Sarah and she was glad this whole thing would soon be behind her.

Her room was the same; Denise Johnson had gone over the mobile home with detailed precision, it was cleaner than she and Joe ever kept it. There was something delicious in the crockpot on the counter. James had colored a picture of flowers; it lay on her pillow. She and Lacey unpacked and caught up.

"What was it like, Sarah? Do you remember any of it?

Sarah had to think before responding, her speech was what it used to be but sometimes it was hard to give descriptions. "I remember riding my bike and feeling afraid like I was being chased. I remember running to the factory parking lot and after that, it's like real fuzzy. When I started coming around and I read all those texts between Davis and me, I remembered seeing Scarface, Davis, I mean Kasov, that's like his real name. Anyway, I believed it was him that actually attacked me."

"Are they sure it wasn't?"

"Now they are, the homeless guy, he lived in the factory, he got a good look at my attacker and described him an' stuff, he identified him from the mug shot and I am pretty sure he's the dude I saw in the park that day." Sarah took a deep breath, "My attacker, I never thought I would say those words! That's the adjective they used, did your attacker talk, did your attacker have any marks, so many questions..."

"Wow, it sure is freaky and all because Scarface was out for revenge. Isn't that what that Ben guy thinks?"

"I guess; he shot him in the army or something. The guy went to a lot of trouble if you ask me; they don't know where he is now. Agent Barone told me I shouldn't be worried. They will keep looking for that Freeman guy but they are sure Kasov has left the country. He doesn't think Freeman will be a problem because like there is nothing in it for him. I sure hope he's right. I don't want to be going through my life like always lookin' around or something."

"Sarah's home," Ben told Ann who had been cleaning the same dish for five minutes.

"I know," It was the second time he'd mentioned it. The tension between them was thick. Ann's sympathy had worn off and resented something, a missed opportunity, a chance at love, unsure she rinsed the dish, threw the cloth in the water, and went to the backroom to see if she needed flour.

He hesitated then followed her. Ann felt the hesitation. The chill between them started yesterday, the day after he told her he was leaving. She coldly accepted his offer, mumbling she hadn't anything better on the horizon and stiffly shook his hand. There had been nothing but polite conversation since—her resentment was as much a mystery to her as it must've seemed to him.

"Can we talk?"

Ann pulled her head out of the pantry and stared at him.

"It's just weird; I would like to know what you're thinking."

"Does it matter?" Ann was not going to put her feelings on the table when it would come to nothing.

"Yes, a lot."

"You first then." There, let him spill his emotions before she had to.

"I don't want to leave…" He said it.

"Why?"

"Because Bingham is everything I want in a small town," it was sarcasm; he always resorted to sarcasm when he was backed in a corner.

Ann put her head back in the pantry and didn't respond. She felt him move behind her. Slowly, she turned to face him.

"Why do you think, you idiot?" He inched closer.

She moved toward him and fell against his chest. The warmth of his body flowed over her; she could feel his heart. His arms wrapped around her, there would be no kiss, Ann wouldn't allow it—but this was enough for now.

"Sometimes you have to go home. I understand."


LEVEL GROUNDS WAS PACKED WITH WOMEN OF ALL AGES and decked out in fall floral arrangements, plenty of streamers, paper globes, and linen clothes on borrowed tables. Ann had a buffet of sliders, various bacon-wrapped hors d'oeuvres, two salads, a chocolate fountain, petit fours, and of course a white layer cake with raspberry filling. For the last two days, she had done nothing but shower prep and planning. Her mind on linens and menus, Ben was a blur in the background, always there, asking if she needed help. He would sneak out for a few hours at a time doing his own thing; she knew it had to do with moving. The shower, a welcome diversion, turned out beautifully. Her mother worked the room with her usual grace, Rachel opened presents while guests munched on dessert.

Last week at this time Ann lay in a hospital bed, the scars still present on her wrists and under her eyes. She glanced at Sarah who seemed out of place in the corner with a cake plate on her lap. They belonged to the same club now, Ann shuddered. Overpowered and hurt by a man. Sarah much worse, Ann moved toward her.

"Can I get you anything, Sarah?"

"Oh no, everything is so nice." Sarah looked down, her hand shaking as she held her plate.

Ann realized this was the first time she had been in public since the beating. "Sarah, will you help me with something, I know you aren't working but I wonder if you would make some coffee."

Sarah jumped up, "Oh yes, I will. Anything else? I'm willing to help."

"Just coffee, for now, I'll serve when you're finished."

Ann watched Sarah quickly disappear behind the counter.

Nana slipped her arm around Ann's waist, "That poor child, she'll need you, Fannie. No mother, she needs us all, I suppose. How are you dear?"

Ann had been asked the question dozens of times throughout the week. Smiling she answered, "I'm fine, Nana, don't worry."

"I know you are physically fine, but otherwise, I don't know and am not sure you do. This animal that tracked you down, he may yet haunt your thoughts, I hope you won't let him. And now Ben is leaving, maybe I'm mistaken; I thought there may be a spark or something there."

*The ever-perceptive Nana,* "It hasn't been the best week." Ann looked around the room and pointed to Rachel, "But this is wonderful, I'm happy to be in the shadow of her happiness and I'm sorry last weekend disrupted it all. As for Ben, it is what it is, he leaves the day after the wedding, his sister needs him." This was what Ann had been telling herself all week.

"Hmmm," Nana squeezed her granddaughter, "I love you, Fannie, so much, so much, so much. It will be all right." She said as she moved to greet an old friend.

"It will Nana," Ann whispered, only half believing.

Nancy said goodbye to the last of the shower guests, Rachel, Sarah, and Ann removed decorations and began putting Level Grounds back together. "Well, that went beautifully, didn't it?" Nancy said as she folded a table cloth. "Ann you did an amazing job!"

Rachel beaming added, "You did, Ann, and in such a short time and with the week you've had." Rachel continued, "Are you sure you're okay?"

Ann had spoken little about John's attack on her the week before. She kept to herself when home and kept busy at Level Grounds and The Flower Shop all week avoiding discussion of it at all costs. Her mother and sister stared at her with anxiety, Ann hated the way they looked at her.

"I'm fine, really."

Nancy and Rachel exchanged a glance.

"What about you Sarah?" Nancy said, "Bet you're glad to be home."

"I sure am, Mrs. Fletcher, thank you all for inviting me," Sarah said looking down.

Ann, after asking her to make coffee had rarely seen her. She kept busy collecting plates, doing dishes, and keeping hidden, Ann supposed from the constant inquiries. Poor Sarah. She looked like a deer caught in the headlights, maybe inviting her had been a mistake.

"You are most welcome, Sarah, I'm just glad you recovered so well and could be here," Rachel's kind words caused Sarah to look away.

"Sarah, let me drive you home. You can leave your bike here till tomorrow." Nancy offered, to Ann's relief. Sarah looked exhausted.

"Ben was going to come get me, but if you don't mind, I'm kinda tired."

Ben and Connor came in shortly after Nancy and Sarah left. Connor with a sly grin on his face sauntered to Rachel and wrapped his arms around her, "I bet I ended up with more loot than you." He pulled a bundle from his pocket.

"From the smell of you, I would guess poker and cigars." Rachel squirmed away holding her nose.

"He cleaned us out, somehow he's been able to get rid of that tell he used to have. I tried to find it all night." Ben said.

Connor laughed and waved his money at Ben. "Any leftovers? The catering at our affair had much to be desired."

"Hey, I ordered the best pizza in town," Ben protested, then looked longingly into the fridge behind the counter. "What are these?" he was holding up the petit fours.

"Petit fours," Ann quickly clarified, "little cakes. Here are some sliders and I think I have a little pasta salad left," she moved closely beside Ben. Her body stiffened as it went into self-protection mode.

He must have felt the same as he straightened and moved away but not without brushing his hand on her shoulder. Ignoring the current it sent through her body, she made two large plates of food that disappeared in a few minutes.

Connor stood and rubbed his abdomen like an old man. Rachel stood also, saying goodbye with a yawn. Ann took that as her cue to leave—staying was out of the question. The more she was around Ben her defenses weakened. Grabbing her jacket, Ann announced she would walk home with them. Shouting goodnight over her shoulder as she went out the door with Rachel and Connor behind her.

It was 1:00 A.M. when Ben looked at the clock for the tenth time. Sleep was not coming; he may as well get up. Several things had plagued his mind since Ann abruptly left Level Grounds. Intellectually he got it, why she left, she had to. If she felt about him the way he did her, it was the only thing to do. She deserved more than what may have happened if she'd stayed, but how he wanted her to stay. It was obvious she was the smarter of the two of them. Starting a relationship right before moving a thousand miles away would be a mistake.

He wondered what his life would be like if she never came home or if he would've moved two months sooner. Would it be better to never have known her at all? His life would be a lot easier. He would leave without looking back; there would be none of this nagging doubt and emptiness. Deciding to go for a run, he put on his running clothes and headed for the door. As he passed the dresser, his gun caught his eye. Something told him to pick it up. He ignored the impulse and got as far as the front door before he turned around. He was not the type to carry; the gun, a single stack luger, was usually kept in the safe at Level Grounds. He brought it home earlier. Now the impulse to strap it on was strong. Not knowing why—he did.

He started with a hard run; maybe it would clear his head to get his heart pumping. Rounding the corner at the school, he continued hard, passing the field, gas station, and Lang's Grocery—at Bingham Place he stopped abruptly; acutely aware it was Ann's neighborhood. He stared down the street, could that be a light on?

Deciding it would be better not to act like a high school boy and stand outside her window he crossed seventy-nine and headed back. He stopped again at Sutter's Grove; a sudden chill hit him. Looking around, all was still, he had not seen a vehicle since he left home but there was a distant hum of an engine. Turning on Sutter's Grove he jogged to the mobile home park entrance and stopped again. The humming was louder, there was a vehicle idling somewhere. He made his way down the street to Sarah and Joe's and stooped behind one of the bushes anchoring the driveway. Quietly he reached for his gun. Joe had several shrubs planted in the yard blocking Ben's view of one side of the home—he now knew someone was near—there were obvious foot-steps. He kept his eyes on the front door where a tall holly bush stood to the left of the door; its leaves moved.

There was a movement in the bush opposite him also. His senses were on high alert. Military training and experience do not expire while on the shelf. Ben felt the enemy and knew he was near. Which bush hid him? Ben turned to the nearest, opposite the driveway. If someone was there it would be an easy target. He inched his way back to the side of the bush that faced the street. Whoever was across the driveway behind the other bush did the same. At the same time, both turned toward one another guns pointed. Ben almost blew his cover, Imogene faced him and put her hand up. She pointed toward the trailer and slowly crept back around the bush. Ben did the same.

Movement in the holly bush was obvious. Ben glimpsing Imogene from his peripheral vision kept his eyes on the porch. A tall figure crept out from between the bush and the mobile home's front porch. He was dressed completely in black wearing a stocking cap, a gun in his hands. As he scaled the porch, Imogene readied her weapon from her hiding place.

"I wouldn't," Imogene shouted.

The stranger turned and searched descending the porch. Imogene was still hidden in the shadows from the stranger's vantage point but Ben could make out her silhouette. Her gun aimed at who he now assumed to be Freeman. Ben, ready to shoot, kept his gun pointed. The stranger took another step.

"Police, drop it." Imogene stepped into view.

Ben saw the flash from the gun and turned in time to see Imogene thrown back and on the ground. His reflexes kicked in and he took him out with one shot, it echoed through the trailer park. Lights came on in each home as he ran to Imogene.

"Imogene! Imogene!" he lifted her wrist and felt for a pulse, which he found quickly to his relief.

"I'm alright, got my vest on," she pointed to her chest. "Did you get him?"

"Why didn't you let me move in? I had him." Ben said helping her sit up.

"I'm the law here, not you; I've been following him since I saw that SUV drive into town. I knew it had something to do with Sarah. Come on, we better see about him." Imogene pulled out her walkie and called Reynolds.

Ben felt Freeman's pulse; it was there but not strong. Sarah and Joe stood at the front door shocked, Joe's arms wrapped around Sarah urging her back into the house. Neighbors began to pour out their doors and Imogene handled crowd control. Soon Mike Reynolds arrived. They determined he was Estaban Ramos Freeman, come to finish the job he started almost two months ago. On the stretcher, he regained consciousness. Ben stayed near, waiting for an opportunity. Hoping he could interrogate him for just a moment—see his face. Reynolds was talking to Imogene near the patrol car. Ben moved closer and when the EMT walked away Ben bent to Freeman's eye level. His gun still in his possession, he discreetly placed the muzzle against his head.

"Where's Kasov?"

Freeman struggled, looking around for help.

"You have two seconds." Ben was bluffing but he knew he wouldn't get an opportunity like this again.

Freeman's eyes were wide now, there was terror behind them. The EMT's were talking to Imogene and the Sheriff; they would be back shortly both men knew this.

Ben pushed the gun harder into his head.

"He's gone, I don't know," Freeman whispered weakly.

"How were you going to get paid then?"

"I don't know," Freeman coughed, blood dripped from his mouth, "he told me to finish the job and I would be rewarded, that's all I know, he's gone, I swear."

Ben was fierce, "Where?" he pushed the gun harder.

"Europe, somewhere, I don't know. Please…" Freeman closed his eyes.

The EMT's approached and Ben discreetly moved back, gun held against his leg. He caught Freeman's gaze as they put him in the ambulance, there was a gruesome, blood-stained, smirk on his mouth. Freeman lifted a shaking finger and pointed to Ben, he mouthed the words, "you're next."

"I'm going to need your gun, Ben," it was Reynolds.

Without taking his eyes off Freeman, Ben handed Reynolds the gun.

"We'll get it back to you after the investigation is over. Thanks for your help. How did you know?"

"I didn't," Ben turned to Reynolds, "I couldn't sleep so I went for a run, I heard an engine idle thought it was weird, came back here on a hunch. Glad I did."

"Bruce found the car, black Cadillac, like the one Kasov brought to JC's. Different plates though. Imogene had a hunch too, better get her a raise." Reynolds moved to his patrol car.

Joe and Sarah still stood at the door. Ben walked to them, they embraced and he followed them inside.

"It's finally over Sarah. I'm sorry."

"How did you know he would be here tonight?" Sarah was visibly shaking as Joe held her hand.

"I didn't, I couldn't sleep…," Ben repeated what he told Reynolds.

"There are no coincidences, that's what my Mama always said," Joe firmly slapped the table, "the Lord brought you and Imogene tonight, I prayed for the Lord to send angels to gather around Sarah, and you and Imogene were angels tonight." Joe was positive in his statement. "The Lord, he did this. They aren't goin to hurt you no more Sarah girl, no more." Joe wrapped his arms around her again.

It was three in the morning by the time Ben left the trailer park. He stood at Sutter's Grove and Seventy-Nine debating which way to turn. He wanted to tell Ann what happened, but he knew he shouldn't he would wake the whole house, maybe they would want to know too. Reaching for his phone, he took a chance.

*"Are you awake?"*

After a few moments, his phone dinged.

*"I am now,"*
*"I'm coming over, have some news."*

Ann, not knowing what news he could possibly have, wouldn't allow herself to believe he decided to stay in Bingham. She put on her robe and ran a brush over her mop of curls, there was no use, bed head had set in. She stacked it on top of her head and made her way downstairs. Opening the door, she found Ben standing there, arms folded across his chest.

"Come in, you'll freeze, what are you doing out at this time?"

Monday morning was busy at Level Grounds, everyone in town wanted to see the hero. By ten Ann had sold most of the baked goods she'd made that morning. It didn't seem to matter that he wasn't there; they all lingered in hopes of patting him on the back and congratulating him. Imogene had cheers when she arrived and Ann gave her coffee on the house. She held court for half-hour or so then went back to work.

Imogene's story was similar to Ben's, she couldn't sleep. She had piddled around the house for a while, a house she bought last year about a mile outside of town facing Highway Seventy-Nine. When the SUV drove by her window, she knew something was wrong, she watched as it crept slowly toward town. She quickly dressed including a bulletproof vest and went straight to the mobile home park. She parked on the side of Sutter's Grove Road and walked to Joe and Sarah's. Like Ben, she heard the hum of the motor but could not see it. Whatever the plan, Estaban Freeman hadn't done himself any favors parking so far away. He was slow and that's really what saved Sarah, that and the hum of the motor. A foreign sound—in the night—in a town the size of Bingham does not go unnoticed.

Imogene admitted she was glad and shocked to see Ben, "It was as if he read my mind," she told the crowd. "I looked up and there he was, course I was worried about him too, that's why I acted when I did but I should have known, his training and all, I should've waited. Thank the Lord for bulletproof vests!"

Ann could scarcely believe what happened herself and while talking with Ben in the early morning hours, she admitted she agreed with Joe—it could be no coincidence. Ben believed too that taking his gun had been preordained—if that's what it was called. He described to Ann his hesitation to walk out the door; it was as if he couldn't move until he picked it up.

Ann spent the busy morning pondering the events of Sarah's beating and her circumstances with John and now the latest. All bad guys but one was accounted for. If there was any justice, that one would soon be behind bars somewhere. Her mother echoed Joe's sentiment, there were no coincidences. No coincidences, Providence as Nana and Millie referred to it. An idea or Being referred to often in her childhood. The will of God. The thought occupied her mind, as morning wore on and the crowd thinned. Her homecoming, Level Grounds, Ben and now his leaving—

what did it have to do with Providence? Why find happiness if it ends up walking out the door? She had not seen him all day and assumed he was still at home sleeping or taking care of moving necessities. Glad of it in a sense. The less she saw the better.

Around noon Nana and Millie came in.

"Has your mother been here?" Nana asked

"No, why?"

"She has an assignment for us and we thought we would sit in here and do it. Supposed to bring in a project for the wedding," Millie eyed Ann. "You look thin, haven't you been eating?"

Ann hadn't had an appetite in a week, she only nibbled at her buffet the day before at the shower, and Millie's question reminded her, she hadn't eaten yet today.

"I'm fine," she gave her standard answer.

"You don't look fine," Nana grumbled. "I bet that dress won't fit, have you tried it on?"

"No, I will later today." Ann looked to the door hoping her mother would come soon. "Can I get you anything?"

"One of your scones, dear," they said in unison.

"They're in the oven, sold out this morning. Half the town was here hoping to see Ben. He's a hero, you know."

"We heard quite a story, going for a jog in the middle of the night and shooting the bad guy. Poor Sarah, she must've been scared out of her wits."

"Yes, I'm sure she was." Ann understood that fear, her nerves had been jumpy all week, she counted two nightmares and when she had slept it was restless and light. She didn't speak of it to anyone; she wanted to see if she could get back to normal on her own. Rachel's wedding in a few days was enough to keep her problems private. Ben leaving hadn't helped; he stayed on her mind constantly. He had been her hero and now he was Sarah's. Her eyes found their way to the door again; she thought he would be in by now.

"I wonder what your mother has up her sleeve," Nana said. "She is under the impression that we feel left out or something and we need to feel useful. I hope she doesn't want any flower arranging, Lord knows she's the only one in the family with that talent. I have heard you have been putting some elegant arrangements together for the nursing home, Ann."

"Yes, Mabel Wesley said you did a wonderful job," Millie chimed in.

At that moment Nancy arrived with a basket of lace fabric and scissors for each of the old women. They were instructed to cut them into four pieces.

"It will be for the table decorations," Nancy said as she set them to work. Both grumbled something about arthritis and stiff hands which Nancy ignored.

"Ann, have you tried on your dress? You look awfully thin." Nancy eyed Ann with concern.

"I will today," she lifted the scones out of the oven, "Scones are finished Millie and Nana, do you want coffee too?"

"You may want to have one of those yourself," Nancy said taking one, wrapping it in a napkin and sliding it her purse, "Put it on my bill, I have to go and meet Rachel at Top Floor to sign off on the menu. Eat something, Ann, please!"

The three cut squares for half an hour, Ann speaking little while Nana and Millie reminisced about their own weddings. Ann wondered how they were so sure; she remembered her grandfathers. Paw, Nana's husband, Ann remembered more. Millie's husband died when she was eight. Paw, her mother's father, reminded Ann of someone who should have been born a hundred years before. She rarely saw him without a suit on and he always had a story to tell. Pop on the other hand was a painter; he dressed casually and had a laugh that could shake the house. As far as Ann knew, both had been happily married but people then never said if they were happy or not, they just stayed married. At least that's what her mother said.

"How did you know Paw and Pop were the ones?" Ann asked.

"You just knew back then," Millie said. "Things were different or I should say the things that mattered were different. You didn't have this nonsense about finding a soulmate or a partner, you fell for the one that made you laugh and who had a good character and reputation. You married and you built a life and family."

"And that's what mattered," Nana added. "Family was important, raising decent human beings, that was important and to do that you knew...we knew children needed both a mom and dad in the home and discipline. None of this dad on the weekend's nonsense. A child can't know if they're comin or goin these days. One set of rules in one house and another in the other one. We stuck together, it wasn't easy but we did, you had to work out all of your problems."

"And when you did everyone was better off," Millie cut in. "If I had left Pop every time I got tired of him, I would've worn a path out the door. That man could be exasperating, but I chose to love him and he chose to love me. None of this fallin' in and out of love, as they say, you just loved. Period!" Millie laughing went on, "Pop would get so mad at me at times, he was a saver and I was a spender. He came home

one day and found a new washing machine in the base-
ment. He was livid. He'd fixed the old one so many times I
lost count, I told him it was that old washer or me—he had
to choose. He walked away mumbling he could've fixed it
again but he supposed he'd keep me instead." Millie went
silent there was a lone tear on her cheek, "I loved that man
and I miss him still."

Nana patted her, "Millie's right, you just loved. You
can't go by what you feel all the time, sometimes you have
to make yourself feel, and if you can't you pray for it. Paw
left me for a while, did you know that?"

Ann, shocked, asked why.

"Some say he went out with a school teacher, anyway I
never wanted to believe it, he may have seen her from time
to time but I don't think it went any further. He moved into
a boarding house that used to be on Main. Never really gave
me a reason for leaving, he was gone oh, about two months."
Nana stacked her cut lace on the pile and picked up another
whole piece, "He came back one night after your mother
and Uncle Peter went to bed. Just stood in the doorway, I
said, 'Peter Spencer, what do you want?' He just looked at
me and said, 'Nadine, I've been a damn fool, I saw you and
the children going into the grocers and I said to myself, Peter,
there goes your world, what the hell are you doin here?'"
Nana held her hands out to her side palms up and shrugged.
"That was it; we never spoke of it again. Back then you lived,
you forgave and you went on, there were no counselors and
therapists. You just did what you were supposed to do. Well,
he made it up to me, gave me everything I wanted for the
next few years and took me to London, I always wanted to
go. Don't know if it was from guilt or what but we went and
had a good time." She laughed at the memory.

"What did you do, Nana, I mean for those two months? Were you upset?" It was beyond Ann how someone could just turn off their feelings.

Nana looked surprised, "well, child, I cried myself to sleep every night, I prayed for him to come back and I prayed if he didn't, I would have the grace I needed to survive. I knew your grandfather; I knew he was not one to shirk his responsibilities, so I left him alone until he came to his senses, which he did, by God's grace."

"After what he put you through, you didn't want to make his life even a little bit miserable?"

"Why should I? I'm sure to up and leave us the way he did, there was plenty of misery in his soul. No, as I said, we never spoke of it again. Once I went to the shed—we kept chickens there—I saw him kneeling. I knew then, whatever tormented him or made him leave, he was taking it to the right place. There was no need for me to punish him."

It was time for Ann's shift to end by the time Millie and Nana left. Still no Ben, Sarah would be in soon. It was for the best, not seeing him today. He texted once to see if things were going okay, made an excuse about getting ready for his move, and had to look over contracts from his new employer. Ann told him not to worry. When he came over at three that morning they talked for an hour, mostly Ben talked. Her desire for him was overwhelming, the more he spoke the more she felt for him. She could sense his guilt over Sarah's beating and she sensed his relief in being able to help her. Ann from lack of sleep—or something outside her—let him talk. His need for it was evident. They said goodbye with a hug, a rather long one and Ann watched him disappear around the Municipal Building. Sleep was out of the question after that, so she waited until the sun rose, went for a jog then went to Level Grounds and began baking. Now she was exhausted, her feet hurt and all she wanted to do was go home and go to bed.

The dress hung on her, this can't be the same dress, she thought.

Nancy walked by, "Ann! Oh, my," she tried to play down her alarm, "well, let me see, this seam would be good to take in, in the back here, yes I think we can manage, let me get my pins." Nancy was gone and back in a moment.

Ann's shoulder bones were obvious. She realized she hadn't eaten all day, not even the scone her mother suggested.

As Nancy pinned the dress, she scolded Ann in a way she hadn't since she was home. "You have to eat, why don't you eat? I'll fix you something when we're finished. I have mac and cheese, how bout' that? Huh? You used to like that."

Her mother sounded desperate which Ann hated. She agreed and found when it was set before her; it was exactly what she needed. With her stomach full she went to bed hoping sleep would not evade her as it had done for the last seven nights. She drifted off immediately with the background noise of her father's television. It was only eight o'clock. It was a solid sleep for several hours and then Ann felt something tighten around her neck, it was dark and she couldn't see, she heard her name but she couldn't cry out. Her mind would not believe this was happening again. She reached for the hands around her neck and pushed them away, she was able to scream, she did, as loud as possible. When she woke, she was sitting up in bed.

"You were having a nightmare, Ann, are you okay?" Stuart was standing next to her.

She looked from her father to her mother to Rachel, all standing in front of her. "I'm okay, it was a bad dream, I'm sorry I woke you." They stood still. "It's okay, go back to bed, I'll be fine."

Rachel walked to the other side of the bed and crawled in. "I'll stay with her," she said to Nancy and Stuart who in turn kissed Ann goodnight. Ann tried to protest but was relieved at the offer. Rachel lay down on her side and put her arm around Ann, "remember when we were kids and when we got scared, we got in the same bed?"

Ann nodded. Nothing else was said, Ann went back to sleep immediately and slept better than she had in nights.

# CHAPTER 16

nn woke the next morning alone. Rachel was about her wedding preparations, Ann was sure. They would go to the city today, LaSalle Street. It was where Nancy bought flowers. For her bouquet, Rachel wanted anemones, ranunculus, and some fall foliage to create a textured look. The car ride down was tense, Ann sat in back sensing the worry. What should have been a joy was wrought with concern for her. Doing what she could to alleviate tension, Ann assured them she had a great night's sleep and felt better than she had in a while, then she asked Rachel about her color choices.

Rachel revealing a preference for blue in the bouquet instigated questions and concerns from Nancy about the time of year and what blue could possibly be found and look appropriate with the vibrant fall colors.

"Blue is not a fall color, there may be some delphinium, I'm not sure." Nancy protested.

They arrived back in Bingham early afternoon. Each agreed to arrange some bouquets and then Rachel would choose.

Ann found the task as therapeutic as preparing for the shower had been. The table of flowers before her was a landscape of color and endless possibilities. Taking into consideration her sister's taste and preferences she worked for almost an hour, stopping only to retrieve ribbon. The final product pleased her. As she looked up, she noticed Nancy and Rachel at the other end of the table working on centerpieces.

"I'm finished," Ann said looking around. "Let's see your bouquets."

They both laughed. "We pick that one," Rachel pointed at Ann's finished product. "I could tell about thirty minutes in I loved what you were doing so we decided to do centerpieces."

"You really like it?"

"Yes, so take a picture so you can duplicate it for Saturday."

Nancy picked it up admiring it, "I didn't think the blue would work, but Ann you pulled it off, just the right amount." She put it in the cooler. "We should go to the church; Denise is there and it will be unlocked. We can figure out what we'll use there, let's bring what's left and I'll grab some tulle and ribbons."

As they passed Level Grounds Ann looked in, Ben was at the counter with a customer. He looked up and waved, she considered going in to say hello but Rachel and Nancy had rounded the corner. It was difficult to move her feet, watching him as he did his work, laughing with someone else increased the longing that already camped in her heart. Smiling, she held her hand up for too long, and reluctantly left the scene.

The Baptist Church was larger than the Presbyterian. Ann had only been inside a few times, once when a classmate committed suicide—the town churches had a meeting to talk to the youth—and once when the Presbyterian and

Baptist congregations hosted a concert. It had been re-done. Gone were the stained plank walls with matching pews and flat, worn red carpet. The walls and ceiling were fresh white. Wainscoting surrounded the perimeter. The pews were both stained walnut and painted white and the red carpet, replaced with a dark hardwood floor. Black chandeliers hung from the white ceiling creating a dramatic contrast, it was modern by Baptist standards.

Rachel's fall wedding colors would pop against the church's white backdrop. Her mother and sister talked with Denise Johnson at the front of the church while Ann lingered in the back imagining a white runner against the dark floor and just the right spray of fall foliage attached to every other pew. It would be magazine-worthy by the time the Fletcher women finished. A sort of sentimental melancholy came over her as she imagined her sister's dream coming to fruition. Ache and grief dominated her heart, not fully understanding why; it must be Ben's leaving but there seemed to be more to it. Her mother's soft voice echoed in the vast space, Ann suddenly needed to sit. The church was cold, she was wearing a light sweater; she cinched it around her, folding her arms around her chest. The emptiness of the church mimicked the hollowness of her spirit. The hunger she felt was not for food and the warmth she desired was not just physical. At twenty-three she felt fifty—like she had lived a lifetime but not really. Looking down at the floor, there was a scrap of paper, someone had taken notes, possibly from the sermon. Only two words were discernable, 'TENDER MERCIES', in capital letters stared up at her. Contemplating the meaning, she had forgotten where she was and why she was there.

"*They are new every morning, new every morning...*" Her mind went to the old hymn.

Her silent reverie came to an abrupt halt with a loud crash. Startled, she let out something between a gasp and scream. A voice from the back apologized; the three in the front of the church turned briefly and Denise waved to someone then appeared to offer an explanation to Nancy and Rachel who were focused on the front of the church.

Ann looked down at her hands, they were shaking. She startled easily since her attack. A chill seized her again, she rubbed her arms. The shaking spread to the rest of her body and she rocked to try and calm herself.

A hand on her shoulder caused her to jump.

"I'm sorry if I startled you." The woman sat next to Ann, "I dropped the music stand. These hardwood floors make everything louder. "I'm Damaris."

Ann stared at the woman; she was about her age with short brown hair and kind eyes.

"I'mmm Ann," *what was wrong with her?*

"You're freezing, Daddy keeps it so cold in here. There is a blanket back here somewhere, Dottie Bingham always keeps one." Damaris said looking suddenly alarmed. She searched the pews and was back in a moment wrapping Ann.

"There that should help. Can I get you some tea or something?"

Ann could not speak, tears welled in her eyes. Not understanding what was happening to her, she tried in vain to stop the shaking and get a hold of herself. She shook her head no.

"Is there something I can do to help?"

Again, her head went back and forth. She stared straight

ahead, her mother and Rachel occupied with their plans, Ann could not move. Tears streaming down her face, she seemed to be losing control. An arm reached around her.

"You've been through a lot, just cry if you want."

And so, Ann did with Damaris' arm around her, overwhelmed by feelings of sorrow and deep longing. The wedding planners continued unaware of what was going on in the back, Ann not sure either what this outpouring of tears meant. John's cruel words echoed in her mind, why was that cruelty surfacing now? His fowl breath she could almost smell—the power of his fist on her face was there again. Her head dropped in her hands and she sobbed.

This drew attention and her mother and sister were upon her, asking what was wrong, speaking to Damaris, wrapping their arms around her shoulder. Denise began to pray out loud, words that had no meaning to Ann. As her body shook with fear, fatigue, anxiety, whatever it was—all her past wrongs accused and shamed her, the longing, she realized was not for Ben nor was it for any other thing she thought would make her happy, the longing was for something else, someone else. The tears and shaking continued, her mother and sister unable to calm her. Ann gave in to it, she was tired, so tired, tired of being fine, tired of being strong for Rachel, tired of hurting. The void was like an open chasm enveloping her soul. She needed something or someone, she knew her mother and her sister could not bring it to her and she knew suddenly who it was. The voice was small at first, Ann believing it was one of the women surrounding her but the second time, it was powerful and clear, *"I'm here."* Startled, Ann looked up. "What?"

"What's the matter, dear?" Nancy looked intently at her daughter.

"Did you hear that?"

"What? Denise is praying."

"No, it wasn't Denise." The tears and shaking left as quickly as they came. Calmness traveled through her being, that voice, it changed everything.

"I think I'm okay, now."

There was considerable activity getting her to her feet, insisting they go home, she needed lunch, when had any of them eaten? Damaris offered to drive them, no, the car was at Nancy's shop, they would walk. When they passed Level Grounds, Ann did not look in but felt Ben's gaze. Nancy and Rachel cradled Ann between them.

"I'm fine go ahead and go. I'm just going to read or something." Ann, embarrassed by her earlier episode persuaded her mother and Rachel to finish the wedding errands. Nancy hesitated to leave her and called Stuart to see if he could leave his class with the teaching assistant and come home, he agreed. Ann went to her room and lay down, if possible, she would sleep, she believed her breakdown was partly to do with fatigue. The voice repeated in her head, it was no mystery who the voice belonged to. "I'm sorry," she whispered. *"I'm here",* came back again and again. *TENDER MERCIES*…She repeated it over and over. When she woke it was dark, her father stood in the door with a tray.

"You started to work and life too soon. I made an appointment for you tomorrow with Dr. Bailey." He put the tray on her nightstand. "It's Millie's chicken soup. A cure-all, according to her. Everyone is worried," he traced his hand around her forehead. "Ben is downstairs."

"What does he know?"

Stuart shrugged, "I didn't say anything, he just stopped by according to him. Do you want me to tell him to shove off?" Stuart's attitude toward Ben had noticeably changed since the news of his leaving.

"No, I'll come down. Give me a few minutes."

"Eat your soup first, while it's hot."

Stuart made his presence known with the clanging of dishes from the kitchen, on occasion he would peer into the living room.

"Do you want to walk? It's not too cold." Ben asked.

Ann said little on the walk to their bench. The lights from a barge moved on the rippling water below. They sat; Ben's gaze laser-like on her face.

"Did something happen today?"

"I had a little breakdown, I guess you would say." Ann was glad for the darkness.

"Do you want to talk about it?" He put his arm around her, drawing her near. She welcomed the warmth and form of his body melting into hers.

"I don't know, not sure what came over me. It was like a load hit all at once, John, my past, coming home, and you. It was all there in front of me kind of mocking and accusing me. A lot of fear mixed in with it all. Am I making sense?"

"Yes," he drew her closer. "Are you okay now?"

Ann remembered the voice, her own silent confessions, and prayers.

"I am, it's hard to explain," it was—she wasn't sure what was happening herself. It was like she was getting to know someone but didn't have the knowledge to talk about him yet. Ben's arms around her felt good in more ways than one. Physical desire was only part of it, comfort in who he was, and his companionship another, yet it was temporary. The word temporary kept coming to the forefront of her mind not because he would be leaving in a few days but because all of this was temporary. Suddenly, being with him did not have the same desperation it had a few nights ago. She felt she could let him go and be at peace. The last two months happened for a reason and she may never know that reason but if she never saw Ben Fontana again it would have to be okay. On the other hand, she didn't believe she would never see him again and her feelings for him were as strong as ever, maybe more so but his leaving felt different somehow.

"I don't want you to work tomorrow."

"Why? You have so much to do, all your packing..." Ann argued. The last thing she wanted was to be a burden to someone else. "I'm already taking half the day Thursday and all of Friday and Saturday."

"I'm going to close on Saturday, remember? Half the town will be at the wedding. I'll ask Sarah to work some extra, she's been wanting to anyway. Just take tomorrow and for that matter, you can take Thursday morning off too."

It was generous, Ann could almost say she loved him but being on guard was vital at this point. She agreed to Wednesday but promised to do baking on Thursday morning. Their goodnight was a disappointment for both. Still no kiss, but it couldn't be helped there was an obstacle; what happened with John, Ann knew, made Ben more careful around her. She was grateful and disappointed at the same time.

The next three days were a whirlwind. Ann cleaned, washed guest linens, and chauffeured family from the airport. Laughter rang through the household as it filled with Fletcher relatives, her Uncle Peter and family were the first to arrive, Bella, his four-year-old daughter, would be a flower girl. She twirled around in the dress and begged Nancy to make flowers for her hair.

There was food from one end of the kitchen to the other. Cousins, friends, well-wishers came and went, dropping off gifts and reminiscing about Rachel as a little girl. Rachel could hardly stand so much attention but bore it well. The rehearsal dinner was at the Country Club. Ann invited Ben but he had packing to do. Eric sat near Ann the entire evening and complimented everything from her dress to the color of her nails. Trying to find something interesting about him proved impossible.

The toasts of the evening brought tears to everyone's eyes. Stuart blubbering like a doting father, obviously not having an easy time of it. Nancy had to stand and take over to which he responded gratefully and lighthearted.

Ann knew she should toast as well but found it difficult to put her feelings into words. All eyes on her meant those staring would be thinking of what happened with John, possibly her breakdown at the church if Denise and Damaris had not been discreet. Loathing the thought of it, she struggled to do what was right and expected and stifled the desire to hide with her head down. Standing, she nervously held her glass, taking in the stares. Sympathy and pity, on some faces, anxiety on others. Nana winked and Millie gave her a thumbs up. Smiling weakly, she began.

"My sister," Ann swallowed hard. "Should have been born first, she has always been the wisest, the prettiest and the best. I am not sure where I would be were it not for her. Rachel has been my touchstone. Always knowing what to do or say even when I refused to listen." At this, Ann lowered her head and bit her lip. Composing herself, she resumed with words from a distant memory, "A word fitly spoken is like apples of gold in a setting of silver. Our Millie used to say that, and it always reminded me of Rachel. It's from

Proverbs, I believe." Ann caught Millie's approving glance. "Connor", turning to him, "I hope you know what a treasure our Rachel is and will spend your life being worthy of her. The Lord bless you both, and keep you…" Ann raised her glass. Her father's voice boomed, 'here, here'. And it was over to Ann's relief.

Nancy caught her glance, winked, and dabbed her eye.

As Ben packed in the bedroom of his home, he noticed a shadow outside his window. It was dusk; he had wanted to join Ann at the dinner but knew time was running out. Most of what he was moving would be shipped and he was still packing boxes and labeling. The shadow moved slowly back and forth, Ben knew he should investigate, he tossed the packing tape on the bed and went to the window, opening it he saw Quigley standing there, head down.

"Quigley, do you want to come inside?"

"No, I jus heard you was leavin'."

"Yes, I am. Are you staying with Lowell?"

"I am. Have to or they said I'd have to go to the home over there."

"I'm glad Quigley, Lowell's a good guy, he'll take care of you."

"I guess." Quigley shoved his toe in the dirt. "I jus wanna thank ya for your kindness and help and say goodbye." He turned to leave.

"Quigley, don't leave, you're welcome." He shouted after him. "Ann will work in the coffee shop, please stop by and see her. I would like to know how you're doing from time to time."

The old man kept walking; he raised his hand goodbye and disappeared around the corner.

The wedding was at four, appetizers and dinner would follow and then the dancing and celebration. The wedding brunch was Fletcher only; Connor would celebrate with his family. There were Fletcher and Spencer cousins, aunts, and uncles scattered in the kitchen, living room, and back porch. Nancy and Ann had worked all morning preparing muffins, scones, ham, roast, baked egg casserole, and an assortment of relishes, vegetables, cheeses, and crackers. Enough to feed a small army but as Nana said, 'we won't eat again until dinner so fill up.'

Children ran and were scolded, the women told stories of their own weddings, men discussed sports and the cost of weddings and Ann basked in the love she felt around her. Nancy had hosted this group for years on holidays and birthdays. In high school Ann would retreat to her room or sneak out to the park to hang with her friends, now as she listened to the sound of family, she understood what she had missed all those years. The look on her grandmothers' faces as they took a small one in their arms, her father's laughter from the patio, Rachel's undeniable glow was all balm to her. Bella ran by and Ann picked her up and kissed her.

The surprised toddler kissed her back, taking Ann's face in her little hands she said, "Fannie, you still sad?" Even the smallest in the family could not escape gossip.

"No love, I'm the happiest I've ever been." Bella was satisfied and squirmed down.

Tanya Wesley arrived on time with the bridesmaids and a basket of curling irons, straighteners, makeup, and all manner of potions and products to curl straighten, smooth, and overall improve the appearance of the wedding party. Stuart and the men of the family made a hasty retreat while the woman set up a makeshift salon in the master bedroom. Nails were touched up as they waited their turn and the steamer went over dresses one last time. Rachel was first; Tanya worked her magic, wrapping Rachel's long dark hair in a braided, twisted creation Ann had never seen. It was agreed they would all wear their hair up; Ann knew hers would be a challenge so she was next.

Bella situated herself on Ann's lap and watched the proceedings with fascination.

"I want mine all curled up too."

"That may not be possible Bella, Ann's comes naturally," Molly, her mother said.

"We'll see what we can do," Tanya replied, running her hand through the toddler's poker-straight hair.

As predicted, the task was monumental but Tanya managed a loose arrangement perfectly framing Ann's face. She finished her with a light foundation and eye color and the perfect shade for her lips.

"Beautiful. Next!"

The three bridesmaids were handled with the same care and finally, Bella climbed in the seat with great expectations, her limp hair hanging in her eyes.

Tanya examined and brushed. "I have something special for you, Bella." Going through her bag, she pulled out a hairpiece and created a seamless blend on Bella's head.

Bella, squealed with delight, "my own curls", she showed her mother, "now I want my princess dress!"

"It's time for all of our princess dresses, the photographer is waiting," Nancy said in a hurry, her own hair still in rollers.

Ann stood at her place in front of the church. Evie serenaded her and the other girls down the aisle with a folksy, contemporary *All Things Bright and Beautiful*. The church packed; Ann found Ben's gaze. Color rose to her face with the intensity of his stare. Smiling, he hesitated then raised his hand. As she moved her gaze from Ben to the back of the church, she spotted Damaris who smiled and gave her a thumbs up. Ann's inside jolted at the thought of her crisis in the back of the church but a few days ago. Damaris must think she's nuts. Her thoughts were interrupted by music.

*Jesu Joy of Man's Desiring* began by the string quartet. It was time, Ann was nervous for her sister, the congregation stood and the large doors in the back opened. Rachel was every bride's dream. Calm, beautiful, full of hope, her father Stuart proudly walked her down the aisle fighting back tears as he went. The church with its spray of fall colors and foliage was the perfect backdrop. Everything went off without a hitch from the music to the vows, even Bella dropped her petals on cue, the reception line was predictable and Ann was asked ten times when it would be her turn.

By the time they reached Top Floor the party had started with hors d'oeuvres, drinks, and background music. Dinner was served, toasts made, traditional dances danced. Ann searched for Ben making eye contact while he danced with Maggie then Imogene. She could not avoid the obligatory dances with Eric, the best man; then her father, her uncle, and a host of suddenly interested high school friends including Tommy Short. They made several attempts to meet up with one another but Ben would be surrounded by one well-wisher and then another. By the time their eyes met again and Ann motioned to the balcony, the crowd had thinned and Bella was asleep on two chairs, her curls and flower wreath both dripping off her head.

It was an unusually warm evening for late October, Ann left her wrap inside. She faced the river; a light breeze caressed her face. Feeling Ben's stare behind her, she turned, he met her with open arms. Falling into his embrace, no words spoken; she went with it, not caring about tomorrow, his leaving, and the uncertainty.

"You look beautiful." He whispered in her ear, his warm breath traveling down her neck.

"Thanks, you're not so bad yourself."

They turned to the river; his arms circled her waist. He drew a long breath, keeping his face close to her neck. They didn't speak. The full moon revealed the slow-moving current of the Mississippi. Ann willed time to stop. In less than twelve hours he would be gone and she had no idea when or how she would see him again. The crowd inside no longer mattered or interested her. His arms held tightly to her and it was all she wanted.

Evie's smooth vocals drifted out to them as she crooned a romantic ballad. Ben turned her to himself and they swayed gently to the music. Her head against his heart; his hand in the small of her back. Swallowing hard, she fought the tightening in her throat. Tears would make it all worse. He guided her to a corner away from the windows, they continued swaying even after the music had stopped.

As they held on, Ann kept her face from his. Sensing his anticipation, she knew what happened next was her call. She also knew making a quick exit with her heart and virtue intact was the right thing to do. The complications of her life, his leaving town and a new awareness or consciousness of faith were enough to keep her from making a huge mistake. As this internal debate raged; the warmth of his body seemed to drown out all arguments her head could come up with. Lifting her head, he was there to meet her, moving his mouth gently around her face, her eyes, forehead, and eventually her mouth. Whispering, as he went how he has waited and imagined.

Giving in to desire, Ann willingly crossed to a place she knew she shouldn't. Caring little about tomorrow, she encouraged and responded. Locked together, arms holding tight, she gave in and followed where he led. His invitation did not surprise her, she whispered her consent. Weaving his fingers in hers, he pulled her to the door.

Still kissing her, he reached for the door handle leading back inside. The realization was abrupt. Turning from her, he tried again; it did not budge. In disbelieve, he tried a third time. Throwing up his hands, he swore under his breath.

"We are locked out."

Ann laughed. An inappropriate response maybe but all of the sudden she felt the joke was on her. Pressing her face to the door, she could see the red glare of an emergency exit was the only light. Her phone, on a table inside, glowed with an incoming message. Her mother no doubt, wondering what happened to her. *Not to worry mom.* She thought. Ann's reality came crashing into her existent dream. Leaving with Ben would have been a mistake and one she would not recover from easily. She looked at him, incredibly handsome, running his hand through his hair in frustration. A frustration she understood. Suddenly aware of the falling temperature, she ran her hands up and down her arms. Ben removed his jacket and wrapped it around her.

In a nearby chair, he pulled her to his lap, holding her close.

"There must be a fire escape…" He glanced the length of the deck.

"Don't you have your phone?"

"At home on the dresser."

"Well, we really are stuck, mine's in there. So, what now, Fontana? I can't climb down a fire escape in these heels and dress."

"This is not how I imagined our last evening together."

"There are no coincidences."

"So, I've heard." He held her tighter as if she might drift away.

Ann leaned her head on his, "It was nice while it lasted."

"Yeah."

There were no words for several moments; each lost in the thought of what might have been and what would be tomorrow. Ann swallowed the rising tightness in her throat. Part of her, only a small part, was thankful that the door was locked. Perhaps as time went on her gratitude would grow and the further she was away from the situation she may become truly grateful for the locked door but for now, it was only half-hearted. No coincidences. Someone was looking out for her; she knew who he was and whispered her halfhearted thank you to him. That was all she could muster; her emotions were still off the tracks and if the lock suddenly unlatched she could still not trust herself. Sitting on his lap, in his coat with his arms around her was probably not the wisest choice. She stood abruptly.

This woke Ben from his thoughts. He smiled a weak understanding smile. "You're thinking, I'm guessing, that you just dodged a bullet."

"I wouldn't put it that way."

He reached for her hand, "It's okay. I know it is for the best. I hate it, but I know it just the same." He stood, "I think the fire escape is that way.

As he turned, Ann saw a shadow inside. She ran to the door and knocked frantically. A light switched on.

A grinning Tommy Short opened the door, "What are you two doing out here?" He winked at Ann.

"Thanks." Ben pushed his way in—glaring at Tommy.

"Good thing I forgot my phone, came back just in time I'd say."

Ann could only nod. Grabbing her shawl and phone, she endured Tommy's snide remarks all the way to the street. From Ben's set jaw, she sensed restraint on his part.

Tommy Short left them on Main, wishing them a good evening with a wink and his boyish grin.

"What now?" Ben ran his finger down her arm.

"I hate goodbyes."

"Me too."

They walked in silence to the Fletcher home but could not part. Ann retrieved a blanket and they walked on through the night until they ended up on their bench; talking over a multitude of scenarios about their future. None of which seemed realistic. They had known one another for only two months. As the night turned to early morning, they huddled under the blanket holding tight to each other. They watched the sunrise over an Illinois farm.

"What time does your phone say?" Ben stood slowly.

"Almost seven."

"My car will be here by eight, I still have packing."

Ann stood. "This is goodbye then."

"I left the keys to the house and jeep in the cash register. JC gave the Jeep the once over, it should be good through the winter." The words caught in his throat. He kept his gaze on the rising sun avoiding her face.

"Mhmm," was all that came out.

"I'll call when I get there."

Again, Ann could only nod.

He raised her head with his hand and kissed her one last time. It was brief and nothing like the night before. Just as quickly, he turned and left. Jogging down the path. She watched until he was out of sight. Her heartbeat seemed undetectable. The sun rising across the river brought the brilliant colors of the surrounding trees and river in view. There was one white cloud against a brilliant blue sky. The remaining leaves from a nearby maple floated gently across the breeze. Ben was long out of sight yet she remained as he left her—almost expecting him to turn around and jog back telling her it was all a joke; he wasn't moving a thousand miles away and he would see her later at the coffee shop. A mournful sigh escaped her lips followed by quiet tears. She walked home feeling more alone than she had ever felt.

The house was quiet.

Rachel gone, her parents and relatives still asleep. Bella's soft breathing from Ann's bed was welcoming. Ann crawled in beside her thankful for the distraction. Brushing a stray hair from the sleeping child's forehead, made her little body stir. Without opening her eyes, the child whispered.

"Ann, do you love Ben?"

Startled, Ann stroked her hair. *Out of the mouths of babes.* Bella rolled over; sound asleep again.

"I do, Bella," it felt good to say it even if the hearer was asleep. "I do." She repeated, then added, "so much, so much, so much."

# ACKNOWLEDGMENTS

Special thanks to Cassidy Stoner, Jessie Flori, Trina Boyer Barchi, and Cindy Redburn whose brilliant editing advice helped me get to publishing. And to my beautiful mom, Patricia Politte Boyer and sisters, Tracy Flori and Trina Boyer Barchi who encouraged me again and again. And to my sweet dad, Leo Boyer Jr., who always told me I was smart.

Also, to all my friends who read and encouraged me along the way.

All Biblical References from ESV translation

Made in the USA
Coppell, TX
18 March 2021